LET THERE BE MOONLIGHT . . .

The Count's voice, barely human, "You should not have—not the light—I will change now—change—"

The curtain fell away and the moonlight streamed in across glittering fields of snow. . . .

The Count . . . his face . . . his nose had elongated into a snout. Even as she watched he was changing. Bristles sprouting on his cheeks. His teeth were lengthening, his mouth widening into the foaming jaws of an animal. The eyes . . . bright yellow now, slitty, implacable. His hands, already covered with hair, were shrinking into paws. With a snarl the Count fell down on all fours. His teeth were slick with drool. The stench intensified. Her gorge rose. She tasted vomit in the back of her throat. Then the wolf leapt.

She was thrown back. She fell down into the patch of moonlight. The beast was ripping away her dress now. It still desires me, she thought. The wolf's spit sprayed her face and ran down her neck. She tried to beat it back but it straddled her now, about to sink its teeth into her throat. . . .

—From S. P. Somtow's
"The Madonna of the
Wolves"

Books in this Series from Ace

ISAAC ASIMOV'S ALIENS
edited by Gardner Dozois
ISAAC ASIMOV'S MARS
edited by Gardner Dozois
ISAAC ASIMOV'S FANTASY!
edited by Shawna McCarthy
ISAAC ASIMOV'S ROBOTS
edited by Gardner Dozois and Sheila Williams
ISAAC ASIMOV'S EARTH
edited by Gardner Dozois and Sheila Williams
ISAAC ASIMOV'S SF LITE
edited by Gardner Dozois
ISAAC ASIMOV'S CYBERDREAMS
edited by Gardner Dozois and Sheila Williams
ISAAC ASIMOV'S SKIN DEEP
edited by Gardner Dozois and Sheila Williams
ISAAC ASIMOV'S GHOSTS
edited by Gardner Dozois and Sheila Williams
ISAAC ASIMOV'S VAMPIRES
edited by Gardner Dozois and Sheila Williams
ISAAC ASIMOV'S CHRISTMAS
edited by Gardner Dozois and Sheila Williams
ISAAC ASIMOV'S DETECTIVES
edited by Gardner Dozois and Sheila Williams
ISAAC ASIMOV'S VALENTINES
edited by Gardner Dozois and Sheila Williams
ISAAC ASIMOV'S WEREWOLVES
edited by Gardner Dozois and Sheila Williams

Isaac Asimov's Werewolves

Edited by
Gardner Dozois
and
Sheila Williams

ACE BOOKS, NEW YORK

ISAAC ASIMOV'S WEREWOLVES

An Ace Book / published by arrangement with
Dell Magazines

PRINTING HISTORY
Ace edition / October 1999

All rights reserved.
Copyright © 1999 by Dell Magazines, Inc.,
a division of Crosstown Publications.
Cover art by Lee MacLeod.
This book may not be reproduced in whole or in part,
by mimeograph or any other means, without permission.
For information address: Dell Magazines,
1270 Avenue of the Americas, New York, New York 10020.

The Penguin Putnam Inc. World Wide Web site address is
http://www.penguinputnam.com

Check out the ACE Science Fiction & Fantasy newsletter,
and much more on the Internet at Club PPI!

ISBN: 0-441-00661-2

ACE®
Ace Books are published
by The Berkley Publishing Group,
a division of Penguin Putnam Inc.,
375 Hudson Street, New York, New York 10014.
ACE and the "A" design are trademarks
belonging to Penguin Putnam Inc.

PRINTED IN THE UNITED STATES OF AMERICA

10 9 8 7 6 5 4 3 2 1

The editors would like to thank the following people for their help and support: Shawna McCarthy, for having the good taste to buy some of this material in the first place; Susan Casper and David Bruce; Jared Goldman and Lori Gerstein; Kathleen Halligan, who set up this deal; and thanks especially to our own editor on this project, Susan Allison.

Asimov's website: www.asimovs.com

For Lynn Irene Williams

CONTENTS

WHAT SEEN BUT THE WOLF
  Gregg Keizer   1
BOOBS
  Suzy McKee Charnas   40
TWO BAD DOGS
  Ronald Anthony Cross   63
THE MADONNA OF THE WOLVES
  S. P. Somtow   84
RED
  Sarah Clemens   143
AN AMERICAN CHILDHOOD
  Pat Murphy   169

WHAT SEEN BUT THE WOLF

Gregg Keizer

"What Seen but the Wolf" was purchased by Shawna McCarthy, and appeared in the February 1984 issue of Asimov's *with a cover by Val Lakey Lindahn and an interior illustration by Gary Freeman. Not a prolific writer, Keizer made a handful of sales to genre publications in the early eighties, to places such as* Asimov's, Omni, Perpetual Light, *and elsewhere, but soon disappeared into the world of computer magazines, working for* Compute! *and other publications, and has subsequently not returned to science fiction, although we keep a hopeful eye on our submission pile, waiting for his byline to turn up again.*

"What Seen but the Wolf" was one of only two sales he made to Asimov's, *but it's a major story, still one of the best of the modern reexaminations of the werewolf legend, as Keizer takes us to the New World at its newest, long before Columbus, for an exciting and suspenseful saga of some Viking explorers who bring an ancient curse to the shores of this new land. . . .*

1

"You should have killed Sverri when you came across him outside Hofstadir, the blood from that farmer on his hands," Bjorn said, looking midships where the pitching deck was open. Sverri's screams still came from there, but they were quieter now. Heltevir, his wife, was by him.

The image came too freely to my eyes. Sverri had been hunched over the warm body of the farmer, his hands dipped over the man's face, as if he was trying to wake him. Blood was everywhere; across Sverri's cheeks and forehead, up to his elbows, down his trousers. His eyes had been mad, their circles too bright in the dim moonlight.

"Kill him for what?" I asked. Bjorn was Sverri's only brother, true, but he had no reason to question my actions. Eight days since the night I'd come upon Sverri, six since we'd sailed, and this the first time we'd talked of it. Perhaps that was part of the problem with the voyage. We should have said all this before we fled Ice Land. "Kill him for murder? That was what it looked like. Kill a friend when he could easily have paid weregeld to the sod's wife? How was I to know Sverri was thought a werewolf?"

Bjorn said nothing, only looked into the rain that clouded the horizon. The storm would be on us quickly. "Yes," he finally said. "You did not see him while he was a wolf, as the farmer's sons swore. If only we'd not found the wolfskin around Sverri's waist." I was silent, tired of trying to explain the wolfshirt Sverri had worn. They believed what they wanted to believe, and nothing I said changed it. "We could have stayed, instead of on our way to beautiful Groenland." The last word was an oath. We'd heard of the lies of Eric the Red, the one who called a land of ice and rock *Groen*.

"It's too late for wishing," I said. "We are all here because of Sverri, but there are few of us who could not have stayed in Hofstadir. A few questions, perhaps some money spent, that would have been all. Everyone had a reason for joining Sverri in exile. Only you," I said, pointing to Bjorn, "and Heltevir had to run with Sverri."

"And you, Halfdan," a tall blond standing beside Bjorn said. I tried to put a name to him, but it took several moments. Thorvin. A friend of Bjorn's from his days gone aviking.

"Yes. It was unfortunate that the farmer's sons decided to fight." I rubbed the back of my head, feeling the lump only now disappearing. They'd held both Sverri and me until Bjorn had hacked his way into their longhouse and pulled us free.

"Enough," said a sharp voice. It was Eirik, his old, weathered face twisted in anger. Or perhaps fear. He leaned a hand on the afterboat, the small boat, large enough for six, perhaps, turned upside down on the deck of the ship. He seemed to touch it with care. Did he expect we would have to flee in it if the ship broke up in the storm approaching? "Enough talk. The storm will be on us soon, and then what? Already we are two days past landfall in Groenland. How are we to reach land if that touches our sail?" He pointed to the dark wall of clouds to the northeast, off our stern.

"Halfdan is sailing master," Bjorn said, looking at me.

"Sailing master?" I asked, wanting to laugh, but finding only fury instead. "On this pig of a boat? It needs a swineherd, not a sailing master." I watched Bjorn, half-expecting him to swing. Tempers were short.

"It was not my idea to sail in this," he said softly, gesturing at the small merchant ship we sailed. It was a knorr, wide and slow, not like the longships I was used to sailing. Its fifty-foot length had seemed enough when we'd left Ice Land, but six days with thirteen and one madman had shortened it by far.

Bjorn was right. We'd had little choice of ships when we'd fled in the night from home. I laughed and the

sound seemed to surprise all those around me. "I have
never sailed this far west," I said. "I only have heard
of this way, that is all. There is a difference between
sailing a passage, and only listening to another's memory of one."

"Four days is the passage," Eirik said, his voice
sounding as if he was afraid of saying it. "We are lost."

"Then we will find land elsewhere," I said, my
laughter forgotten, my anger again tight in my throat.
"*Vikingr* have sailed around the world, and there always
was land to be found. If we are lost from Groenland,
what matter is that? Ice and bare mountains and little
food is something I can do without. You?"

"We will try to find Groenland, Halfdan," Bjorn said,
his voice an order that even I wanted to obey, for all
my brave words. "I would not wish to be alone in the
wilderness with my brother." He almost whispered the
words. Those clustered around us glanced towards midships. I noticed Thorvin cross himself and wanted to
spit. Christians among us, too. Wasn't Sverri Tryggvason, our werewolf, enough?

"Someone should stay with him when the storm
hits," Eirik said nervously. He glanced towards me, then
looked back to where Sverri was bound below the deck.
"In case he is afraid, one of us could comfort him." It
was too quiet when his words were gone.

"To watch him, you mean," I said loudly. "In case
he breaks the bindings?" Eirik would not look at me.
The men began to drift away, each to his own task before the storm. None stayed too long near midships.

"What of the animals?" I asked. There were two
cows and four sheep huddled in the open well midships,
their backs gray from the salt spray.

"Hope that they do not die of fright," Bjorn said,
smiling slightly. "Hope that none of us die of fright."
I smiled, but there was no laughter in me at his wish.

I looked at Bjorn and shook my head. "We'll live through this," I said.

"Will we?"

I listened to Sverri's distant screaming and wondered if I was right.

The storm came on us full of fury and horrible seas. The winds drove us south for three days, our ship wallowing in the troughs of the huge waves. It was impossible to calculate our course, for the sun was gone, hidden by the clouds, and the wind seemed to be backing; it came from a different direction than the sea ran. Then the fog smothered us. We were trapped in it for almost a day.

That was when we lost Ingolf, a cousin to Sverri and Bjorn. He went to the stern to piss, shrieked in a voice that made my heart cold, and was gone. We shouted for him, but the fog seemed to swallow our words. Bjorn found a spot or two of blood on the deck beside the steering oar, but that was all. Thorvin was at the oar, but he heard only a low moan before Ingolf yelled. Thorvin said it sounded like a pained animal, but it must have been only the wind, I thought. I stumbled in the dimness to Sverri's side, but the bindings were all in place, tight as before. It could not have been him. No one wanted to talk of it.

We let the ship ride before the wind, the sail furled and all of us sick from the gale. One of the sheep died and since there was no way to cook it, we had to simply skin it and heave the carcass overboard. Sverri quieted finally; the storm silenced his madness.

"Sverri, do you hear me?" I whispered to the shape in the dark. He stirred, then tried to sit up. I helped him edge back until he was against one of the knorr's ribs. "Sverri?" I asked, loud enough for only him to hear. I didn't think the others would want me talking to our werewolf.

"Hello, Halfdan," Sverri said, his voice even and sane. Where was his madness now?

"Do you remember?" I asked, sitting in front of him. Even so, it was impossible to see his face, for the clouds were still thick above us.

"How long has it been?" he asked.

"Eleven days since I found you on that farmer. Nine since we sailed."

He was quiet. For some reason, I wanted a light, so I could see his face. What if he was a wolf even now? I reached out my hand to touch his face, but stopped, unable to wish my arm to move further. My hand trembled, and I let it drop to clasp my axe.

"Groenland?" Sverri asked.

"We are off course," I said. "I don't think we will see Groenland soon." Again, Sverri was silent. "We are old friends. You have always been everything a friend should be," I said finally. "We have gone aviking together and you saved my throat that day in Frisia." I swallowed hard. "Did you kill Ingolf?" I put both hands on the axe. For the third time Sverri said nothing. "Sverri? Did you kill him as you killed that farmer?"

"Am I a simple murderer to you, Halfdan?" he asked quietly. "Is that all I am? Not even a madman?" I could not force the words to answer. "I have heard the others whisper of it, Halfdan. They think me mad, or worse. Do you?"

I shook my head, realized he could not see in the darkness and grunted a reply. Mad? I could not believe it. A murderer, yes, for I'd seen him hunched over the farmer's corpse. He had even had the madness in his eyes then, but all killings bring that on in a man. I'd killed, and knew that brief madness had glittered in my face as well. I remembered the sounds my voice had somehow made when the berserker madness caught me in battle. Sverri a madman? No. He had killed, but that did not make one insane, did not make one dangerous to old friends. How could Sverri be a madman for doing what I had done? How could he be mad, when I knew I was sane?

"Why don't you free me from these?" Sverri asked, and I heard the rustle of cloth as his hands appeared in front of my face. The bindings were tight, and even in the dimness I could see they cut his skin.

"Do you believe I am a wolf, Halfdan?" I did not know what to believe. Everyone else seemed sure Sverri was a werewolf; the farmer's sons, Bjorn, all the rest of those on the ship. But we'd lived and sailed and fought together too many years for me to believe he could be a shape-shifter without my knowledge. The two years since we'd returned from Norway, where we'd been *ulfhednar*, wolf-shirted warriors for the King, had been filled with whispers of the frightened rustics of Ice Land. Sverri had not laid aside his wolfskin, as I had, and so the sods thought him strange. I knew him truly, and even though I too believed in the power of the wolf-shirt in battle, had proved it to myself more than once while fighting for the King, I knew it did not make one a shape-shifter. His *ulfhednar* wolfshirt was what they found on Sverri after his murder, and though I had tried to tell them it was nothing, they hadn't listened to me.

Yet, even still, in the darkness and quiet sound of the sea, I wondered and had small doubts. Could he be a werewolf? How could I not have those doubts. Only a god can be sure.

"Do you believe, Halfdan?" he asked again. Did he lean toward me in the dark? Were those shapes before me his hands? No, he was bound tight, I tried to remember. "If you believe I am a wolf, Halfdan, then that is what I am."

I left him then, afraid of his answers if I asked more questions. Did I believe?

• • •

"We are seven doegr south of the Groenland Western Settlement," I said, still holding the husanotra in my hand. Bjorn was in front of me, but in the darkness, even though the sky was clear, I could only see his outline. He took the husanotra, the quarter circle of wood, from my outstretched hand and held it up so that its bottom edge was level with the horizon, the line where the stars disappeared into the sea. He lined the Pole Star with the curved edge of the husanotra, marked the place with his finger, then counted the notches back to the straight edge.

"Seven doegr." He sighed. "Seven days of good sailing," he said, finally agreeing with me that we were far from Groenland. "Where are we?" he asked, his voice quiet. More out of secrecy from the rest than for fear of disturbing their snorings.

I shrugged my shoulders, then realized he could not have seen the gesture. "West of Groenland, south of Groenland, I would say. Lost."

"Still no land," Bjorn said.

"There are plenty of birds. We'll see land in a day, perhaps two."

"Go north when we come to land, than back east?" he asked. I wondered if he would let me make the decision, or if he was only asking me to soothe my injured pride. We were lost, after all.

"What if we left Sverri here, then sailed north to the Western Settlement?" I asked. The thought came suddenly. Even if Sverri was no danger to me, he was to the others. His kin and closest friend he might still smile on. But the others? Wouldn't it be simpler to exile one, even though a friend, than to risk the death of several?

Bjorn snorted loudly, the sound waking the closest sleeper. I couldn't see who moved on the deck beside our feet.

"No?" I said. "Ingolf would disagree, I think."

"Ingolf fell overboard. The man could not hold his

bladder." Bjorn's outline moved in the darkness. "Sverri had nothing to do with his death. He will come out of his magic once we are in Groenland. When he knows we are far from any of that farmer's kinfolk, he will cease his shape-shifting. Sverri is kin to me, remember that. I could not strand him."

I was silent. I'd decided Sverri had somehow murdered Ingolf. How, I didn't know; the asking of why was simpler to answer. Ingolf had most strongly claimed Sverri a werewolf. Sverri had not liked those accusations. That was what I'd decided. But it was not the time to argue, not when we were lost in an unknown sea none had heard spoken of.

"Sverri is inhabited by the White Christ's devil," a voice from the deck said quietly. Thorvin's voice. "That is what made him attack that farmer. That is what made him a werewolf." The voice was sure. I heard Bjorn swear under his breath.

"Only Christians could believe such foolishness," Bjorn said. Like myself, Bjorn had refused to take the cross in his hands and the White Christ into his heart. Thorvin, however, had not refused.

"Sverri is a murderer. Perhaps he is even mad enough to wear the wolfskin and think he could murder and not be found out that way. Perhaps he even thinks himself a wolf. But he has no devil within him." I had let my voice carry too loud, and more of the crew were waking. But I had little patience for Christians, even for the ones on board, the ones I knew.

"I will pray for him," Thorvin said. "I will pray for you as well, Halfdan Haukadale and Bjorn Tryggvason, so you will take the White Christ into you. Someday you will see that your gods are false." I heard Bjorn snort again. How many of the twelve sane on our knorr were Christian? I wondered. "If you had prayed for a safe voyage before we left home, as we asked, this would not have happened." Bjorn did not answer then, but I could feel his hatred in the air.

"I do not believe you are the same man who went aviking with me," Bjorn said after several moments. "You were not so pious then, Thorvin, for I saw you slit more than one Irish monk's throat. You have had more than one Irish nun under you."

Thorvin was on his feet, his voice roaring in the darkness, the skittering sound of a blade pulling free of its scabbard filling my ears. But Bjorn already had a hand on his lance. He must have touched it before he spit his words on Thorvin. I stepped back, towards the edge of the deck, one hand grabbing a walrus-hide line to steady myself, the other reaching for the only weapon I had with me, my hand axe. It was unnecessary, for as quickly as it had started, it was finished.

Bjorn was standing, his foot planted on Thorvin's chest, his lance through Thorvin's shoulder, pinning him to the deck. Thorvin moaned softly; that was the only sound. I wondered if any of us even breathed during those moments. Then it was past, for Bjorn jerked out his lance point and threw the weapon to the deck. He was kneeling beside his friend, his hands wrapped around the man's chest. No one moved to help, or interfere, when Bjorn hefted Thorvin in his arms and carried him to the hold midships, then gently lifted him under the forward deck. Someone in the dark muttered under the sigh of the wind on the sail. Whether it was a curse, or a prayer to the White Christ, I could not tell.

It was not as if we did not have troubles enough to last us this voyage, I thought. Now we had to worry about this sudden division, as well as what Sverri had become, and the fact that we were far from the known world. It was too much for even a saga. Too much to live through.

●   ●   ●

The dawn came on us too slowly, for Sverri woke and began screaming once more, adding to the cries of Thorvín as he lay dying on a pallet below deck. Heltevir, Sverri's wife, tried to stem the blood from Thorvin's shoulder, but it was of little use. Bjorn's lance had probed too deeply. Bjorn stayed at the steering oar the remainder of the night, telling everyone who came near to go away. He would not even listen to me when I came to talk about our course.

My nose had been right, for when the light was strong enough, land loomed before us. It was not Groenland, for my sailing directions had said I would see high mountains with huge glaciers behind them. A coastline much like Ice Land, the man had said. But this land was low, only an occasional hill showing above the trees. That was the first thing I saw: the heavy green of the forests that stretched down all the way to the highwater mark, all the way to the cliffs that dropped into the sea. Even in the small bay before us, the trees walked almost into the very water, as if they were thirsty, or hungered for our ship.

"Thorvin is dead," a woman's voice behind me said. Heltevir would not look at me when I turned to her. Instead, her eyes were on the coastline off the port quarter. I could think of nothing to say.

"We will want to bury him here, I think," I finally said, to no one really, though Heltevir heard and nodded slowly. For some reason, though we had been out of sight of land for thirteen days, I did not want to step out of the ship onto that darkness of trees. Stupidity, I thought to myself, touching the hand axe next to me. There was no smoke curling above the trees, no savage Skraelings, the fierce natives the stories had warned about.

Then Sverri screamed again, and I touched Heltevir's arm; gently caressing it. What had we to fear from the

land when there was a werewolf among us? I could not
help but smile at the thought.

Bjorn threw the first handful of dirt into the grave. I
watched as it covered the hilt of Thorvin's sword and
splashed onto his sleeve. We'd laid him in a hole hacked
among the roots of the trees towering all around us, and
put the few things he'd brought with him alongside his
body. A sword, two spears, his leather cap and shield,
his axe, some meager food that we could ill spare.
Bjarni, a Christian like Thorvin, had asked to bury his
friend in their custom, but Bjorn had only stared him
into silence.

"Could I say a prayer for his soul?" Bjarni asked.
His words seemed to echo through the thick woods.
Bjorn was silent, only watched as two of the crew, Kare
and Ari, pushed the dirt back into the grave, then shoved
more on top to make the mound. We'd gathered rocks
earlier and I stooped down to set the first one in the soft
earth, pushing it until it was half covered. Bjorn and the
others helped make the outline of the boat that would
carry Thorvin to Valholl, but three of the men, Bjarni,
Thorstein, and Gudlief, stood to one side. Only three
Christians still with us, I thought. Unless some of the
others helping set the rocks had changed their beliefs
suddenly. It didn't matter, I decided, as long as they
didn't try to bury me in Christus style when I died.

"Say your prayer if you wish," Bjorn said to the three
Christians. "Thorvin is safe from the eaters of the dead,
and on his way to Odin's house. Nothing you mutter
now will hurt him." And he walked toward the beach
where the small afterboat was pulled clear of the water.
I watched him, glanced at the ship riding on the short
swells in the bay, and wondered if I should follow.

"Please, O Christ, listen to my prayer," Bjarni said,
his voice too pleading for my liking. "Save Thorvin's
soul so that he may see the gold of Heaven. Carry him

to your heart and protect him from your devil. Save, also, the soul of Sverri Tryggvason and return him to the living. Banish the devil in his soul." I could listen no longer, and left the grave then, pausing only to kick a stone deeper into the dirt.

The air was cleaner once I left the shadow of the woods, and I could breathe easier. Bjorn was sitting on the rock-strewn beach, flinging pebbles into the water.

"It's as if Sverri has cast a troll's spell over all of us," he said as I sat beside him. "Ingolf drowned, Thorvin murdered by my own hands. What will be next?" I shrugged my shoulders. "What is next, sailing master?"

"North, then east to Groenland," I said.

"Thorvin is the first one I have killed in manslaughter," Bjorn said. "Plenty of Irishmen, a few of those strange people south of Frisia, but those died when I went aviking. Not like Thorvin." I remembered the faces of those I'd killed, of the many that had perished under an *ulfhednar*'s axe. Only Sverri had made so many deaths, and again I wondered if he was truly a werewolf. Here, in the light, the thought almost made me laugh. In the darkness, I knew I might think different. Bjorn paused for a few moments, throwing more pebbles into the water. "Thorvin has two brothers and a father in Groenland."

That was why he worried. Not so much because he had murdered a friend, though that was enough to bother any man, but because of where we were to go. If Thorvin had living kin in Groenland, and they found out what had happened, as they surely would from Bjarni and the other Christians, then there would be a blood feud. Thorvin's kin would not rest until Bjorn and his family were dead. If it became bloody enough, it could extend even to those who had traveled and befriended a Tryggvason. Perhaps even me.

"I don't think the others will want to hear this," I said. The rest who had rowed with us from the knorr were still in the woods. How could they stand the darkness?

"You will stand with me," Bjorn said. "For Sverri, you will." He was right. I had left Ice Land because of my friendship with Sverri; I had done this much and could see little profit in stopping now. "We cannot go to Groenland," he said.

"What if we went to the Eastern Settlement instead?" I asked. Bjorn shook his head. I sighed and said, "They would find us eventually, I suppose."

"South?" he said, looking out into the bay at the ship. I could hear the voices of those returning from Thorvin's grave.

"If we did not have Sverri around our necks, we could go home. None of Thorvin's kin are there."

"You do not mean that," Bjorn said softly. I wondered if he was right; for Sverri's voice came back to me as it had two nights before, when we'd talked. A shadow fell over us and I squinted into the harsh light to see Bjarni. "Did you want to talk to me?" Bjorn asked him.

Bjarni, Thorstein, and Gudlief stood close together. Bjorn and I stood as well, and my hand went on its own to the hand axe in my belt. I noticed the others in the background, Heltevir in their front. She was brushing her hand through her long hair. Not for the first time, I thought of her hair in my hands, but thrust the thought aside. She was married, married to my friend, married to our werewolf.

"What is it, Bjarni?" Bjorn asked, his hands crossed over his chest.

"What matter is this of yours, sailing master?" Bjarni said, looking at me. "You are not standing with this murderer, are you?" I said nothing.

"You will be left to rot here, Bjarni," Bjorn said. "Put away your madness, and everything will be forgotten."

"Thorvin was buried a pagan, not as a follower of the White Christ should be. He was murdered by a pagan. We are here because of a pagan's crime in Ice Land. Thorvin has avengers in Groenland, Bjorn. You would not live long even if you did reach the Western Settlement." Bjarni stepped forward and pulled his sword free from his belt. Its blade glittered in the sunlight.

"Stop it!" a woman's voice shouted, and I saw Heltevir push her way through the three Christians. "Do you think this is Ireland, and you are all gone aviking? Listen then," she said as she stood between us, her eyes almost as dangerous as Bjarni's blade. I held my breath to listen, and heard Sverri's screams from the knorr riding in the bay. The sound echoed off the short cliffs bordering the sides of the bay, bounced from each of the thousands of trees. "Listen, stupid *vikingr*. That is why we are here in this wilderness. Do you think they will greet us with open arms in Groenland once they discover my husband? Do you think that they will welcome any of those who sailed with a werewolf? It doesn't matter if they are Christian or not, they will think the same. That we, too, may be like Sverri. We were stupid to think that we could escape. The first ship from home would tell them stories. It doesn't matter if Thorvin has kin or not; no one would have wanted us even if he was standing next to us now," she said.

Bjarni still held his sword, though the point had dropped until its tip was close to the rock and sand of the beach. Heltevir exhaled softly.

"We can only go south," Bjorn said. "We cannot go to Groenland, nor back home to Ice Land. We must go south, where it will be warmer for the winter. It will be here soon enough, two months, perhaps more if we sail far south." Bjarni still stood quietly. "If you wish, you may take the afterboat and sail north to Groenland, the three of you. Any others who wish to join them, as well," he said, his voice carrying over the water. "You can have your share of food, your weapons—''

His words were interrupted by another scream from the ship. It was almost a howl, Sverri's cry, almost like the sound of a wolf from the edge of the glaciers back home. But that was not what stopped Bjorn's words, for the screaming howl was not alone.

An answering cry came from across the bay, from deep in the woods it seemed. The answer was even throatier than Sverri's, and the hairs on my arms moved of their own will.

''Another?'' Bjarni whispered, and all I could think of was the memory of Sverri bent over the body of the farmer he'd murdered, yet now the face was different on the corpse. I tried to wipe my mind clean, but the face remained. It was my face. By Thor, mine.

''More wood, Eirik,'' a voice from the other side of the fire said, and the old man tossed another twisted piece of driftwood onto the blaze. Sparks climbed into the night air and I moved closer to the warmth. We had slept on ship the past four nights, and even though I had been glad, had felt safer with water between us and the noises that crowded the shores, the fire was comforting. Perhaps it had been only my imagination, but each night on ship I had believed I heard replies to Sverri's wolf howls. None of the others would talk of it, but each day everyone was more nervous than the last.

Heltevir was curled beside me, asleep, her woolen cloak tucked around her. I recognized it. Sverri had taken the red piece of cloth from a girl we'd not been able to force in our boat. Sverri had killed her quickly, a blade thrust through her stomach, and laughed. Two years ago and more. It seemed like it had never happened.

''How many on guard tonight?'' I asked the shape across the fire. We had seen no sign of Skraelings, the stooped and dark-skinned savages rumored to inhabit the unknown lands, but we would still post guard. There were other things besides savages to fear. Bjorn answered softly.

"Three. One by the afterboat, one near the fire, one by the treeline," he said. "Three hours and then wake another to take your place." The way he said "your," I knew he wanted me to take one of the first turns. But it was better than being on the ship another night.

The man next to me shuddered in the darkness. Not from the cold, for we were so far south that when the midday sun shone it was almost straight above us. "I never believed in trolls," he said. It was Bjarni. He and his Christians were still with us. Heltevir had been right; no one would have welcomed us with a werewolf in our company. Bjarni knew her reasoning had been sound. "It was not a devil of the White Christ, it had no horns like the priests have told me, so it had to be a troll. Am I right?" he asked. I didn't know what to say to him, for I had only heard the screams the night before, not seen what had crept on board.

"It was a troll," Eirik said, throwing more wood on the fire. Heltevir stirred beside me. "I saw it plain in the moonlight. It had huge shoulders, and long, stinking hair. Like the underside of turf when you dig it up for buildings. And his hands . . ."

"Shut up," Bjorn said, and in the sudden flame from the new wood, I saw his face. He was afraid.

"Let him talk," said Thorstein, the young man near Eirik. Even in the dim light, I could see Thorstein's auburn hair gleam from the oils he smeared into it each morning. He was a distant kin to Sverri, but a Christian friend to the dead Thorvin.

"It may help us all to talk of it," I said quickly, hoping to get my words out before Bjorn swore. But he was quiet this time.

"Trolls, yes, they were trolls," Eirik said again after some time. "And they had troll blades that gleamed in the dark.'' The old man was telling a story, that was plain. Who should know better than another saga teller? He had seen *something*, of that there was no doubt, but he was stretching details to hold us in his story. What matter, I thought, for the end was the same. Trolls or not, something had come aboard our ship the night before and slit two throats.

''. . . and the blades seemed alive, in a way. I heard Ari cry out, struggle against the troll, but before I could get to him, he was dead. Then Thorvold screamed, but everyone heard that,'' Eirik whispered. ''The trolls leaped back into the water and that was that.''

''Perhaps they were Skraelings,'' I said, wondering at the same time if it had been Sverri. But I said nothing of that fear. He'd been bound with leather thongs since we'd sailed. How could he have done this?

''We've seen no signs of anyone,'' Eirik said. He was not going to give up on his troll stories so easily.

''That doesn't mean there is no one there. Just because we see no smoke, nor houses, doesn't mean Skraelings couldn't be about,'' I said. I stared into the flames for a moment, then jerked my head up as I heard a scream-howl from the ship. We'd left Sverri alone on the knorr. No one could stand his sounds any longer. Perhaps a troll, or whatever had killed Ari and Thorvold, would creep aboard again and rid us of our werewolf. That was not a friend's way of thinking, I knew, but I wondered how many of us still thought of ourselves as friends of Sverri.

''It doesn't matter who they were,'' Bjorn said and Bjarni muttered agreement. ''We can't stay on the ship any longer. There's not enough room to swing a blade on it.'' He looked at the fire. *That* was something else we couldn't have on the knorr. The fire's warmth was comforting after so long sleeping cold, but the light was what made me feel safe. We might see what came to attack us this time.

"I'll take the treeline," I said as I stood and reached for my axe. Its haft felt good in my hand. The light from the fire quickly dimmed as I walked up the beach and towards the trees. The wall of them was complete; there was no break in their solidness. What kind of men crept onto your ship and murdered you in your sleep, I wondered as I sat on a fallen tree and tried to see through the darkness. Not a brave man. Not a man that had been aviking. Like one of those in Wales, who shot at you from afar with those strange bows of theirs.

Away from the voices of the others, I could hear Sverri's screams more plainly. Every time he howled, I winced, trying to will myself to stop, but it was impossible. The sough of the trees only half-covered his noises, and even when I pressed my hands over my ears, I could still hear him. For a moment, I thought of swimming out to the ship and slitting his throat, knowing that the others would think another troll came to us. But the thought passed by, and eventually, I fell asleep.

I must have fallen asleep. I must have been dreaming when Sverri walked from the treeline and sat down beside me on the downed log. I was dreaming, so I did not fear him, even when he smiled and spoke to me.

"Halfdan, my friend," he said, "how is it that you are out here?"

Since I was dreaming, I answered. What harm in that? "Guard for the others," I said.

"Don't you want to know how I escaped the bindings?" he asked. I shook my head. "Ah, you believe this is a nightmare. It isn't, you know."

My axe was not in my hand; it must have fallen to the ground when I dozed. Now I wished it was in my hand, for something in Sverri's voice made me believe him. I touched his shoulder with my hand, and it was solid under his woolen shirt. He was no dream.

"How did you get off the ship?" I asked. I tried to

look from the corners of my eyes for my axe, but I couldn't see it in the darkness.

"Do you believe, Halfdan?" Again the question of believing.

"In what?"

"In what I am."

"You talk with riddles, Sverri," I said, wondering if I could shout out for the others.

"It is in here, you know," he said, pointing to his head. There was light enough from the moon to see that. "Your belief is in here," he said again.

"Did you kill Ari and Thorvold?" Perhaps there were no trolls, nor Skraelings, who slit throats.

"Do you think I did?" It was useless, Sverri would never answer straight. My fright was past, and though I wished to feel my axe in my hand, I was not afraid of Sverri. How could I be? His voice was soft and sane, the same voice that had spoken to me for long years of friendship, the same voice that had comforted me in crazed battle for the King. What reason would he have to harm me? Even if he killed Ari and Thorvold—for whatever reason—I was safe. My friendship was my shield.

He stood and walked towards the trees, leaving me on the fallen log. Before he stepped into the woods, he turned back and looked at me. The shadows flickered over him, seeming to change his shape with every moment.

"I am what you believe me to be, that is all," he said and the shadows changed again as the trees behind him moved. For the span of a breath, as my doubts returned, I stared and thought I saw a wolf, the gray hairs on its neck gleaming in the moonlight, its eyes yellow and blinking, but then it was gone. I rubbed my eyes hard, but there was nothing there; only trees and shadows.

Shouts reached me. The night was bright, too bright even for the full moon. Then I saw it. The knorr was ablaze from bow to stern, and the only thing I could think of was how strange the woodsmoke smelled as it waved towards the beach.

"Get the boat into the water," Bjorn's voice shouted. "Fast, before it's to the keel!" I could see several figures shove the afterboat from the beach and then jump into it as it slammed through the breakers.

I ran to the beach and grabbed the first man I came to. It was Thorstein, and he stammered from the excitement.

"Sverri's l-loose," he said, pointing to the ship. "Bjarni said he saw him leap over the side and swim for shore, just before the ship caught fire. Who would have thought . . ." he said, but I didn't let him finish, and instead ran down the shore. It was too late for me to help fight the fire on board; the men in the afterboat would have to do. I had to find Sverri.

My eyes were wide now, not half-closed by sleep. But it was useless looking for him here on the beach. He had struck for the trees, away from the light and the fire he'd set to hide his escape. I began calling for him, yelling his name out every few moments. Perhaps he was sane enough still to come to his name.

A screech of a howl answered me, and I turned to the sound, my arms suddenly far colder than they should have been. He was there, in the forest.

"Sverri!" I shouted. "Sverri, it's Halfdan. It's safe. Sverri!" I waited, and within a moment, his howl reached me. It was farther away this time. He was moving deeper into the woods.

He was truly a werewolf. Until this moment, I had not believed it. No matter what those farmer's sons had said they'd seen attack their father; no matter what Bjorn said about the wolfskin around Sverri's waist. Even Sverri's own words had not convinced me. Until now I had thought it all just troll-stories, like the tales I'd spun enough times in a safe and dry longhouse. But for that brief moment I believed in werewolves.

I stood beside the first tree at the edge of the woods, and wanted to go in after him, but I could not force myself to do it. My legs were weak, and my throat was dry, and the axe in my hand was almost too heavy to hold. So I turned away from the dark trees, and walked back to the beach, my eyes on the knorr, the fire still burning in it. Sverri's screams continued to weaken in the distance.

I joined the three who stood on the beach and watched as the ship burned. There were five fighting the blaze, then, for now there were only nine of us. Though the light from the fire was bright, it seemed smaller since I'd first seen it.

"I think it was only the sail," Heltevir's voice said beside me in the dark. "Hope that is all he did," she said. A man next to her grunted a reply. I put my hand on Heltevir's arm and she moved closer to me, her warmth pressed against my side. "What will we do for Sverri?" she asked quietly. No one answered her.

We waited on the shore, watching the fire dwindle on the knorr, then looked hard into the half-dawn as the afterboat rowed toward us. The five men in it were soot-stained and singed around their eyes. Bjorn climbed over the afterboat's thwart slowly, almost falling into the water. I moved to help him and we stumbled onto the sand. He fell to the ground, rolled over on his back, and breathed deeply.

"Can she sail?" I asked him, kneeling on the sand next to him. It took him moments to catch his breath.

"In time," he finally said. "The sail is gone, the mast is charred and weakened. It will have to be replaced. The animals are dead and part of the foredeck is burned through. It could have been worse." He paused. "Where is Sverri?" Bjorn asked, looking up at me. The light

was enough to see his face now, though the sun had yet
to rise over the water.

"Gone into the woods," I said. "I tried to follow
him." Bjorn was silent. "I did not want to go into the
trees to follow him," I said, and breathed easier when
Bjorn and the others nodded. They would not have followed him, either.

"Sverri will return," Heltevir said in a whisper, her
gaze on the forest to our backs. She was still pressed
against me. "He will get lonely and come back to us
before we leave."

I remembered my certainty that he was a true werewolf, and again had doubts. How could he be a shape-
shifter when we had spent our lives together? How could
he have hidden it from me? I recalled his voice, and the
vision of the wolf I'd seen, and wondered which was
true. What should I believe? Yet I knew that if Sverri
came back to us, it would not be because he was lonely.
If he was sane, and only a murderer, it would be because
he was angry at the bindings he'd worn since we'd
sailed; if he was truly a werewolf, it would be because
he was hungry and could not find anthing else to feed
on. For the first time since we'd sighted this terrible
land, I wished it held Skraelings. Sverri would prey on
those before he came to us, I hoped.

The winds swept over the bay and thundered against the
turf walls of the longhouse we crowded in. There had
been little to do since the storms had come for the winter
except spend our time telling stories, talking about the
voyage and what we had done and seen. That was the
only consolation; that we had done and seen things no
other dreamed of. We listened to the wind, listened to
the noises from the woods that were still troll-filled to
us, listened to the howls of the wolves that roamed the
edges of the forest. Whether the howls were from real
wolves, or from Sverri, it was impossible to tell. I tried

to believe they were real, but it was not always easy.

We had pulled the knorr onto the shore long before and built low walls around her to keep the water out. It took several days, but we finally got her turned over and a vessel shed made so the ice would not split the strakes and make her unable to hold water. The new mast was cut and shaped, but not fitted. It would have to wait until spring.

The longhouse was not large enough for us all, especially since it was dangerous to venture outside for more than a few minutes at a time. The two benches that ran along the walls were barely large enough to hold us all when we slept, even when we had two guards awake during the dark hours.

Thorstein said he saw Sverri near the cliffs on the far side of the bay. He was in his human shape, Thorstein said, but he changed before his eyes into a wolf. I did not doubt his word. Signs of Skraelings were all about as well. Footprints along the shore, the glint of something bright moving in the hills behind us, a butchered caribou far in the trees. We had not been quiet as we cut wood, or fished from the afterboat. They knew we were here, but they did not show themselves. Perhaps they were afraid of us; though I wagered they were more afraid of the werewolf that haunted the edge of our camp.

"He has been gone too long," Bjarni said. I chewed on a piece of dried fish. "Three hours is too long," he said, looking at each of us in turn.

"Snorri can take care of himself," Bjorn said. Bjorn should know; Snorri was *his* house slave. "He has good reason to be gone this long. The snow is deep."

"We could look for him," Bjarni said.

"And get lost as well?" Thorstein asked, looking up from the piece of bone he whittled on.

"Something should be done," Bjarni said again, his

voice quivering slightly. I wondered if he had renounced his faith in the White Christ yet. The other two Christians, Thorstein and Gudlief, had. Cold winds and werewolves were too strong for the White Christ, it seemed.

Another howl came from outside the turf walls and everyone looked up. It was close, that one. Very close.

I reached for my axe and went for the door. Bjorn was right behind me, and the others grabbed their weapons to follow us. The wind held the door closed for a moment, but I pushed hard and forced it open, then stepped into the snow. Light and powdery, it flattened easily, though even one step was work. The paths we'd beaten down in the snow before were covered by the recent fall. The howl came again, off to the left, in the trees not twenty paces away.

"What are you waiting for?" Bjorn's voice asked from behind me. I had stopped and not known it. My arms were cold, even through the thick furs.

"What?" I said, looking into the dimness of the trees, believing that I saw two points of light blink once, twice, three times.

"Move aside if you are going to stand and shake," Bjorn said loudly, pushing me to one side as he lunged through the snow for the trees. His lance was pointed up and in front of him, but still he was lucky when the wolf leaped from the woods.

I closed my eyes for only a moment, my heart thick in my mouth from my fear. I heard screams behind me, and the sound of teeth in front of me. Then I was myself, my axe lifted high above my shoulder, my eyes wide open.

The wolf had leaped onto Bjorn's lance point, and was struggling to escape. I could see the dull point jutting from the wolf's back. Bjorn was under the wolf, his hands in front of his face, warding off the death snaps of the wolf's mouth. I stepped forward, and swung the axe hard onto the wolf's neck. The axe was still sharp and cleaved the head from the body easily. Only then did I realize I was screaming like a beserker, only then did I feel the sweat slipping down my back and sides under my thick furs.

Bjorn wiggled from underneath the dead wolf, and yanked his lance from the carcass. We all waited for the shape-shifting that we thought would come when the dead wolf flickered into the form of Sverri, for we all believed at that moment that the dead animal was no more wolf than any of us. But the beast's shape remained constant, and it was growing colder by the minute. The wolf's open neck finished steaming and still it was only a wolf.

A howl sounded across the ice of the bay. A dim chorus of the sounds reached us all, repeated. The blood on my axe was frozen, I noticed.

"Snorri is still out there," Bjarni said, his breath billowing in the cold air. "We must find him before dark."

"Before more of these find him, you mean," I said, pointing to the wolf on the snow.

"He is dead," Bjorn said. His voice was final.

"You cannot be sure," Bjarni said. "He could be close by, hurt perhaps by a wolf."

"Bjorn is right," I said. "Snorri is dead. He has been gone almost four hours. There are too many wolves to count around us." My unsaid words were clear to all; *Sverri may be near, Sverri may have killed again.* Was our friendship enough to protect me now?

"We could make sledges from the wood of the afterboat and pull them across the ice," Thorstein said, his oily hair glistening with the snow that continued to fall. The idea was ridiculous, but we were desperate. In the background, Eirik coughed quietly. He coughed too often, lately, and I wondered how long he would live before an illness took him.

"None of us would see home," I said, turning for the house almost lost in the swirlings of the snow. It was too cold, too dangerous, to remain here and talk. Sverri could be listening behind the nearest tree, he could be calling his new-found friends down on us within the span of a breath. I walked for the house, past the men who, like myself, had once called themselves *vibingr*, but who now whispered for fears of trolls and were-wolves. If I had not been so frightened, I would have taken the temptation and laughed.

The next three days we spent inside, not daring to venture where the wolves could get to us. We even pissed in the corner, throwing dirt into the hole after each use. The smell was enough to force tears, but the fear was stronger. None of us wanted to end like Snorri, more likely than not buried somewhere in the forest under a snowdrift. We talked louder with each passing night, trying to drown out the sounds of the wolves, but it did no good, for sooner or later we had to sleep, or pretend to, and then the noises came through the walls.

"It's mad to sit here and listen to them, all the night and day," shouted Bjarni from his bedroll. It was dark in the house, the only light from the hearth at the center of the room. All of us were awake now. "They've got to stop!" he yelled, louder this time. "Stop it, make them stop it!" I was up and out of my furs, but there was already someone leaning over Bjarni, soothing him. Heltevir, perhaps. But it was doing no good. "Leave me be," Bjarni screamed and there was a thud of a body on the dirt floor. Then the door burst open and a needle-like spray of snow swept into the room. Bjarni was outlined in the doorway by the light of the moon on the snow. He had his sword in his hands, its tip pointed into the air.

"Sverri!" he screamed. "Sverri, you pagan, come to me. Come give your soul to the Christ, Sverri. You will thank me for it." He yelled each word into the wind, then ran from the doorway into the storm. By the time I reached the door, he was invisible in the snow, his tracks before the doorway already drifting shut. Thorstein, one of his once-Christian friends, wanted to push past me and follow, but I held him tightly.

"Are you as mad as he? He will be dead before he can breathe and shout another curse. Do you want to join the White Christ that much?" Thorstein struggled briefly, but not seriously. He knew I was right.

It was not as crowded in the long house now that there were only seven of us. We sat, most of the time in silence, and listened to the sounds from outside. Increasingly, we were on each others' nerves, taunting each other with silly things that should not have mattered.

Finally, the weather broke and the wolves disappeared with the storms. The snow melted quickly, faster than I had ever seen it in Ice Land. The ground seemed to swallow the snow in great gulps. It left acres of mud where the beach's sand and rocks ended. But at least Sverri and his kind were gone.

It was not yet spring, for the sun was not climbing high enough for that, but the clear, cold air made us feel human again, and we used the time well, getting things ready to sail once the ice in the bay broke. The sail was pieced together with what spare cloth we'd been able to salvage from the knorr, the hull was tarred with seal fat, and we split some of the immense birch trees for planking on the foredeck. Bjorn and I checked the knorr, looking for places where ice had gotten between the hull strakes, but the ship was sound.

We went nowhere without our weapons. Skraeling signs were everywhere, as well as wolf tracks that crisscrossed the mud and ended in the trees. Of Bjarni we found no trace, though we found Snorri's lances thrust in the ground at the edge of the forest. One was broken, another had pieces of fur and feather tied to its shaft. Both the fur and feather were colored red, the color of dried blood, Bjorn thought. It was not actually blood, for it flaked off too easily. It was some sort of smeared paint. Skraelings? We could not decide.

The fifth day after the weather broke, I was gathering firewood at the edge of the trees, one eye watching the green darkness, one hand on my axe. But he still surprised me. Sverri had walked up behind me, and I hadn't heard a sound.

"Hello, Halfdan," he said, and I shouted and whirled all in one moment, swinging my axe in front of me. He was several feet out of reach, and he smiled as I let the axe drop. It was Sverri, by the gods, and he wore an *ulfhednar's* wolfshirt around his waist.

"Sverri," was all I could manage to croak.

"You do not believe still, Halfdan?" he asked. He spread his arms wide, as if he was inviting attack, then the smile still on his face, let his arms fall to his sides, his thumbs hooked in the wolfskin. I turned to see if there was any other in sight, but they were all in the longhouse, or the vessel shed. I did not want to cry out.

"What of Snorri and Bjarni?" I asked. "What have you done with them?" Sverri said nothing, only smiled. "Are you werewolf?" Again, no answer. I pulled my axe up to my chest and stepped forward toward him, but he only danced back lightly.

"I am what you believe I am," he said, speaking in riddles. Normally, I take fun at a riddle as easily as the next man, but not from this thing that was Sverri.

"And if I believe you to be a harmless rabbit that I can split with this," I said, holding my axe higher, "then that is what you are?"

"If you believe." He paused. "But you will not believe that I am a rabbit. I know you too well, Halfdan. You believe me a friend who will not harm you. But not a rabbit." He was right. No matter how I tried to imagine it, he was not a rabbit. In the bright sun I could not even believe he was a werewolf. He seemed too much like the friend he had always been. I realized, even with my brief doubts, that I'd always thought him this. Perhaps mad at times, but a friend.

"Why did you burn the ship, Sverri?" I asked. I had the feeling that if I did not keep his attention with questions, he would flee. Or worse.

"The Skraelings think me a god," he said, ignoring my question. "They are like children, in a way. I am going to stay with them, did you know that?" I shook my head. "You will leave when the ice breaks?"

"If the ship is ready."

"With only six men and a woman to sail her?" He did know Snorri and Bjarni were dead. We stared at each other for a long while before he spoke again. "Leave as quickly as you're able. Do not linger here. Tell Bjorn that for me." And he turned and was gone, almost as if into the air, for he moved so quickly into the trees that he was gone before I'd taken one breath.

I told no one of speaking with Sverri, just as I had not said anything of the first two times. No one felt love for Sverri, and I did not think any would take kindly to one talking to a madman. The madness might spread, they would certainly think.

But I thought long of what Sverri had said. He had spoken as sane as any of us, though his words and eyes had been unsettling. Why did he treasure the Skraelings so? What did they give him that he needed? What was it that we could not provide him?

"Halfdan! Halfdan, here!" Heltevir shouted from the low doorway. I turned from the broken lance I was tying together and the look of fear on her face made me stand and run to her. She looked out the door, and I followed her gaze. Down on the beach Bjorn and the others stood uneasily as a crowd of Skraelings walked towards them. At least three dozen, I thought.

They halted once they were within a score of steps from my friends. I reached behind me for an axe and ran to Bjorn, but the Skraelings did not seem to even notice me.

"We will be killed if they want it," Bjorn said to me. He held his sword in one hand, a shield in the other. At least everyone was armed, I saw, looking down the short line to Eirik, Kare, Thorstein, and Gudlief. Six against thirty-six; a battle would not last long.

The Skraelings were tall, almost as tall as I. Their hair was dark and hung loose about their shoulders, as mine did. There the likeness ended. They were red, completely red, for they had smeared something over their hair, their faces, and their bodies. Its color reminded me of the paint spread on the feather and fur we'd found tied to Bjarni's broken lance. And their eyes. They were wide, wider than any I had seen, the brown circle inside the eye wider than my thumb.

One walked apart from the others, and as he stepped forward, I heard Thorstein hiss. "Kill him now," were the only words I could catch. But Bjorn stayed where he was and did not even raise his sword, for the Skraeling was stepping carefully to us, his hands held in front of him, the palms pointed up to show he held no weapon. He spoke in some savage tongue that I could not comprehend. Pointing to the ground, then to the forest, he nodded several times, then pointed back to us, all the while talking quickly as if we understood. He smiled, shook his head, smiled again, then pointed to the woods again.

"What does he say?" Heltevir asked from behind me. She had followed me from the longhouse. I wanted to tell her to go back, but I saw she held a lance. If the Skraelings decided to kill us, she would be as dead in the longhouse as here. Perhaps she might kill some herself if they threw themselves on us, so I said nothing. She wore the red cloak Sverri had given her long ago.

The Skraeling talked quickly, pointing to us again, then to himself. We were nervous, for it seemed he

would order his people to attack, but he only motioned
one man forward. The second Skraeling threw a pile of
furs on the ground before us, then stepped back. Eirik
leaned down and felt one of the pelts. "I've never seen
anything like this," he said, and the first Skraeling
grated a word or two out. The name of the beast whose
fur it was?

I reached behind me to Heltevir, and pulled the cloak
from her shoulders. Ripping a small piece from it before
she could say anything, I walked to the Skraeling and
handed it to him. He stared at the red cloth, held it
against his own red skin, then waved it above his head.
The red of the cloak was far brighter than the paint
they'd smeared themselves with. The Skraeling seemed
to think highly of the cloth, for he motioned another man
forward who threw more pelts onto the ground. We were
already wealthy men, for I knew the furs would bring
us enough silver to last a season of drinking.

The red cloth was quickly torn into enough pieces for
all the Skraelings, and they in turn made piles of furs in
front of each of us. One by one, each of the furs were
named by the Skraelings, but the sounds were too
strange and did not stick in my mind. Until the leader
of the savages stepped forward, a wolfskin held out in
front of him, and said "Sverri," loud enough for all to
hear.

It was suddenly silent, the only noise the waves on
the sand to our right. Gudlief crossed himself in the
manner of the White Christ; Bjorn muttered under his
breath and stepped backward without knowing it.

"Sverri," the Skraeling said again. The word was gar-
bled, but understandable. It was certainly the name of
our friend. The Skraeling held out the wolfskin again,
expecting us to take it, I thought.

Thorstein and Gudlief whispered to each other, and I
felt Heltevir's hand on my arm. "Can that be his skin?"
I heard Bjorn ask, but no one answered.

"Sverri?" the Skraeling said, stepping forward and thrusting the wolf's pelt into Bjorn's face.

"By Thor . . ." Bjorn hissed, then moved back under the Skraeling's pressure. I saw Bjorn's sword moving in his hand.

"Sverri, Sverri, Sverri," said the Skraeling, stepping forward with each word. He pointed to us, then to the forest, then back to us, shaking his head, saying the name over and over.

"They want Sverri," I said, suddenly understanding the Skraeling's actions. He wanted to trade the wolfskin for our werewolf, for Sverri. The wolfskin they tried to give us was payment for Sverri, *was* Sverri in their minds. "Bjorn, they want to take Sverri from us," I said, turning to our werewolf's brother, but it was too late.

Bjorn was silent, but his face was blue with anger. His sword was above his shoulder and already arcing to the Skraeling's throat. I tried to reach for Bjorn's arm, but he was too fast, and before I could suck in a breath, the Skraeling's head was cut from his neck. Blood flew onto my shirt and the madness was on us.

The Skraelings screamed, and threw their hands into the air, but we gave them no quarter. At first I tried to stop Bjorn and the others, but it was useless, for the blood lust was in them and they were mad. Then the Skraelings broke for the trees, and quickly the air was filled with arrows like the ones the Welsh shoot with their bows. Eirik went to ground, an arrow through his throat, and he flopped as a fish does before he died. Gudlief caught two in his legs and he screamed as he fell.

It was over as easily as it had started. The Skraelings were gone, all fled into the woods, all except the ones dead on the beach. Eight, I counted altogether. One stirred, pierced by a lance, but Thorstein drew his knife and put the man to sleep. Bjorn leaned over his knees and breathed heavily. His shield was full of arrows, and his hands were red from the dead Skraelings. I let my axe drop into the sand and knelt beside it and I was sick. I'd killed two of them, and they had not even raised their hands to shield their faces. Somehow it was different than killing Irishmen.

I dimly heard Gudlief moaning in the distance, and Kare's voice trying to comfort him, but did not concern myself with it. We had to leave as soon as possible, I knew now. The Skraelings would be back for revenge, that was certain, and with their numbers, we would not live long in their attack.

"They have killed Sverri," I heard Bjorn say. I looked up, and he was talking to Heltevir. "That was his skin they cut from him."

"No," I said, wiping my mouth and the sourness from it. "They wished to trade for Sverri. The wolfskin was ours if we would leave Sverri with them. They think Sverri is a god."

Bjorn looked at me. "How do you know this?"

What could I tell him? The truth, that Sverri himself had told me this? Or some lie Bjorn would surely see through? "I've spoken with Sverri three times since we sailed. Last night he told me this. He said they thought him a god, and warned us to leave." It was the truth, though it did not sound like it, even to my own ears, when I said it aloud. But Bjorn believed it; his face showed that he did.

Heltevir spoke next. "You talked with him?" I nodded. "Then he was not mad?"

"Not always," I said.

"We must leave in the morning," Bjorn said.

"The ship isn't ready. We have the mast to fit . . ." I began.

"The afterboat will do. Four men could not sail the knorr. If we ran into any storms, we would drown." He was right. With Eirik dead and Gudlief unable to stand, for his legs were surely broken by the arrows, we did not have enough hands for the knorr. The six of us would fit into the afterboat, though it would be a tight sailing. "Everything but food and water and weapons must be left," Bjorn said. "Even those," he said, pointing to the furs still piled on the beach. A pity, for they would have made us rich.

We spent the rest of the day burying Eirik and readying the afterboat for the morning. All our possessions that we could not take with us we threw in a heap next to the longhouse. The furs from the Skraelings were tossed on top, then we added a layer of wood. When we left, we would put the torch to it all. There was no use leaving it for the Skraelings.

Night came too quickly, and we huddled in the longhouse, the fire bright, our weapons in our hands. We tried to talk of the battle, Bjorn even started to draw up a verse or two for it, but his heart was not in it. We all thought too often of Sverri and the Skraelings.

I waited until they were all asleep. Only Gudlief was awake, but his pain occupied him. I didn't think he saw me slip outside.

The moon was new, and the darkness was thick around my eyes. I waited until I was used to it, then stepped away from the longhouse towards the woods. The trees were impossible to see. I could tell where they were only because they were darker than everything else. I stumbled many times, hitting my shins on logs, but I finally decided I'd come far enough from the house, and found a dead tree to sit on. I was not sure what I was waiting for, but I knew I had to wait.

"Sverri, old friend," I said to the shadow that moved in front of me. My arms were cold, and the axe heavy in my hands, but I kept my voice level. What if it was not Sverri, but a real wolf, or a vengeful Skraeling?

"Halfdan Haukadale," he said. It was Sverri, and I breathed easier. "You did not take my advice, Halfdan."

"We leave in the morning," I said.

"I told them that you would be dangerous," Sverri said. "But they wanted to see their god's companions, and trade."

"They offered skins for you," I whispered.

"I told them you were dangerous, but I didn't try to stop them. A god cannot stop his children from foolishness, can he?" Sverri paused. "Yet I did not expect your thirst . . ."

"It was over before it started. Bjorn thought the skin was yours, and he went mad. I could not stop him . . ."

"You tried so hard you killed as well," Sverri said.

He had been watching from the woods that morning, then. "We leave in the morning," I said again.

"The ship is not ready."

"We leave it behind. The afterboat will take us east. Perhaps all the way to Ireland. If we do not talk in our drink, no one there will know we sailed with a werewolf."

Sverri was quiet there in the darkness before me. He sighed and I wondered what he thought.

"Come with us," I said. "You are sane, Sverri. Come with us."

"Is that what you believe, Halfdan? That I am sane?" Still, the talk of believing. "The Skraelings believe me to be a god. A god who can alter his shape at will," Sverri said. In the darkness, it was difficult to see, but I can swear I saw Sverri's outline shiver, then slip into that of a wolf. Hot, sour breath came to my nose and the sound of an animal panting to my ears. Then the outline shivered again, and Sverri was there. "I am what is believed, Halfdan. In Ice Land, or Groenland, or even Ireland, what would they believe? That I was a god? I do not think so. A murderer, perhaps, like those farmers thought me, but no god. It would be the same everywhere. Werewolves do not kill for food; they kill for pleasure. That is what I would have to do, then."

I began to understand his concern with believing. "Then Snorri and Bjarni, Ari and Thorvold?" I asked softly.

"Their beliefs were too strong to ignore," Sverri said. "They died of what they believed would harm them here. Ari and Thorvold wondered of trolls, Snorri and Bjarni believed I was a werewolf. They believed they would be murdered, so that was what happened."

"And the Skraelings do not," I said. I thought I saw Sverri nod in the dark. "You wish to remain here, where you will not have to kill." Again, I thought I saw movement. "What *are* you, Sverri?"

"What you believe," he whispered. "You believe me to be a friend, a man, a sane man, so that is what I am for you."

"For Bjorn? And Heltevir?"

"They believe other things. I would murder Bjorn and become a madman for my wife. That is what they believe."

"Were you ever a man, Sverri?" I remembered the days long ago when we'd gone aviking and he had laughed as he killed a girl in Ireland. "Were you ever human, Sverri?"

"While that is what everyone thought of me, I was a man," He was quiet for some time. "While we were *ulfhednar* for the King, I changed, Halfdan. Too many enemies of the King believed the *ulfhednar* power, that we were truly werewolves in battle, and so it all began. Too many believed to ignore. Home to Ice Land was no different. Even Heltevir thought me changed from those two years with the *ulfhednar*. I was a man until the King called for me. But beliefs change, Halfdan."

So they did, for in the darkness there with Sverri, I wondered what would happen if I had doubts of my beliefs. I thought him a sane man, a friend who would not harm me, and so he was. What if that belief slipped from me and I thought him a werewolf, as Bjorn so

obviously did? My answer came swiftly, for the hot
breath reached my nose again, and a low growl came
from the shape I knew would be that of a wolf, if only
I had light enough to see. The image passed, and again
it was only Sverri.

"Your belief is strong, Halfdan."

"Luck to you, Sverri." I stood and held out my hand,
groping for his shoulder. Then it was there and I felt his
hand on my shoulder. His fingers gripped my shirt tight.

"Thank you, Halfdan Haukadale. You always thought
me a friend. I had no desire to be anything else for you."
And his hand slipped from me and he was gone, through
the trees, heading to the Skraelings who thought him a
god. And so he was one.

It was near dawn and I felt more tired than I had ever
felt before. I wanted to sleep, forget everything Sverri
had said. I knew I would not, and that thought tired me
even more.

The wind and the currents were strong and though it had
been only eighteen days since we sailed from Sverri's
Land, already we had seen hints of land. First there was
green moss in the water, and then several birds. They
were the kind who lived in the south of Ireland, so that
was where we would make landfall, I believed.

I believed. Two small words, but the difference between living and dying in the wilderness. I had tried to
tell Bjorn, Heltevir, Kare, Thorstein, even crippled Gudlief, of what I knew, but the words always came out
wrong, and they only looked at me strangely, as if I was
a Skraeling and spoke an unknown tongue. Whether they
believed me was not my concern. Their beliefs were
their own, after all.

As we neared landfall, I could only remember when
we left Sverri's Land. It was gray, and colder than it
should have been, but we waded into the water, pushing
the afterboat in front of us. When the water was deep

enough, we each climbed in. Bjorn set the sail while I held the steering oar.

We each looked back one last time, seeing the smoke from the pile of goods we had set afire rather than leave to the Skraelings. There was movement in the trees, and then a figure stepped out of the darkness and onto the beach. Heltevir cried out, and Bjorn swore, but I only looked.

It was Sverri, waving farewell to us, a group of Skraelings behind him in the woods. He had on his leather helmet, a lance in his hand. He was just as when we went aviking together so many years ago, before the King called us to become *ulfhednar*, and forced the change on Sverri.

What Bjorn and the rest saw, I had no way of knowing, though I had guesses I thought would have been on the mark. A wolf, a madman, what did it matter? He was what he was, that was all. Each according to his own desires.

I was happy with what I believed, and would not exchange it for all the gold crosses in the White Christ's heaven. *Beliefs change, Halfdan,* Sverri had said to me in the dark that lastnight. *I hope not, old friend.*

For if they do, who then would you be?

BOOBS

Suzy McKee Charnas

"Boobs" was purchased by Gardner Dozois, and appeared in the July 1989 issue of Asimov's, *with an interior illustration by Laura Lakey. Charnas has only made two sales to* Asimov's *to date, but they've both been memorable, and critically acclaimed, stories. Her most recent* Asimov's *story, "Beauty and the Opera or the Phantom Beast," was a finalist for the World Fantasy Award, and her first sale to us, the controversial story that follows—a compelling and unflinching look at a troubled young girl's bizarre Coming-Of-Age—won her a well-deserved Hugo Award in 1989.*

Born in Manhattan, Suzy McKee Charnas spent some time with the Peace Corps in Nigeria, and now resides in New Mexico with her family. She first made her reputation with the well-known SF novel Walk to the End of the World *and its sequel* Motherlines. *Her fantasy novel/collection* The Vampire Tapestry *(one of the first "revisionist" looks at the vampire legend, and still one of the best) was one of the most popular and critically acclaimed fantasies of the seventies; a novella from it, "Unicorn Tapestry," won her a Nebula Award in 1980. Her other books include the novels* Dorothea Dreams, The Bronze King, The Silver Glove, *and* The Golden Thread, *and a chapbook collection,* Moonstone and Tiger Eye.

The thing is, it's like your brain wants to go on thinking about the miserable history midterm you have to take tomorrow, but your body takes over. And what a body! You can see in the dark and run like the wind and leap parked cars in a single bound.

Of course you pay for it next morning (but it's worth it). I always wake up stiff and sore, with dirty hands and feet and face, and I have to jump in the shower fast so Hilda won't see me like that.

Not that she would know what it was about, but why take chances? So I pretend it's the other thing that's bothering me. So she goes, "Come on, sweetie, everybody gets cramps, that's no reason to go around moaning and groaning. What are you doing, trying to get out of school just because you've got your period?"

If I didn't like Hilda, which I do even though she is only a stepmother instead of my real mother, I would show her something that would keep me out of school forever, and it's not fake, either.

But there are plenty of people I'd rather show that to.

I already showed that dork Billy Linden.

"Hey, Boobs!" he goes, in the hall right outside Homeroom. A lot of kids laughed, naturally, though Rita Frye called him an asshole.

Billy is the one that started it, sort of, because he always started everything, him with his big mouth. At the beginning of term, he came barreling down on me hollering, "Hey, look at Bornstein, something musta happened to her over the summer! What happened, Bornstein? Hey, everybody, look at Boobs Bornstein!"

He made a grab at my chest, and I socked him in the shoulder, and he punched me in the face, which made me dizzy and shocked and made me cry, too, in front of everybody.

I mean, I always used to wrestle and fight with the boys, being that I was strong for a girl. All of a sudden it was different. He hit me hard, to really hurt, and the shock sort of got me in the pit of my stomach and made me feel nauseous, too, as well as mad and embarrassed to death.

I had to go home with a bloody nose and lie with my head back and ice wrapped in a towel on my face and dripping down into my hair.

Hilda sat on the couch next to me and patted me. She goes, "I'm sorry about this, honey, but really, you have to learn it sometime. You're all growing up and the boys are getting stronger than you'll ever be. If you fight with boys, you're bound to get hurt. You have to find other ways to handle them."

To make things worse, the next morning I started to bleed down there, which Hilda had explained carefully to me a couple of times, so at least I knew what was going on. Hilda really tried extra hard without being icky about it, but I hated when she talked about how it was all part of these exciting changes in my body that are so important and how terrific it is to "become a young woman."

Sure. The whole thing was so messy and disgusting, worse than she had said, worse than I could imagine, with these black clots of gunk coming out in a smear of pink blood—I thought I would throw up. That's just the lining of your uterus, Hilda said. Big deal. It was still gross.

And plus, the *smell*.

Hilda tried to make me feel better, she really did. She said we should "mark the occasion" like primitive people do, so it's something special, not just a nasty thing that just sort of falls on you.

So we decided to put poor old Pinkie away, my stuffed dog that I've slept with since I was three. Pinkie is bald and sort of hard and lumpy, since he got put in the washing machine by mistake, and you would never know he was all soft plush when he was new, or even that he was pink.

Last time my friend Gerry-Anne came over, before the summer, she saw Pinky laying on my pillow and though she didn't say anything, I could tell she was thinking that was kind of babyish. So I'd been thinking about not keeping Pinky around anymore.

Hilda and I made him this nice box lined with pretty scraps from her quilting class, and I thanked him out loud for being my friend for so many years, and we put him up in the closet, on the top shelf.

I felt terrible, but if Gerry-Anne decided I was too babyish to be friends with anymore, I could end up with no friends at all. When you have never been popular since the time you were skinny and fast and everybody wanted you on their team, you have that kind of thing on your mind.

Hilda and Dad made me go to school the next morning so nobody would think I was scared of Billy Linden (which I was) or that I would let him keep me away just by being such a dork.

Everybody kept sneaking funny looks at me and whispering, and I was sure it was because I couldn't help walking funny with the pad between my legs and because they could smell what was happening, which as far as I knew hadn't happened to anybody else in Eight A yet. Just like nobody else in the whole grade had anything real in their stupid training bras except me, thanks a lot.

Anyway I stayed away from everybody as much as I could and wouldn't talk to Gerry-Anne, even, because I was scared she would ask me why I walked funny and smelled bad.

Billy Linden avoided me just like everybody else, except one of his stupid buddies purposely bumped into me so I stumbled into Billy on the lunch-line. Billy turns around and he goes, real loud, ''Hey, Boobs, when did you start wearing black and blue makeup?''

I didn't give him the satisfaction of knowing that he had actually broken my nose, which the doctor said. Good thing they don't have to bandage you up for that. Billy would be hollering up a storm about how I had my nose in a sling as well as my boobs.

That night I got up after I was supposed to be asleep and took off my underpants and T-shirt that I sleep in and stood looking at myself in the mirror. I didn't need to turn a light on. The moon was full and it was shining right into my bedroom through the big dormer window.

I crossed my arms and pinched myself hard to sort of punish my body for what it was doing to me.

As if that could make it stop.

No wonder Edie Siler had starved herself to death in the tenth grade! I understood her perfectly. She was trying to keep her body down, keep it normal-looking, thin and strong, like I was too, back when I looked like a person, not a cartoon that somebody would call "Boobs."

And then something warm trickled in a little line down the inside of my leg, and I knew it was blood and I couldn't stand it anymore. I pressed my thighs together and shut my eyes hard, and I did something.

I mean I felt it happening. I felt myself shrink down to a hard core of sort of cold fire inside my bones, and all the flesh part, the muscles and the squishy insides and the skin, went sort of glowing and free-floating, all shining with moonlight, and I felt a sort of shifting and balance-changing going on.

I thought I was fainting on account of my stupid period. So I turned around and threw myself on my bed, only by the time I hit it, I knew something was seriously wrong.

For one thing, my nose and my head were crammed with these crazy, rich sensations that it took me a second to even figure out were smells, they were so much stronger than any smells I'd ever smelled. And they were—I don't know—*interesting* instead of just stinky, even the rotten ones.

I opened my mouth to get the smells a little better, and heard myself panting in a funny way as if I'd been running, which I hadn't, and then there was this long part of my face sticking out and something moving there—my tongue.

I was licking my chops.

Well, there was this moment of complete and utter panic. I tore around the room whining and panting and hearing my toenails clicking on the floorboards, and then I huddled down and crouched in the corner because I was scared Dad and Hilda would hear me and come to find out what was making all this racket.

Because I could hear them. I could hear their bed creak when one of them turned over, and Dad's breath whistling a little in an almost snore, and I could smell them too, each one with a perfectly clear bunch of smells, kind of like those desserts of mixed ice cream they call a medley.

My body was twitching and jumping with fear and energy, and my room—it's a converted attic-space, wide but with a ceiling that's low in places—my room felt like a jail. And plus, I was terrified of catching a glimpse of myself in the mirror. I had a pretty good idea of what I would see, and I didn't want to see it.

Besides, I had to pee, and I couldn't face trying to deal with the toilet in the state I was in.

So I eased the bedroom door open with my shoulder and nearly fell down the stairs trying to work them with four legs and thinking about it, instead of letting my body just do it. I put my hands on the front door to open it, but my hands weren't hands, they were paws with long knobby toes covered with fur, and the toes had thick black claws sticking out of the ends of them.

The pit of my stomach sort of exploded with horror,

and I yelled. It came out this wavery "woo" noise that echoed eerily in my skullbones. Upstairs, Hilda goes, "Jack, what was that?" I bolted for the basement as I heard Dad hit the floor of their bedroom.

The basement door slips its latch all the time, so I just shoved it open and down I went, doing better on the stairs this time because I was too scared to think. I spent the rest of the night down there, moaning to myself (which meant whining through my nose, really) and trotting around rubbing against the walls trying to rub off this crazy shape I had, or just moving around because I couldn't sit still. The place was thick with stinks and these slow-swirling currents of hot and cold air. I couldn't handle all the input.

As for having to pee, in the end I managed to sort of hike my butt up over the edge of the slop-sink by Dad's workbench and let go in there. The only problem was that I couldn't turn the taps on to rinse out the smell because of my paws.

Then about three A.M. I woke up from a doze curled up in a bare place on the floor where the spiders weren't so likely to walk, and I couldn't see a thing or smell anything either, so I knew I was okay again even before I checked and found fingers on my hands again instead of claws.

I zipped upstairs and stood under the shower so long that Hilda yelled at me for using up the hot water when she had a load of wash to do that morning. I was only trying to steam some of the stiffness out of my muscles, but I couldn't tell her that.

It was real weird to just dress and go to school after a night like that. One good thing, I stopped bleeding after only one day, which Hilda said wasn't so strange for the first time. So it had to be the huge greenish bruise on my face from Billy's punch that everybody was staring at.

That and the usual thing, of course. Well, why not?

They didn't know I'd spent the night as a wolf.

So Fat Joey grabbed my book bag in the hallway out-side science class and tossed it to some kid from Eight B. I had to run after them to get it back, which of course was set up so the boys could cheer the jouncing of my boobs under my shirt.

I was so mad I almost caught Fat Joey, except I was afraid if I grabbed him, maybe he would sock me like Billy had.

Dad had told me, Don't let it get you, kid, all boys are jerks at that age.

Hilda had been saying all summer, Look, it doesn't do any good to walk around all hunched up with your arms crossed, you should just throw your shoulders back and walk like a proud person who's pleased that she's growing up. You're just a little early, that's all, and I bet the other girls are secretly envious of you, with their cute little training bras, for Chrissake, as if there was something that needed to be *trained*.

It's okay for her, she's not in school, she doesn't re-member what it's like.

So I quit running and walked after Joey until the bell rang, and then I got my book bag back from the bushes outside where he threw it. I was crying a little, and I ducked into the girls' room.

Stacey Buhl was in there doing her lipstick like usual and wouldn't talk to me like usual, but Rita came bus-tling in and said somebody should off that dumb dork Joey, except of course it was really Billy that put him up to it. Like usual.

Rita is okay except she's an outsider herself, being that her kid brother has AIDS, and lots of kids' parents don't think she should even be in the school. So I don't hang around with her a lot. I've got enough trouble, and anyway I was late for Math.

I had to talk to somebody, though. After school I told Gerry-Anne, who's been my best friend on and off since fourth grade. She was off at the moment, but I found her in the library and I told her I'd had a weird dream about being a wolf. She wants to be a psychiatrist like her mother, so of course she listened.

She told me I was nuts. That was a big help.

That night I made sure the back door wasn't exactly closed, and then I got in bed with no clothes on—imagine turning into a wolf in your underpants and T-shirt— and just shivered, waiting for something to happen.

The moon came up and shone in my window, and I changed again, just like before, which is not one bit like how it is in the movies—all struggling and screaming and bones snapping out with horrible cracking and tearing noises, just the way I guess you would imagine it to be, if you knew it had to be done by building special machines to do that for the camera and make it look real: if you were a special effects man, instead of a werewolf.

For me, it didn't have to look real, it was real. It was this melting and drifting thing, which I got sort of excited by this time. I mean it felt—interesting. Like something I was doing, instead of just another dumb body-mess happening to me because some brainless hormones said so.

I must have made a noise. Hilda came upstairs to the door of my bedroom, but luckily she didn't come in. She's tall, and my ceiling is low for her, so she often talks to me from the landing.

Anyway I'd heard her coming, so I was in my bed with my whole head shoved under my pillow, praying frantically that nothing showed.

I could smell her, it was the wildest thing—her own smell, sort of sweaty but sweet, and then on top of it her perfume, like an ice-pick stuck in my nose. I didn't actually hear a word she said, I was too scared, and also I had this ripply shaking feeling inside me, a high that was only partly terror.

See, I realized all of a sudden, with this big blossom of surprise, that I didn't have to be scared of Hilda, or anybody. I was strong, my wolf-body was strong, and anyhow one clear look at me and she would drop dead.

What a relief, though, when she went away. I was dying to get out from under the weight of the covers, and besides I had to sneeze. Also I recognized that part of the energy roaring around inside me was hunger.

They went to bed—I heard their voices even in their bedroom, though not exactly what they said, which was fine. The words weren't important anymore, I could tell more from the tone of what they were saying.

Like I knew they were going to do it, and I was right. I could hear them messing around right through the walls, which was also something new, and I have never been so embarrassed in my life. I couldn't even put my hands over my ears, because my hands were paws.

So while I was waiting for them to go to sleep, I looked myself over in the big mirror on my closet door.

There was the big wolf head with a long slim muzzle and a thick ruff around my neck. The ruff stood up as I growled and backed up a little.

Which was silly of course, there was no wolf in the bedroom but me. But I was all strung out, I guess, and one wolf, me in my wolf body, was as much as I could handle the idea of let alone two wolves, me and my reflection.

After that first shock, it was great. I kept turning one way and another for different views.

I was thin, with these long, slender legs but strong, you could see the muscles, and feet a little bigger than I would have picked. But I'll take four big feet over two big boobs any day.

My face was terrific, with jaggedy white ripsaw teeth and eyes that were small and clear and gleaming in the moonlight. The tail was a little bizarre, but I got used to it, and actually it had a nice plumy shape. My shoul-

ders were big and covered with long, glossy-looking fur,
and I had this neat coloring, dark on the back and a sort
of melting silver on my front and underparts.

The thing was, though, my tongue, hanging out. I had
a lot of trouble with that, it looked gross and silly at the
same time. I mean, that was *my tongue*, about a foot
long and neatly draped over the points of my bottom
canines. That was when I realized that I didn't have a
whole lot of expressions to use, not with that face, which
was more like a mask.

But it was alive, it was my face, those were my own
long black lips that my tongue licked.

No doubt about it, this was *me*. I was a werewolf, like
in the movies they showed over Halloween weekend.
But it wasn't anything like your ugly movie werewolf
that's just some guy loaded up with pounds and pounds
of make-up. I was *gorgeous*.

I didn't want to just hang around admiring myself in
the mirror, though. I couldn't stand being cooped up in
that stuffy, smell-crowded room.

When everything settled down and I could hear Dad
and Hilda breathing the way they do when they're sleeping, I snuck out.

The dark wasn't very dark to me, and the cold felt
sharp like vinegar, but not in a hurting way. Everyplace
I went, there were these currents like waves in the air,
and I could draw them in through my long wolf nose
and roll the smell of them over the back of my tongue.
It was like a whole different world, with bright sounds
everywhere and rich, strong smells.

And I could run.

I started running because a car came by while I was
sniffing at the garbage bags on the curb, and I was really
scared of being seen in the headlights. So I took off
down the dirt alley between our house and the Morri-
sons' next door, and holy cow, I could tear along with
hardly a sound, I could jump their picket fence without

even thinking about it. My back legs were like steel springs and I came down solid and square on four legs with almost no shock at all, let alone worrying about losing my balance or twisting an ankle.

Man, I could run through that chilly air all thick and moisty with smells, I could almost fly. It was like last year, when I didn't have boobs bouncing and yanking in front even when *I'm* only walking fast.

Just two rows of neat little bumps down the curve of my belly. I sat down and looked.

I tore open garbage bags to find out about the smells in them, but I didn't eat anything from them. I wasn't about to chow down on other people's stale hotdog-ends and pizza crusts and fat and bones scraped off their plates and all mixed in with mashed potatoes and stuff.

When I found places where dogs had stopped and made their mark, I squatted down and pissed there too, right on top, I just wiped them *out*.

I bounded across that enormous lawn around the Wanscombe place, where nobody but the Oriental gardener ever sets foot, and walked up the back and over the top of their BMW, leaving big fat pawprints all over it. Nobody saw me, nobody heard me, I was a shadow.

Well, except for the dogs, of course.

There was a lot of barking when I went by, real hysterics, which at first I was really scared about. But then I popped out of an alley up on Ridge Road, where the big houses are, right in front of about six dogs that run together. Their owners let them out all night and don't care if they get hit by a car.

They'd been trotting along with the wind behind them, checking out all the garbage bags set out for pickup the next morning. When they saw me, one of them let out a yelp of surprise, and they all skidded to a stop.

Six of them. I was scared. I growled.

The dogs turned fast, banging into each other in their hurry, and trotted away.

I don't know what they would have done if they met a real wolf, but I was something special, I guess.

I followed them.

They scattered and ran.

Well, I ran too, and this was a different kind of running. I mean, I stretched, and I raced, and there was this joy. I chased one of them

Zig, zag, this little terrier-kind of dog tried to cut left and dive under the gate of somebody's front walk, all without a sound—he was running too hard to yell, and I was happy running quiet.

Just before he could ooze under the gate, I caught up with him and without thinking I grabbed the back of his neck and pulled him off his feet and gave him a shake as hard as I could, from side to side.

I felt his neck crack, the sound vibrated through all the bones of my face.

I picked him up in my mouth, and it was like he hardly weighed a thing. I trotted away holding him up off the ground, and under a bush in Baker's Park I held him down with my paws and I bit into his belly, that was still warm and quivering.

Like I said, I was hungry.

The blood gave me this rush like you wouldn't believe. I stood there a minute looking around and licking my lips, just sort of panting and tasting the taste because I was stunned by it, it was like eating honey or the best chocolate malted you ever had.

So I put my head down and chomped that little dog, like shoving your face into a pizza and inhaling it. God, I was *starved*, so I didn't mind that the meat was tough and rank-tasting after that first wonderful bite. I even licked blood off the ground after, never mind the grit mixed in.

I ate two more dogs that night, one that was tied up

on a clothesline in a cruddy yard full of rusted-out car
parts down on the South side, and one fat old yellow
dog out snuffling around on his own and way too slow.
He tasted pretty bad, and by then I was feeling full, so
I left a lot.

I strolled around the park, shoving the swings with
my big black wolf nose, and I found the bench where
Mr. Granby sits and feeds the pigeons every day, never
mind that nobody else wants the dirty birds around crap-
ping on their cars. I took a dump there, right where he
sits.

Then I gave the setting moon a goodnight, which
came out quavery and wild, "Loo-loo-loo!" And I loped
toward home, springing off the thick pads of my paws
and letting my tongue loll out and feeling generally su-
per.

I slipped inside and trotted upstairs, and in my room
I stopped to look at myself in the mirror.

As gorgeous as before, and only a few dabs of blood
on me, which I took time to lick off. I did get a little
worried—I mean, suppose that was it, suppose having
killed and eaten what I'd killed in my wolf shape, I was
stuck in this shape forever? Like, if you wander into a
fairy castle and eat or drink anything, that's it, you can't
ever leave. Suppose when the morning came I didn't
change back?

Well, there wasn't much I could do about that one
way or the other, and to tell the truth, I felt like I
wouldn't mind; it had been worth it.

When I was nice and clean, including licking off my
own bottom which seemed like a perfectly normal and
nice thing to do at the time, I jumped up on the bed,
curled up, and corked right off. When I woke up with
the sun in my eyes, there I was, my own self again.

It was very strange, grabbing breakfast and wearing
my old sweatshirt that wallowed all over me so I didn't
stick out so much, while Hilda yawned and shuffled

around in her robe and slippers and acted like her and Dad hadn't been doing it last night, which I knew different.

And plus, it was perfectly clear that she didn't have a clue about what *I* had been doing, which gave me a strange feeling.

One of the things about growing up they're careful not to tell you is, you start having more things you don't talk to your parents about. And I had a doozie.

Hilda goes, "What's the matter, are you off Sugar Pops now? Honestly, Kelsey, I can't keep up with you! And why can't you wear something nicer than that old shirt to school? Oh, I get it: disguise, right?"

She sighed and looked at me kind of sad but smiling, her hands on her hips. "Kelsey, Kelsey," she goes, "if only I'd had half of what you've got when *I* was a girl— I was flat as an ironing board, and it made me so miserable, I can't tell you."

She's still real thin and neat-looking, so what does she know about it? But she meant well, and anyhow I was feeling so good I didn't argue.

I didn't change my shirt, though.

That night I didn't turn into a wolf. I laid there waiting, but though the moon came up, nothing happened no matter how hard I tried, and after a while I went and looked out the window and realized that the moon wasn't really full anymore, it was getting smaller.

I wasn't so much relieved as sorry. I bought a calendar at the school book sale two weeks later, and I checked the full moon nights coming up and waited anxiously to see what would happen.

Meantime, things rolled along as usual. I got a rash of zits on my chin. I would look in the mirror and think about my wolf-face, which had beautiful sleek fur instead of zits.

Zits and all I went to Angela Durkin's party, and next day Billy Linden told everybody that I went in one of the bedrooms at Angela's and made out with him, which I did not. But since no grown-ups were home and Fat Joey brought grass to the party, most of the kids were stoned and didn't know who did what or where anyhow.

As a matter of fact, Billy once actually did get a girl in Seven B high one time out in his parents' garage, and him and two of his friends did it to her while she was zonked out of her mind, or anyway they said they did, and she was too embarrassed to say anything one way or the other, and a little while later she changed schools.

How I know about it is the same way everybody else does, which is because Billy was the biggest boaster in the whole school, and you could never tell if he was lying or not.

So I guess it wasn't so surprising that some people believed what Billy said about me. Gerry-Anne quit talking to me after that. Meantime Hilda got pregnant.

This turned into a huge discussion about how Hilda had been worried about her biological clock so she and Dad had decided to have a kid, and I shouldn't mind, it would be fun for me and good preparation for being a mother myself later on, when I found some nice guy and got married.

Sure. Great preparation. Like Mary O'Hare in my class, who gets to change her youngest baby sister's diapers all the time, yick. She jokes about it, but you can tell she really hates it. Now it looked like it was my turn coming up, as usual.

The only thing that made life bearable was my secret.

"You're laid back today," Devon Brown said to me in the lunchroom one day after Billy had been specially obnoxious, trying to flick rolled up pieces of bread from his table so they would land on my chest. Devon was sitting with me because he was bad at French, my only good subject, and I was helping him out with some verbs. I guess he wanted to know why I wasn't upset because of Billy picking on me. He goes, "How come?"

"That's a secret," I said, thinking about what Devon would say if he knew a werewolf was helping him with his French: *loup. Manger.*

He goes, "What secret?" Devon has freckles and is actually kind of cute-looking.

"*A secret,*" I go, "so I can't tell you, dummy."

He looks real superior and he goes, "Well, it can't be much of a secret, because girls can't keep secrets, everybody knows that."

Sure, like that kid Sara in Eight B who it turned out her own father had been molesting her for years, but she never told anybody until some psychologist caught on from some tests we all had to take in seventh grade. Up till then, Sara kept her secret fine.

And I kept mine, marking off the days on the calendar. The only part I didn't look forward to was having a period again, which last time came right before the change.

When the time came, I got crampy and more zits popped out on my face, but I didn't have a period.

I changed, though.

The next morning they were talking in school about a couple of prize miniature Schnauzers at the Wanscombes that had been hauled out of their yard by somebody and killed, and almost nothing left of them.

Well, my stomach turned a little when I heard some kids describing what Mr. Wanscombe had found over in Baker's Park, "the remains," as people said. I felt a little guilty, too, because Mrs. Wanscombe had really loved those little dogs, which somehow I didn't think about at all when I was a wolf the night before, trotting around hungry in the moonlight.

I knew those Schnauzers personally, so I was sorry, even if they were irritating little mutts that made a lot of noise.

But heck, the Wanscombes shouldn't have left them

out all night in the cold. Anyhow, they were rich, they could buy new ones if they wanted.

Still and all, though. I mean, dogs are just dumb animals. If they're mean, it's because they're wired that way or somebody made them mean, they can't help it. They can't just decide to be nice, like a person can. And plus, they don't taste so great, I think because they put so much junk in commercial dog-foods—anti-worm medicine and ashes and ground up fish, stuff like that. Ick.

In fact after the second schnauzer I had felt sort of sick and I didn't sleep real well that night. So I was not in a great mood to start with; and that was the day that my new brassiere disappeared while I was in gym. Later on I got passed a note telling me where to find it: stapled to the bulletin board outside the Principal's office, where everybody could see that I was trying a bra with an underwire.

Naturally, it had to be Stacey Buhl who grabbed my bra while I was changing for gym and my back was turned, since she was now hanging out with Billy and his friends.

Billy went around all day making bets at the top of his lungs on how soon I would be wearing a D-cup.

Stacey didn't matter, she was just a jerk. Billy mattered. He had wrecked me in that school forever, with his nasty mind and his big, fat mouth. I was past crying or fighting and getting punched out. I was boiling, I had had enough crap from him, and I had an idea.

I followed Billy home and waited on his porch until his mom came home and she made him come down and talk to me. He stood in the doorway and talked through the screen door, eating a banana and lounging around like he didn't have a care in the world.

So he goes, "Whatcha want, Boobs?"

I stammered a lot, being I was so nervous about telling such big lies, but that probably made me sound more believable.

I told him that I would make a deal with him: I would meet him that night in Baker's Park, late, and take off my shirt and bra and let him do whatever he wanted with my boobs if that would satisfy his curiosity and he would find somebody else to pick on and leave me alone.

"What?" he said, staring at my chest with his mouth open. His voice squeaked and he was practically drooling on the floor. He couldn't believe his good luck.

I said the same thing over again.

He almost came out onto the porch to try it right then and there. "Well, shit," he goes, lowering his voice a lot, "why didn't you say something before? You really mean it?"

I go, "Sure," though I couldn't look at him.

After a minute he goes, "Okay, it's a deal. Listen, Kelsey, if you like it, can we, uh, do it again, you know?"

I go, "Sure. But Billy, one thing: this is a secret, between just you and me. If you tell anybody, if there's one other person hanging around out there tonight—"

"Oh no," he goes, real fast, "I won't say a thing to anybody, honest. Not a word, I promise!"

Not until afterward, of course, was what he meant, which if there was one thing Billy Linden couldn't do, it was to keep quiet if he knew something bad about another person.

"You're gonna like it, I know you are," he goes, speaking strictly for himself as usual. "Jeez. I can't believe this!"

But he did, the dork.

I couldn't eat much for dinner that night, I was too excited, and I went upstairs early to do homework, I told Dad and Hilda.

Then I waited for the moon, and when it came, I changed.

Billy was in the park. I caught a whiff of him, very sweaty and excited, but I stayed cool. I snuck around for a while, as quiet as I could—which was real quiet—making sure none of his stupid friends were lurking around. I mean, I wouldn't have trusted just his promise for a million dollars.

I passed up half a hamburger lying in the gutter where somebody had parked for lunch next to Baker's Park. My mouth watered, but I didn't want to spoil my appetite. I was hungry and happy, sort of singing inside my own head, "Shoo, fly, pie, and an apple-pan-dowdie . . ."

Without any sound, of course.

Billy had been sitting on a bench, his hands in his pockets, twisting around to look this way and that way, watching for me—for my human self—to come join him. He had a jacket on, being it was very chilly out.

Which he didn't stop to think that maybe a sane person wouldn't be crazy enough to sit out there and take off her top leaving her naked skin bare to the breeze. But that was Billy all right, totally fixed on his own greedy self and without a single thought for somebody else. I bet all he could think about was what a great scam this was, to feel up old Boobs in the park and then crow about it all over school.

Now he was walking around the park, kicking at the sprinkler-heads and glancing up every once in a while, frowning and looking sulky.

I could see he was starting to think that I might stand him up. Maybe he even suspected that old Boobs was lurking around watching him and laughing to herself because he had fallen for a trick. Maybe old Boobs had even brought some kids from school with her to see what a jerk he was.

Actually that would have been pretty good, except

Billy probably would have broken my nose for me
again, or worse, if I'd tried it.

"Kelsey?" he goes, sounding mad.

I didn't want him stomping off home in a huff. I
moved up closer, and I let the bushes swish a little
around my shoulders.

He goes, "Hey, Kelse, it's late, where've you been?"

I listened to the words, but mostly I listened to the
little thread of worry flickering in his voice, low and
high, high and low, as he tried to figure out what was
going on.

I let out the whisper of a growl.

He stood real still, staring at the bushes, and he goes,
"That you, Kelse? Answer me."

I was wild inside. I couldn't wait another second. I
tore through the bushes and leaped for him, flying.

He stumbled backward with a squawk—"What!"—
jerking his hands up in front of his face, and he was just
sucking in a big breath to yell with when I hit him like
a demo-derby truck.

I jammed my nose past his feeble claws and chomped
down hard on his face.

No sound came out of him except this wet, thick gur-
gle, which I could more taste than hear because the
sound came right into my mouth with the gush of his
blood and the hot mess of meat and skin that I tore away
and swallowed.

He thrashed around, hitting at me, but I hardly felt
anything through my fur. I mean, he wasn't so big and
strong laying there on the ground with me straddling him
all lean and wiry with wolf-muscle. And plus, he was in
shock. I got a strong whiff from below as he let go of
everything right into his pants.

Dogs were barking, but so many people around
Baker's Park have dogs to keep out burglars, and the
dogs make such a racket all the time, that nobody pays

any attention. I wasn't worried. Anyway, I was too busy to care.

I nosed in under what was left of Billy's jaw and I bit his throat out.

Now let him go around telling lies about people.

His clothes were a lot of trouble and I really missed having hands. I managed to drag his shirt out of his belt with my teeth, though, and it was easy to tear his belly open. Pretty messy, but once I got in there, it was better than Thanksgiving dinner. Who would think that somebody as horrible as Billy Linden could taste so *good*?

He was barely moving by then, and I quit thinking about him as Billy Linden anymore. I quit thinking at all, I just pushed my head in and pulled out delicious steaming chunks and ate until I was picking at tidbits, and everything was getting cold.

On the way home I saw a police car cruising the neighborhood the way they do sometimes. I hid in the shadows and of course they never saw me.

There was a lot of washing up to do in the morning, and when Hilda saw my sheets she shook her head and she goes, "You should be more careful about keeping track of your period so as not to get caught by surprise."

Everybody in school knew something had happened to Billy Linden, but it wasn't until the day after that that they got the word. Kids stood around in little huddles trading rumors about how some wild animal had chewed Billy up. I would walk up and listen in and add a really gross remark or two, like part of the game of thrilling each other green and nauseous with made-up details to see who would upchuck first.

Not me, that's for sure. I mean, when somebody went on about how Billy's whole head was gnawed down to the skull and they didn't even know who he was except from the bus pass in his wallet, I got a little urpy. It's amazing the things people will dream up. But when I thought about what I had actually done to Billy, I had to smile.

It felt totally wonderful to walk through the halls without having anybody yelling, "Hey, Boobs!"

Even my social life is looking up. Gerry-Anne is not only talking to me again, she invited me out on a double-date with her. Some guy she met at a party asked her to go to the movies with him next weekend, and he has a friend. They're both from Fawcett Junior High across town, which will be a change. I was nervous when she asked me, but finally I said yes. My first real date!

I am still pretty nervous, to tell the truth. I have to keep promising myself that I will not worry about my chest, I will not be self-conscious, even if the guy stares.

Actually things at school are not completely hunky-dory. Hilda says "That's Life" when I complain about things, and I am beginning to believe her. Fat Joey somehow got to be my lab-partner in Science, and if he doesn't quit trying to grab a feel whenever we have to stand close together to do an experiment, he is going to be sorry.

He doesn't know it, but he's got until the next full moon.

TWO BAD DOGS

Ronald Anthony Cross

"Two Bad Dogs" was purchased by Gardner Do-
zois, and appeared in the September 1990 issue
of Asimov's, *with an illustration by Ron and Val*
Lakey Lindahn. Cross made his first sale to Asi-
mov's under Shawna McCarthy in 1983, and has
since sold a number of other stories to the mag-
azine, including another odd adventure of Eddie
Zuckos, the intrepid hero of "Two Bad Dogs."
He is also a frequent contributor to The Magazine
of Fantasy and Science Fiction, *and has sold to*
Universe, New Worlds, Orbit, Pulphouse, Weird
Tales, Far Frontiers, In the Fields of Fire, New
Pathways, The Berkley Showcase, *and elsewhere.*
His only novel to date, Prisoners of Paradise, *ap-*
peared in 1988. He lives in Santa Monica, Cali-
fornia.

Here he treats us to a wild and funny look at
the unexpected hazards of life as a tabloid jour-
nalist. . . .

I: My Story

You have to understand that, while it is true that I do
not particularly like dogs, I would never kick one. But
if I were to make an exception, little Charlie Dog, as

Melissa so lovingly calls him, would probably still be out there, blazing across the sky like a doggie meteor.

Like most people of sensitivity, I had made the aesthetic decision at an early age to admire the cat and disdain the lowly servile panting dog. Man's best friend, my ass; more like man's best groveling lackey.

Anyway, home from a hard day's work interviewing maniacs (I am a reporter for the *National Revealer*), I opened the door to my duplex apartment, prepared for another bout with the wretched little creature.

Since I had been unable to talk—no, beg—Melissa out of leaving the nasty wee beastie with me while she rushed off to the bedside of her ailing father somewhere in Iowa, I could only pray each night that he would die quickly (and painlessly, of course). (Either the dog or the father would do.)

So I peeked in my doorway—no sign of the little bugger. I called out my usual greeting, "Bad dog!" and waited for the reaction. Tiny as he was, it was always wise to locate him before entering a room. No reply.

I tried "Charlie, where are you, you little swine, you miniature pig, you ugly little minute gargoyle?"

I heard the low growling that is his trademark. Sounded like the bedroom. So I confidently entered the house, scrutinizing the living room rug for dog shit. No—perhaps I hadn't fed him enough.

Might as well get it over with, I figured, heading into the bedroom.

"Where are you? Reveal thy ugly self, oh pigdog."

A creature resembling a rat with curly hair popped out from under my bed, growling, furiously shaking something white as if it were a small animal (smaller than even itself) that it wished fervently to dismember. It took me a moment to recognize my underpants.

I shuddered to think what the nasty little creature had been doing all day long with my underwear. And as if in answer, Charlie Dog tossed them to the floor and hunched over them, attempting sexual union. Luckily my underwear had no more interest in the disgusting little creature than any small dog would have had, so the marriage pretty much went unconsummated.

"Ah, Charlie, true love at last, eh? Give me my underwear."

Charlie crouched down over my underpants, growling, his little lip raised perfectly in a snarl.

With what must have been divine inspiration, I jerked the spread off the bed and threw it over him like a net. The small lump squirmed and thrashed about, barking in his sharp staccato style, either in panic or delight. I can't tell the difference, and I doubt whether Charlie Dog can either.

With some pleasure, I watched him going through his little fit, pleasantly muffled by the bedspread, until the image of myself springing off the bed and landing on that pathetic little lump appeared in my consciousness: I went swiftly out into the living room before it became too compelling for me to resist. (Not long, I'll bet!)

I sat down on the shabby old couch. (Was it my imagination, or did it bear the slight odor of Charlie's special perfume?) I closed my eyes. Started to drowse. Was of course awakened by another fusillade of earsplitting little barks. The creature was prancing up and down stifflegged in front of me on the rug. When he was convinced that he had gained my full attention, he ran into the kitchen. It was especially irritating to hear the little clippity-scratchy noise of his toenails on the linoleum. Dinner.

"He'll only eat hamburger, cooked well done—Oh, I almost forgot, must be heavily salted," Melissa had informed me as she was going out the door. *Sure he will, he'd probably eat Purina rat chow and think it was a gourmet meal*, I figured. As usual, I had figured wrong. I'd started out with canned dog food. "Dig right in,

Charlie Dog. Good boy, good dog. Eat. Sit. Sit. Eat. Stand up and eat.''

Charlie always wore an aggravated expression—aggravation was the key to his cuteness—but in this case it had surged clearly over the line and well into the territory of revulsion. No go. As was the attempt to feed him the hamburger raw. As was the attempt to feed him the hamburger well done, until I realized that I had forgotten to salt it.

I had recently interviewed a woman for the *Revealer* who claimed to have been five hundred years old. ''Never touch meat,'' she had told me, ''that's the secret.''

''You've never eaten meat,'' I said, ''in five hundred years?''

''You miss the point.'' She shook her head at me. ''I said, 'Never *touch* meat.' Filthy stuff. Rotting away, dead as a doornail. Once you touch it, it *infects* you. It's too late then to worry about whether you eat it or not. You might as well do anything you want with it *then*. Rub it all over your body,'' she suggested. ''Stuff it up your nose. Who cares?

''Have a brief but merry life,'' she had mumbled to me as I went out the door. She had died within the week. Perhaps even talking about it had de-immortalized her.

Anyhow, I always thought about her as I prepared Charlie's repast. I'm not a vegetarian, far from it. But there's something in mucking about with raw hamburger that gives me the creeps. As apparently it also did to Charlie Dog. He wouldn't go near it until it was thoroughly cooked and salted. But once its aroma informed him that it had reached its proper state of preparation, he would relay the info to me by frantically leaping into the air and, of course, barking. Barking, barking, barking.

All this would be followed by a brief respite as the tiny beast from hell ate its din din. That night I was particularly tired, as I've already pointed out. I made it back to the couch and had barely closed my eyes—or so it seemed—when, guess what? Bark, bark, bark.

Now it was time for the familiar ritual of Charlie Dog convincing me of the necessity of taking him on his nightly walk.

If the dinner routine required a lot of passionate barking and leaping about, the after-dinner ''go for a walk'' number might have been choreographed by some top Russian gymnast, and Charlie performed it as if he were competing for the doggie gold medal. First he would bark, then he would *bark*, etc.), then he would throw himself down and writhe on the carpet as if in his death throes (I wish), then spring up in the air, twisting around and around; he practically did handsprings—I expected to find myself jumping up to my feet and holding out a sign that read ''9.5.''

Outside for our walk next, where Charlie would finally settle on the perfect spot and make a big scene in order to draw attention to himself as he performed the wonderful (to him) art of defecation. Tonight, under the careful scrutiny of a very angry-looking old lady.

''Young man,'' she said to me after the sordid little affair was over, ''have you no respect for the rights of others? You should pick it up and take it home with you, and dispose of it properly.''

''You may have it,'' I snarled back at her. ''Do with it as you wish.''

Back home I sank down on the couch and closed my eyes again. *I've been working too hard*, I thought to myself. Working for the *National Revealer* was turning into more and more of a Herculean chore, and I was a small Hercules. A very small Hercules. A very, *very* small Hercules. In fact, in my drowsy state of consciousness, I allowed myself to wonder for a moment if part of the reason for my intense dislike of Charlie Dog didn't have something to do with my own diminutive

size. A spry little (albeit incredibly handsome) fellow
with a feisty little toy poodle seemed to present an in-
surmountable barrier to whatever the hell it was I was
trying to prove to the world. But what if Charlie had
been a big macho stud pit bull dog? Named Duke?

I drowsed. Images of all the maniacs and movie stars
I had interviewed lately poured through my mind. (The
difference between the movie stars and the maniacs had
turned out to be more a matter of degree than kind. The
movie stars, like the emperors of that other Hollywood
in old Italy, were suffering from the severest possible
form of mental illness: public-supported insanity.)

Suddenly I awoke with a start. Something small but
heavy and warm was curled up on my chest. Charlie
Dog. When I looked at him, he growled menacingly.

I jumped up, and Charlie did a doggie flip, landing
quite skillfully, I must admit, but complaining nonethe-
less in his bitter way. Bark bark, etc.

"Late for my interview, Charlie. At least it's not a
movie star this time. Thank God."

Charlie said, or anyway seemed to say: Interview, *this*
time of night? Who do you think you're kidding? But
quick as a wink, I was out the door and on my way.
Walking. Someone in L.A. actually lived close enough
for me to walk to her house.

Soon there I was, in her house, sitting there comfy
and cozy on her plush sofa, holding my pad, pen, and
getting ready to fire off some of those deep questions
the *National Revealer* is so famous for, such as: "What
makes you think the bugs in your kitchen are actually
advanced beings from Mars?" or "Then what happened
to the *real* Mike Tyson?" or "If everyone is under their
spell, then how come we don't *know* it?" Tonight it was,
"Well, I hear you've had an unfortunate accident with
your dog." But I figured I'd break one of my long-
standing rules and use a little finesse with this one. Lead
into it.

"Lovely place you've got here." (Slight exaggeration, but what the hell.) Actually, the woman was making me a little nervous. Big (well—bigger than me), rangy, and with kind of a fey look in her huge dark eyes. Not at all unlike some of those whacko movie stars I had been interviewing of late. And restless. She kept moving about the living room, picking things up and putting them down, lifting up the blind, and peeking out into the dark.

"Do you live near here?" she said. And there was a strange intensity in her voice.

"Not too near," I lied carefully.

"Do you want a drink? I think we should have a drink. Sort of break the ice between us."

"I'm sorry," I said, "I don't drink."

"But you should, you really should. People who drink live longer, you know."

It only seems longer, I said to myself.

"Here's just a little bitty one I made for you." She loped across the expanse of rug and shoved a glass in my hand. I caught a whiff of it and practically reeled—rubbing alcohol and soda?

"There," she said quite forcefully, "that's better, isn't it?"

I nodded. Then she did a very odd thing. She turned around in a circle a couple of times before she sat down next to me on the couch, and curled up with her knees up to her chest; her feet were bare.

"Much better," she said, and I thought, not for the first time, what a strange husky voice she had.

"I really like being here with you, Eddie, feeling so relaxed, well, I feel like I can just let my hair out, you know?"

"Down," I said.

"What?" she said, looking angry again.

"It's 'let your hair down,' Ms. Lombardo."

"Oh, please call me Cindy," she said. "Drink up."

I pretended to sip from the glass—Jesus, the fumes burned my eyes.

"Well, Cindy, I have some questions I have to ask. We might as well get started."

"Sure," she said, "I'm ready to let my hair out—I mean down. Silly me. Wonder why I keep saying that?"

"What exactly was it that happened between you and your dog?"

She said coyly, "I told you over the phone. Don't you want to drink up?"

I had put my drink down on the coffee table in order to pick up my pad and pen.

"I want to be sure I got it right. Would you mind telling me again?"

"I killed my dog," she said. "I bit him to death."

"Was he a bad dog?—Sorry. I mean, was he a big dog?"

"Doberman pinscher," she said, and she smiled wickedly. "I'm quite strong, you know."

"I believe you," I said, noticing a bit of trepidation creeping into my tone of voice. Was I imagining it, or was there more hair on her arms and legs than I had noticed before?

"But it's not the strength, you know it's something else. Sometimes a kind of wildness comes over me, and—I don't know how to describe it. It's as if someone else is doing those things."

"A kind of wildness came over you, Cindy," I said, writing it down. "Then exactly what happened?"

"I don't really remember it that clearly." She looked away, got up and crossed the room, and peeked out the window again. What did she see out there in the dark?

"Prince was barking at me, for some reason. I . . . I just can't remember why. Barking and snarling, but backing up. Then we were fighting, and I was biting into his neck. I remember that for sure. I was just so damn furious. I remember the taste of his blood."

She licked her lips. Oh my God, she licked her fucking lips! I felt hair rise up all over my body. In places
where I probably didn't even *have* hair. Suddenly I was
seriously frightened. But at the same time I was writing
it down. Digging it. Thinking, *"Woman Bites Dog to
Death": great headline*. It's what I do.

"This . . . uh . . . wildness that comes over you, have
you noticed when it occurs, by chance?"

"Always at night," she said. "Let me think for a
minute." She got up, loped over, looked out the window.

"What's out there?"

"Full moon."

Jesus! My hair fluttered all over my body again.

"Does the full moon have . . ."

"You know," she said, looking astonished, "I do believe it might have something to do with it at that."

Came back over and sat down next to me, and smiled
and knocked down the huge drink she had made herself,
and then said: "Full moon, drinking whiskey, stuff like
that."

I had stopped writing, stopped breathing. For a while
we just sat there in silence. Then I said, "Uh, probably
PMS."

"Do you know what I want you to do?" she said.

"Uh, write up your story and publish . . ."

Her expression became very angry very suddenly.

"Shut up," she said. "I want you to shut up and drink
your drink and stand up without saying another word
and take off all your clothes and then tear mine off of
me. Just rip them off."

"Oh," I said. "Oh, oh, oh."

"You *bastard*. You men are all alike," she said. "All
you can think about is sex, sex, sex."

But it was death, death, death that I was thinking
about. All I could manage to say was "Oh." I couldn't
even get out the "my God" part. And yes, her arms and

legs were definitely getting hairier, and her face—oh my *God*, her face was changing shape, and hair was now growing on it too. Thick, dark hair.

"Sex, sex, sex." That hoarse low voice of hers was practically growling now. "You're all panting like dogs with your tongues all hanging out." She began to pant in order to illustrate her lovely simile, tongue lolling out, and it was too long—way too long.

"Oh shit, it's happening, it's happening!" she shouted suddenly. "Yes, *yes*, let it, I *want* it to happen! Oh, oh shit."

Now she curled up and rolled off the couch and down onto the carpet.

"Come here," I think she said. But I could no longer understand her. She lay there writhing and groaning.

I broke out of my trance, threw down my drink, and tried to make a dash for the front door. But she came out of it enough to spring at me, causing me to turn and run the other way. The kitchen! But the back door was locked. Dead bolt. Oh Jesus, Jesus! I just froze up again, pushing at the door. Got to think think think.

The swinging door that led to the living room opened, and there she was, growling at me. The transformation was complete now, and strangely enough, she didn't look anything like a wolf, but a lot like werewolves look on TV or in the movies. I think maybe she could have changed into any form she wanted, but, not knowing this, patterned herself after the movie version. Figures!

Oh my God, what am I going to do? She took a step toward me. Growling. Stalking me. Playing with me, actually. I scanned the kitchen frantically for a weapon. There was poor Prince's food dish. A Doberman! And on the shelf next to me, a few cans of his food and a can opener.

So I grabbed the opener and frantically started opening a can. The creature growled, but clearly was puzzled.

"Good dog," I said. "Good Cindy. Eat, Cindy. Eat. Good dog."

I practically ripped the can open, and just dumped the food on the floor in front of me. "Eat, Cindy. Eat," I said again.

Her growl changed to a whining noise.

"Yes, yes. Good dog. Eat, Cindy. Good Cindy."

The creature took another step toward me, then suddenly dropped down on the shiny yellow kitchen linoleum floor and began to scarf up the dog food. To tell you the truth, it smelled pretty good to me, too.

But she was gobbling it up too fast. Like most animals, she had atrocious manners.

I opened another can and tossed it on the floor. Then I carefully edged my way around her and tip-toed out through the kitchen door. Then I ran like hell for the front door, and then I ran like hell all the way home. We're talking a couple of miles here. Probably three-minute ones.

For the first time in my life I was glad to see Charlie. Home sweet home.

"Thank God I didn't tell her where I lived, Charlie." *Is there some way she could get my address?* I thought. *Calm down. You've got to think it out.* But there was no way. It's the middle of the night. And anyhow, it's the *Revealer*'s policy never to give out any reporter's home address. Very strict policy. My breathing began to slow down. I was safe. Really safe.

Now I was feeling better. Still too shook up to sleep, but much better. I sat down in my chair again, and flicked on the TV, changed a few channels with my remote until I found a suitably dull sitcom, and put my feet up, shoes and all, on my coffee table, since there was no one to tell me not to. Pretty soon I started to doze again.

Suddenly there came a pounding at the front door, accompanied by Charlie Dog's frantic barking.

"Eddie, are you in there? It's me, Cindy. I've come to apologize. Won't you open the door, Eddie?"

"No!" I shouted. "No, I won't open the door. How the hell did you get my address?"

"I called the *Revealer* and your boss was there, working late. I simply asked him."

"But that's against the *Revealer* policy," I whined.

"I know, he told me that, but I explained to him that I was very upset and all, and that I would find him and tear his throat out if he didn't tell me, and he just said, 'Sure, better him than *me*.' Now will you please open this door, Eddie, because I'm starting to get very angry again, and I'm afraid I'll lose control out here and do something that might embarrass you in front of your neighbors."

And do you know, the funny thing, the absolutely insane thing, is that I did open the door. Because somehow I couldn't stand the thought of her changing into an animal in front of my neighbors. I almost felt that I would rather be killed than get thrown out of my apartment in disgrace. But I only opened the door a crack.

"What do you want?"

A crack was enough. With astonishing ease she shoved the door the rest of the way open, popping off the little chain, and knocking me clear off my feet.

"I want *you*, you son of a bitch," she said. Her fists were clenched, and yes, her garden of hair was beginning to sprout again.

"You think you can just take advantage of me and then throw me aside like an old used—" she searched wildly for a simile "—tampax. Just leave me laying there, right there where you'd had your way with me. Right there on the kitchen linoleum floor."

She was changing fast. I scanned the living room desperately for silver bullets or crucifixes, and had just about the kind of luck you'd imagine I'd have.

For once, Charlie Dog was not barking. He was just

frozen there with his mouth, or snout or whatever you like to call it, open. Wide open.

I ran over and scooped him up. "Here, Cindy. *Eat*. Good Cindy." I tossed Charlie toward her.

Sure enough, the little demon quickly mastered his uncharacteristic reticence, scampered over, and tried to couple with one of her now-quite-hairy legs. Jesus, what a sex maniac.

"Sorry, Charlie, but you've been such a bad dog," I whispered as way of good-bye, while edging my way toward the bedroom door.

And . . . tender last scene, the last thing I saw as I carefully inched through the doorway was the bitch growling down at Charlie, who, of course, was still lost in the raptures of love.

Then I was hiding under the bed, praying to whatever God there was (or wasn't) that she'd be satisfied with the little snack I'd offered her.

Hours later, when I was finally able to drum up the courage to go back out and check, the front door was open, and the two bad dogs were gone. Charlie, I was sure, forever. If only I would be so fortunate with Cindy.

In fact, I was so certain she had eaten him, that he no longer existed, that I put him totally and completely out of my mind, so that when my girlfriend Melissa called me on the phone and asked about her little—ugh—poo-chie pie, I was stunned. What do I do now?

"Oh, poochie pie's fine. Just fine. We're getting along just great, aren't we, Charlie Dog?"

I held the phone away from me and attempted to imitate his annoying little bark.

Strangely enough, she said, "Yeah, he sounds okay, I guess. You're not forgetting to take him for his walk, are you? And remember, he likes to be brushed around 7:15 in the morning," etc., etc. Daddy, it appeared, was still busy dragging out his death scene. (Positively Shakespearean!) Well, okay. I'd postpone telling her

about Charlie till the last possible moment. I breathed a
sigh of relief. I always feel so much better once I come
up with a plan.

A few nights later came a thumping at my door. Not a
pounding. But a thumping and a scratching.

    Panic. "Who's there? Cindy, is that you?"

    "No, it's not Cindy, you fool. Open the door. It's
me."

    "Ah, who's 'me'?"

    "It's *me*, damn it. Charlie."

    "Sure it is," I said. I opened the door and looked out.
What I saw was the body of a poodle—yes, it could be
Charlie's—the tiny little body of a toy poodle, but gro-
tesquely crowned with a pale white, puffy, ugly human
face.

    "I've become a were-human," it whined in an an-
guished tone.

II: Charlie's Story

"Right at first I have only dog's memories. Feelings.
Impressions. Odors. Anger. Fear. More emotions. In
short, like a human's memories, only without the neu-
rotic ability to fantasize and make a little story out of
the whole affair with me at the center of it. And then
tell it to myself over and over until I believe it. Well,
those simple sweet doggie days are gone.

    "I ran with the bitch. I wanted to screw her, but I
couldn't reach her." (Yeah, it was Charlie, all right.)
"But really the excitement was enough. The running,
the hunting, the odors.

    "During the day she was like an ordinary human be-
ing with a hangover. But not quite. She was always on
the verge. She reeked of fury. I loved to smell her. Human on the outside, wolf within. She would wander
about the house, pretending to be a human, but with the

restlessness of a wolf, prowling her territory, pacing back and forth, muttering to herself, emitting little electrical surges of anger from time to time. Trying to be human. But really, she was just waiting for the night. The hunt. The kill. The blood.

"The two of us would corner our victims, slowly and tantalizingly advancing, driving them farther and farther out of themselves and into the limitless void of pure panic. How we would drink in those perfumed clouds of panic and despair. Then, when it was so delicious that we could stand it no more, we would attack: She, going for the throat; I, the *foot*.

"How I loved the bitch. But as always, each dog kills the thing he loves. Or, as in my case, tries. Driven over the edge by bloodlust, I turned on her, savagely going for the ankle.

"The next thing I knew, I was swimming, semi-conscious; in a sea of pain, captured tightly in a vise of needle-sharp teeth and being shaken as if I were a rat.

"If she hadn't tried to swallow me, I wouldn't have escaped. But luckily for me, she was invested with the strange power to alter her structure to a most amazing degree. In my case, she stretched out and widened her jaws, and made the ludicrous attempt to swallow me whole. Of course she choked, gagged, and coughed me out. I was shot out of her mouth like a projectile, and the shock of hitting the cold concrete floor of the alley forced me back into consciousness. I managed to scramble between some trash cans stacked up in the alley and make a run for it. I heard her smash into the trash cans and go down. When I glanced back I could see she had momentarily forgotten all about me, and was now venting her rage upon the trash.

I almost died. But the wound inflicted by a werewolf is a supernatural wound, and it either kills you or it heals supernaturally fast. I found myself another alley nearby

and crawled into it, and hid myself as best I could and
prepared to die.

"By the next night, I was coming out of it, but something else was happening. Something weird. All of my
memories were being sorted out and put into order. Not
necessarily proper order, you understand? It was rather
an arbitrary order, chosen to make the past more pleasant
and meaningful. Some memories were suppressed, others exaggerated, emphasized. It was an attempt to make
something more important than it really was. Me. The
concept of me-I was what the process was trying to em-
phasize, what it was making into the center of the universe. And the universe, and the center, the 'I,' were
both only a part of that process. It was all illusion, but
it was inevitable, inexorable illusion that forced you to
accept it as the truth. It was later that I realized what it
was: I was becoming human.

"I was now able to put together the proper set of
memories and attempt to find my way back to your
apartment. Well, here I am. Feed me."

I fed him. And he gobbled the well-done, highly
salted hamburger down, same as always. But when he
was finished he did a strange thing. He wept, loud and
long. It was an eerie sight to see: The puffy white lu-
gubrious face distorted in anguish, the sniffling, snuffling, sobbing, and wailing emitting from it, while the
nasty little poodle body scampered back and forth, back
and forth restlessly bearing its awful burden.

"Why are you crying?" I said.

"It is a terrible thing to be human," he said, "trapped
in your own deceit. It is a tragedy."

"Well, Charlie," I said, "it is indeed a tragedy. But
if you could see yourself from my eyes, you would realize that it's a comedy, too."

But no, Charlie could not see it. It seems to be another
sad or funny fact of human existence that it's only a
comedy when someone *else* is suffering it.

Charlie paced back and forth anxiously in front of me, still weeping, while I did what I could—sat down on the sofa and dozed off again.

What woke me up was the silence. I live in L.A. There is *always* noise here: The hysterical scream of a siren, the angry honking of automobile horns (many of them blaring out novelty tunes such as "I Won't Be Home Until Morning"), the rumbling of earthquakes, the screams of your next door neighbor's wife, the crisp thunk of his fist connecting, the ripe thud of her body hitting the floor (or sometimes vice versa), the occasional punctuation of an assault rifle on full automatic.

It makes no difference what time it is; you go outside in the middle of the night and drive somewhere and you will find the freeways jammed with swearing sweating psychotics, leaning on their horns. It is always rush hour in L.A.

And even my apartment makes noise. It sways and grumbles and creaks and whispers and constantly shifts and moves about. Perhaps this is due to the jelly-like motion of the earth here: It is more like living on the ocean than near it.

At any rate, whether due to Charlie's new powers, me tuning in to his mystical brainwave broadcast, or whether it was just one of those freak L.A. accidents embellished with a touch of synchronicity, I awoke enveloped in a cloud of silence. Startled, I looked around the room. Charlie had reverted back to his dog form, and was asleep on the rug. I couldn't even hear him breathe. I couldn't see anything unusual. I thought, *What does this mean?* And the answer, the overwhelming answer, came flooding into my mind: *Get up and run!*

But I couldn't move, couldn't scream, couldn't even breathe, because I was frozen with fear. Oh yes, because I *knew* what was coming through the door. Now. Now. *Now*.

I just sat there, mouth open, eyes opening wider and

wider, staring at that door, and listening to the first sound in that sea of silence: Not the howl of a wolf, but a keening, high-pitched shriek of an unknown carnivore closing in fast upon its quarry. And I watched the door explode off its hinges—I saw this so clearly that it appeared to me as if it were a film on television being played in slow motion. And then *she* was in the room, and I began to breathe, only too fast. Too fast.

And now she reared back and spread her hairy arms in a world-encompassing gesture and howled, not anything like the howl of a wolf, but so high-pitched, loud, and uncanny that you could feel the sound vibrations coursing through your body like a paralyzing charge of electricity. You just sat there, breathing, breathing, waiting, panting.

And suddenly something floated between us, something so ludicrous that I couldn't register it at first, and just saw it as a distortion of vision between me and the werewolf. Then I felt the pressure, a terrible surging pressure like an instant migraine headache, complete with flashing lights. And things in the room started exploding: One by one, the glasses on the shelf, followed by the decanter and the lamp on the coffee table (the table flew up and smashed into the wall); the little thirteen-inch TV blew to smithereens; and last, the lightbulb in the ceiling fixture popped.

And now I could see what it was that had come floating between the bitch and her prey: It was Charlie Dog in his were-human form, and the reason I could see it was because the white puffy pliable face was radiating a sickly cloud of brilliant light.

I could see him, and I could see the bitch struggling as if against an unseen barrier, and I could hear her roar in rage and *frustration*, and then, still struggling, emit a series of nasty growls and snarls; and finally, in what sounded like the severely damaged voice of someone suffering from some awful disease, she grunted something that I thought could have been "Fucking men and their dogs, fucking dogs and their men. Kill, kill, kill . . ."

"Put your hand in your mouth," Charlie said in his strange, small, shrill, but sweet voice.

Slowly, but inexorably, struggling wildly like a fish in a net, she put her hairy hand in her mouth.

"Bite down," Charlie said. And as she did it, he shouted in a crisp tone of voice, "Bad dog!"

She bit down hard; there was a loud crunching sound, and blood poured out, a lot of it. And Charlie shouted out once again, "Bad, *bad* dog. Go home, bad dog!"

And she turned and ran out the door.

"Is that all you can do?" Charlie said, "Just sit there and hyperventilate?" As if released from a spell, I jumped up and ran into the bathroom and threw up. When I came back out, he said: "Don't worry, she won't come back. It's simply a matter of knowing how to train a dog."

Then he circled wearily around and around and curled up on the rug. For a few moments he lay there, weeping softly; and as I watched, his puffy white face disassembled like a cloud, and reformed into the face of Melissa's darling little Charlie doggie. He looked at me imploringly and whined, and then closed his great sad eyes and slept.

And that should have been the end of the story. You would think it was enough, but no such luck. Things keep on happening even when you think they just ought to stop and give you a break for a while. Especially then.

Of course I called the police. "Jeez, too bad, we're all out of silver bullets," the voice over the phone snarled, as the cop slammed down the receiver.

"We can't just leave her loose, out there," I said.

"What else can we do?" Charlie answered. "We saved ourselves from the evil that attempted to destroy

us. The world outside is full of killers. What else can
we do?''

But there was something I could do. I could print the
truth. I couldn't force anyone to believe it, but I could
get it into print.

"Hey, Eddie," my boss said enthusiastically over the
phone, " 'Liz Takes Bath in Front of Millions of Ador-
ing Fans.'—Is that lead or is that *lead?*''

"How 'bout *this?*'' I shot right back at him:
" 'Woman Bites Dog, Bites Man, Bites Self.' '' So it
wasn't a lead story, but I got it in print. (The rest of it's
up to you.)

And as for Charlie, as with the rest of the world, there
was a whole lot too much going on, with no time-outs
included in the deal. He was changing every night now.
Developing into . . . we knew not what. He did not seem
to be held back by any constraints emanating from the
werewolf legend. It made no difference to him whether
it was full moon or not, and garlic was fine as long as
it was mixed in with properly prepared hamburger:
Charlie was something brand new.

It was a few days later that I got the call. Charlie was
in his doggie phase. But, as with Cindy, he was never
quite all the way in one stage or the other: There was
dog in the human, human in the dog. So he knew something was up with the phone call. He kept barking at
me, staring at me with those huge dark inquisitive eyes.
He was, of course, trying to speak.

"It was Melissa," I said, hesitantly. "She, uh . . .
well, Charlie, she was lying. Her father's not dying. He's
not her father, he's some young stud she met at the
disco. She's not coming back." I choked up, and for a
moment I couldn't speak. Then I said: "I guess she's
ditched us both."

Charlie whined and scampered out of the room. I
could hear his little claws on the kitchen linoleum, the

sound of him pacing back and forth. Back and forth. But later, when I drowsed off as usual, and woke up to find him curled up asleep in my lap, his face was once again the face of a human: But not the same human.

"Not to worry, Charlie," I was amazed to hear myself say. "We'll stick together, you and me. Ride it out. All of it, to the very end."

The eyes blinked open, and the human face yawned. The tortured eyes stared into mine for what seemed to me like a very long time.

"You poor human sap, don't you know that there's no such *thing* as an end?" he said finally. And then closed his weary eyes again. And slept.

THE MADONNA OF THE WOLVES

S. P. Somtow

*"The Madonna of the Wolves" was purchased by
Gardner Dozois, and appeared in the November
1988 issue of* Asimov's *with an interior illustration by Laura Lakey. Somtow, who has also written under the name of Somtow Sucharitkul, made
his first sale here to George Scithers in 1978, and
has since contributed a long string of stories to
the magazine under several different regimes. In
the moody, atmospheric, and very scary story that
follows, he takes us along on a sinister journey
through nineteenth-century Europe on the old
Orient Express, through snow-choked forests and
across the desolate, moonlit expanses of the
moors, as a young woman hurtles relentlessly toward a destiny that will be far stranger than she
could possibly imagine. . . .*

*Born in Bangkok, Thailand, S. P. Somtow has
lived in six countries and was educated at Eton
and Cambridge. Multitalented as well as multilin-
gual, he has an international reputation as an
avant-garde composer, and his works have been
performed in more than a dozen countries on four
continents. Among his compositions are "Gon-
gula 3 for Thai and Western Instruments" and*

"The Cosmic Trilogy." He's also dabbled in the film world, acting as writer, director, and composer for such horror movies as The Laughing Dead *and an updated version of* A Midsummer Night's Dream *called* Ill Met By Moonlight. *Back in the print world, his book publications include the novels* Starship and Haiku, Mallworld, Light on the Sound, The Aquiliad, The Darkling Wind, The Shattered Horse, *and* The Fallen Country. *In the last few years, he's become even better known as a horror writer than as an SF writer with major horror novels such as the landmark* Vampire Junction *and* Valentine, *as well as a memorable werewolf novel,* Moon Dance. *His most recent books are the semi-autobiographical novel of a boyhood in Thailand,* Jasmine Nights, *and a new book in his "Vampire" series,* Vanitas. *In 1986, he received the Daedalus Award for* The Shattered Horse. *A resident of the United States for many years, he now makes his home in California.*

"Excuse me. Might I respectfully inquire . . . are you . . . might you possibly be . . . Mademoiselle Martinique?"

"Sir, this is the ladies' waiting room. I trust that you will recognize the impropriety of your presence amongst these unescorted ladies, and that you will retire a few paces beyond the entrance and state your request without the forwardness you have just exhibited."

"I say. Awfully sorry, I'm sure."

Overhearing this conversation and her own name, Speranza Martinique looked up from her Bible. A corpulent woman, whose feathery hat ill suited her belligerent demeanor, was having an altercation with a bearded gentleman in morning dress. Perhaps this was the messenger that his lordship's secretary had mentioned in his letter to her. She rose and tugged at the fat woman's sleeve. "Your pardon, madam, but I think the gentleman is looking for me."

The woman turned on her with a look of sheer disdain. She shuddered, and her unnatural plumage shuddered with her. "A railway station waiting room is hardly the place for a furtive encounter," she said. "I find the fact that you seek to disguise your unnatural intentions behind a *Bible* most revolting."

Mildly, Speranza said to the aggravating woman: "Look to the mote in your own eye, madam; it is the best way, I have found, of alleviating the harm that a prolonged meditation on the world's evils can afflict upon a lady's refined sensibilities."

"I never!" the fat woman said, as Speranza swept past her and accosted the bearded gentleman, who was waiting by the entrance. She could see that he was amused by their exchange; but seeing her approach, he suppressed his laughter and was all gravity.

"Mademoiselle," he began in atrocious French, pulling a sealed paper from his waistcoat pocket, "j'ai l'honneur de vous présenter cette lettre écrite par—"

"Heavens!" the fat woman remarked, eavesdropping at the door. "I should have known. A Frenchwoman. What an unprincipled lot, those frogs!"

"Only half French, actually," Speranza said, "and half Italian. Oh, sir, do let's continue this conversation elsewhere! Certain people are becoming most tiresome! Surely the crowds that are gathered here will render a chaperone unnecessary."

"I say, you speak English awfully well, what."

"I do," Speranza said, "and if it is not too forward of me, might I ask that we use English from now on? I think my command of that tongue might be a little . . ." She tried to say it tactfully, but could not; so she changed the subject slightly. "I was, after all, the governess of the son of Lord Slatterthwaite, the Hon. Michael Bridgewater, before he was unfortunately taken from us—"

"Consumption, I understand," said the messenger,

shaking his head. "But I have neglected to introduce myself. My name is Cornelius Quaid. I represent . . . a certain party, whose name I am not presently at liberty to divulge."

"Lord Slatterthwaite assured me that this party's credentials are impeccable. I will take him at his word, Mr. Quaid. And where is the boy?"

"Soft, soft, Mademoiselle Martinique. All in good time. First let me go over the plans with you. Here is the letter I spoke of; it will allow you and the lad safe passage to your destination. Attached to it is a banker's note which, you will find, will cover any emergency you may encounter; I trust you will not abuse it. The traveling papers, tickets, itineraries, and other paraphernalia are here as well. You depart in a little over an hour. Your things are at the left luggage office, I presume? I shall have my man see to them. Furthermore—" he reached into a capacious trouser pocket and pulled out a small purse "—I have been authorized to give you a small advance." Speranza was very grateful for this, for her dismissal from Lord Slatterthwaite's service, though no fault of hers, would have left her destitute, had it not been for this rather mysterious new development. "Count it at your leisure, mademoiselle. You will find that it contains one hundred guineas in gold. The rest, you may be sure, will be forthcoming upon the safe delivery of the boy to a certain Dr. Szymanowski, in Vienna."

"I will take your word on it, Mr. Quaid," Speranza said, tucking the purse into an inside pocket of her coat. Where was the child? His lordship had told her that her new duties would involve escorting a young lad across Europe, for which, he said, she was eminently suited; for not only was she trained in the care of children, but she was well acquainted not only with French, English, and Italian, but had a smattering of the many languages of the Austro-Hungarian Empire. There was no more

information about the boy, however, and Speranza was
anxious to learn all she could. She was regretting having
left the relative warmth of the ladies' waiting room. Victoria Station, imposing though it was, was not well
heated; and she could see, clinging to the hair of beggars
and urchins and to the hats and overcoats of those who
could afford them, evidence of the snowstorm that was
raging without. It was a veritable bedlam here: flower
girls, newspaper vendors, old women hawking steak and
kidney pies, and of course the passengers themselves.
Rich and poor, they shuffled about, their expressions
bearing that self-imposed bleakness which Speranza
found all too common amongst the English.

"The boy?" she said at last.

"Ah yes, the boy." For the first time, a look of trepidation seemed to cross the face of Cornelius Quaid.
Was the boy ill? Consumptive, perhaps, and capable of
spreading the disease? But Speranza had remained at
poor little Michael's bedside day and night for many
weeks. Surely, if she were going to catch it, she would
have done so already.

She said, "Sir, I am not afraid of catching a disease.
I take it that disease is at issue here, since you desire
me to deliver him to this doctor. A specialist, I assume?
I assure you I will take the greatest pains to—"

"Mademoiselle, the boy's affliction is not physical. It
is of the soul."

"Ah, one of the newfangled *dementiae*?" Speranza
was aware that certain research was being done into the
dark recesses of the mind; but of course such subjects
were not within the boundaries of decent discourse.

"No, I mean the soul, mademoiselle, not the mind."

She stiffened a little at this, for the fat lady had been
unwittingly right in one thing; the Bible that Speranza
Martinique carried upon her person was a purely cos-
metic device. For Speranza suffered constantly from
thoughts that, she felt, should correctly be suppressed;

her severe dress and her Bible were intended to deflect the suspicions of strangers, who she was certain could see into her very soul did she not stand constant guard against discovery.

"The boy is possessed," Mr. Quaid said in profound earnest. "Sometimes, when the moon is full . . ."

"Tush, Mr. Quaid! This is the nineteenth century; we don't believe such superstitions any more, do we?" she said, a little uncomfortably, shivering a little, thinking to herself: I have every right to shiver, do I not? It is the dead of winter, and these beastly English do enjoy the cold so. "Let us just say that the boy is . . . ill."

"Very well, then. I am no expert on the young. But I will tell you this. The boy's parents are dead. They were killed under most unpleasant circumstances. I wasn't made privy to the details, but there was . . ." he lowered his voice, and Speranza had to strain to hear him, "devil worship. Heathen rites. Mutilation, I believe. Terrible, terrible!"

"If so, then the boy's distress is perfectly understandable. Possession, indeed! Grief, confusion, perhaps a misunderstanding of the nature of good and evil . . . nothing that proper, attentive care won't heal," Speranza said. She did not add—though she almost blurted it out—that she found the English notion of loving care most astonishing, consisting as it did of little more than an assiduous application of the birch to the behind. Ah, where do they get their love of flagellation from? she mused.

"Well," Mr. Quaid said, interrupting her reverie, "it is time you met your charge."

He gestured. So imperious was his gesture that the crowd seemed to part. Two men came forward; they appeared to be footmen from some well-established household. The boy was between them. The shame of it, Speranza thought, having him escorted like a prisoner! After all he has suffered!

"Come, Johnny," said Mr. Quaid. "This is Mademoiselle Martinique, who will assume the responsibility for your welfare until you are safely in the hands of Dr. Szymanowski."

He makes him sound like a sacrificial animal, Speranza thought. And she looked at the boy who walked towards her with his eyes downcast. She had expected a rich, pampered-looking child; but Johnny wore clothes that, had they not recently been cleaned, might have come from a poorhouse; his coat, she noticed with her practiced eye, had been clumsily mended. He was blond and blue-eyed; his hair was clipped short; only prisoners and denizens of lunatic asylums had their hair that short, because they had sold it to wigmakers. She wondered where Johnny had been living before his nameless benefactor found him. And no more than seven years old! Or perhaps he was small for his age, improperly fed. He came closer but continued to stare steadfastly at the ground. His face, she noticed, was scarred in a dozen places. He had clearly been mistreated. Those English! she thought bitterly, remembering that even in the final stages of his consumption the Hon. Michael Bridgewater had occasionally been subjected to the rod.

And to the fresh air, she remembered. That fresh air that they love so much here, freezing though it might be. She was sure that the fresh air had driven little Michael to his death. She was determined that no such thing would happen to this Johnny. Already she felt a fierce protectiveness towards him.

"Johnny Kindred," Cornelius Quaid said, "you are to obey your new guardian in all ways. Understood?"

"Yes, sir," the boy mumbled.

"You may shake Mademoiselle Martinique's hand. Bow smartly. There. Now say, 'How do you do, Mademoiselle Martinique.' "

Speranza grew impatient. "Mr. Quaid, I trust you will allow me to exercise my particular speciality now." She

turned to the child and took his hand. It was shaking
with terror. She gripped it affirmatively, reassuringly.
"You may call me Speranza," she said to him. "And
you needn't shake my hand. You may kiss me on the
cheek, if you like."

Mr. Quaid rolled his eyes disapprovingly.

"Speranza," the boy said, looking at her for the first
time.

She did not wait for Mr. Quaid to harangue her. Without further ado, still grasping the boy's hand, she steered
him towards the platform. Soon they would reach the
sea. Soon they would cross the English Channel and
reach a land where men did not hesitate to show their
feelings.

Already she had begun to love the child they had entrusted to her care. Already she was determined to heal
his anguish. Affliction of the soul indeed, the poor boy!
Speranza believed that love could cure most every illness. And though she was a woman possessed of many
accomplishments, it was love that was her greatest tal-
ent.

On the train from London, on the ferry across the Channel, the boy said nothing at all. In France he merely
asked for food and drink at the appropriate times. Their
benefactor had bought them second class tickets; Speranza was glad of that, for she had had occasion to travel
by third class, and she knew that it would be crowded
and cold and crammed to bursting with unpleasant char-
acters.

When they crossed the German border, the two old
priests who had been occupying their compartment left,
and she and the boy had it to themselves. His mood
lightened a little. There was not much to watch but fields
and fields of snow, and now and then a country station
with an ornate, wrought-iron sign and a bench or two.
Speranza decided that the best tactic would be to wait;

when the boy was ready, he would doubtless begin to talk. He was afraid of everything; she already knew that, for whenever she tried to touch him, he flinched violently away from her as though she were on fire.

A few kilometers into Germany, the boy asked her, "Have you any games, Mademoiselle?"

At last, she thought, he is giving me an opening. Another part of her reflected: Yet I must not become too attached to him; he is mine for only a few more days. And in the back of her mind she saw Michael Bridgewater's pathetically small coffin being lowered into the ground. That too had been in the snow.

"Speranza," she said to him, reminding him that they were to be companions, not opponents. She opened a valise which Quaid's people had provided, labeled *Entertainments*; it contained, she saw, a pack of cards, a backgammon set, and a snakes and ladders board. "Shall we play this?" she said, pulling it out and setting it down on the middle seat, between them. Steadily the fields of snow unreeled. The game was not printed on cardboard, but handpainted on a silken surface. The snakes were very realistically depicted. There was a velvet pouch with a pair of ivory dice and a tortoiseshell die-cup.

The boy nodded.

"Good, Johnny," she said. She wished she could pat his cheek, but knew that he would flinch again. Instead she handed him the dice.

He threw a 3 and eagerly moved his counter three squares. There was a ladder, and he clambered up to the third row. Speranza threw a 5, and was stuck on the bottom. They played for a few minutes, until Speranza encountered her first snake and slid back down almost to square one. Johnny laughed.

Then he said, "Those snakes, they're just like a man's prick, aren't they, Speranza?"

Speranza did not quite believe she had heard him say

that. She was flustered for a moment, then said, "Why, where did you learn a word like that from, Johnny?"

"Jonas taught me."

"And who might Jonas be?" Speranza asked, intrigued. Clearly the boy's upbringing had had almost nothing to commend it.

The boy said nothing; he had a guilty look, and Speranza felt that to probe further would perhaps be inopportune. They went on playing. Johnny's counter hit a snake and slid. He cackled. "Right through to the snake's bleeding arsehole!" he said. His voice seemed different; harsher, more grownup.

"Johnny, I am a rather unorthodox woman, but even I find your language a trifle indecent," she said mildly.

"Fuck you!" Johnny said. He looked her straight in the eye. There was anger in those eyes, blazing, unconscionable anger. "Fuck, fuck, fuck, fuck, fuck!"

"Johnny!"

He started to cry. "I'm sorry," he sobbed, "I'm sorry, sorry, sorry. Jonas told me to do it, it wasn't me, honestly it wasn't." He crumpled into her arms, dashing the snakes and ladders board to the floor. Seeing how much he needed affection made Speranza hug him tightly to her. But as he buried his face in her breast she heard him growl, she *felt* his growl reverberate against the squeezing of her corsets. It was like the purring of a cat, but far more vehement, far more menacing. She thought: I cannot be afraid of him; he is only a child, a poor hurt child, and she clasped him to her bosom, struggling not to disclose her anxiety.

They crossed the Rhine. At Karlsruhe, they waited for several hours; part of the train was detached and sent north, and they were to be joined by another segment that had come up from Basle. Thinking to give the boy some exercise, Speranza took him for a walk, up and down the platform. Although the station was canopied, there was some snow and slush on the cars and on the tracks, and many of the passengers milling around outside had snow in their hair and on their coats. The car that joined theirs was elaborate, and bore on its sides the crest of some aristocratic family. Of course, Speranza thought, we have to wait for those high-and-mighty types.

"Let's go and see!" Johnny said. There was nothing in him now of the obscene, deep-voiced child that had emerged earlier. He was all innocence. She was convinced now that his problem was some kind of division within his soul, some combat between the forces of light and darkness. Taking his hand, she took him up to the carriage.

Heavy drapes prevented one from seeing inside. The car seemed dilapidated, and the coat-of-arms had not been painted lately; beneath it was the legend:

von Bächl-Wölfing

in the *fraktur* script which Speranza found difficult to read. The arms themselves were fairly ordinary looking. Two silver wolf's heads glared at each other across a crimson field. Argent, she reminded herself, and gules. Little Michael had always been very particular about heraldry. But then he had been the son of a peer of the realm. As she mused on her former life as the young aristocrat's governess, she saw that Johnny had stepped up very close to the track, that he was shaking his fist at the coat-of-arms . . . that the same menacing growl was issuing from his throat.

Then, to her alarm, Johnny pulled down his trousers and urinated onto the side of the train.

"Johnny, you must stop!"

"I am Jonas!" He turned; their eyes met once; she saw that his eyes were slitty-golden . . . like the eyes of a wild animal! Terrified, she started to follow him, but he growled and sprinted to the front of the train, across the track, clambered up to the other side of the platform.

She called after him. Then she started to run after him.

I'll have to take a short cut, she thought. She dived into the train. An old peasant woman with two hens in a basket looked up at her. She tried to open the door on the other side, but it would not come open.

She pressed her face against the window, called his name again. He was urinating again, on the track, on the steps into the train, and shouting, "This is my place I'll not run in your pack I'm me I'm me leave me alone alone alone!"

"Help me," Speranza whispered. "If you please, though I can't speak your language . . . au secours, j'ai perdu mon enfant . . ."

Some of the others in the carriage were looking out, too. A burly man said to her, "Is' es Ihr Kind dort aufm Gleis?"

She nodded, not understanding. The man began shouting, and an official in uniform came and opened the door. Speranza and some of the others leapt down onto the side of the track.

"I'll not run in it I'll not I'll not!" Johnny screamed, spraying them with piss.

"Was sagt er denn?" The strange man caught the boy and held him tight as he wriggled. "Beruhe dich," he said softly to him, and stroked him gently on the neck and head. Johnny grew still.

"Thank you." Speranza reached out to take him from the man. He was curled up in fetal position, sucking his thumb. His clothes and his face and arms were stained and foul-smelling; it was an unfamiliar odor, as though his urine were somehow not quite human.

In the compartment, she filled a jug with water, moistened a towel, and began to swab his face. He did not stir. A whistle sounded, and the train began to ease itself away from the station. The odor was pungent, choking. But Speranza had cleaned and washed little Michael every day in the last weeks of his consumption, and her stomach was not easily turned. The boy seemed to be fast asleep. She did not want to embarrass him. She took off his coat and laid him on it. Very gently she began to undo his back and front collar-stud and to pull his shirt over his head, and to unbutton his braces so that she could unfasten his trousers. The shirt tore as it came away. The backs of the child's hands were covered with fine, shiny hair. His back was unusually hairy, too; when she started to wipe it it gleamed like sealskin. There were welts and scars all over him; she knew from this that he had been beaten, probably habitually, since many of the marks were white and smooth. She wrung out the cloth, soaked it in water again, and cleansed him as best she could. Though she tried to look away, she could not help seeing his tiny penis, quite erect above a tuft of silverwhite hair. She did not think little Michael had had hair down there. This boy definitely had some minor physical abnormalities as well as his obvious emotional ones.

The sun began to set behind distant white hills. She managed to get him into a nightgown that had been starched stiff; clearly it had never been used before, like all the other clothes in the trunk that Quaid's men had loaded onto the train. The sharpness of the fabric must have disturbed him. He opened his eyes and said, "Tell me a story, please, Speranza. Then I'll be fast asleep and Jonas won't come, he never comes when I'm asleep."

She was going to ask him about Jonas, but she was afraid her questioning might bring more strange behavior; so she merely said, easing back into the padded seat and allowing him to lie with his head against the lace and black satin of her skirts, "What story would you like? A story about a prince in a castle?A beautiful princess? A dragon, perhaps? Or would that be too frightening?"

"I want Little Red Riding Hood," he said in a small

voice. "But make Little Red Riding Hood a boy."

She tried not to show how startled she was at his request. She felt a strange indecency about what he had asked, though she could not put into words why she would feel that way. She did not look at him while she spoke; she watched the fields go by, the snow slowly blooded by the setting sun. "Once upon a time there was a girl—"

"A boy."

"—named Little Red Riding Hood who lived by the edge of the forest." When she reached the part about the wolf dressed in the grandmother's clothing, the boy clung to her in terror, but that terror was also something a little bit like lust . . . she had always known that children are not pure and innocent, as the English liked to believe. But the idea that the boy was enjoying her discomfiture, actually, in some inchoate way, taking advantage of her person . . . and yet, she could tell already, he loved her. So she went on: "And the wolf said, 'The better to eat you with, my darling boy.' And ate the little boy up. In one gulp. And then the hunters—"

"That's enough. They just put the hunters in so little children won't be frightened. But you and I know the truth, don't we?"

"The truth?"

"The hunters don't care. And even if the boy was still alive inside the wolf, then the hunters' rifles would just rip them both apart anyway, wouldn't they, Speranza?"

"It's only a story," she said. The sexual tension had passed away; perhaps, Speranza thought, it was just in herself, she had imagined it; how could a seven-year-old boy, even a profoundly disturbed one, manipulate me in this fashion?

"It's not a story, Speranza. Believe me. And if you can't quite make yourself believe me, maybe you'll talk to Jonas one day." And he drifted into sleep, lulled by the repetitive clanging, and she covered him and sat thinking for a long time. She had forgotten, after all the day's commotion, that they had missed the early session in the dining car.

There was a knock at the door.

"Dar fich herein, bitte?" A slimy voice; the sort of man used to toadying; not the kind of voice she expected for a railway official. Her heart beat faster.

"Je m'excuse," she said in French, "je ne comprends pas l'allemand." Then she added in English, "Please, sir, I have no German."

She unlatched the door of the compartment.

It was a man in evening dress, very stiff and proper, bearing a silver tray. "May it please you, Fräulein Martinique," he said, "my master would very much enjoy the pleasure of your company at dinner, now that the boy is asleep."

"How does he know—"

"He felt it, gnädiges Fräulein. In his heart."

"Sir, I do not think it is quite proper for a man to invite a woman to whom he has not been properly introduced—"

The steward, or butler, or whoever it was, handed her the little platter. There was a calling card on it, printed on rag paper, with a gold border. It contained only the name:

Graf Hartmut von Bächl-Wölfing

Speranza knew that the word *Graf* meant Count or Earl or some such title. What did this man know about her and the boy? How could he have felt the boy's waking and sleeping? And why did Johnny try to urinate all over the Count's railway carriage? She was afraid of what this might be leading to. She felt a premonition of something . . . unnatural. Perhaps even supernatural. But Speranza was not superstitious, and curiosity vanquished her fear.

The Count's servant was waiting for her reply.

"I will be glad to come," she said, "if you will send

someone to watch the child while I dine; and perhaps the Count's cook could prepare some small tidbit for me to bring back to him. Poor Johnny is worn out, but he hasn't had his supper, and I think he may wake up hungry in the middle of the night.''

The servant paused, perhaps translating her comments to himself; the train clattered as it negotiated a curve. "Yes, gnädiges Fräulein," he said at last.

"Now leave me so that I can dress. If I am to meet a Count, I ought perhaps to try not to look so shabby," she said, feeling suddenly frail.

When the man departed, Speranza looked through her trunk and found little to wear; she changed into a somewhat cleaner black dress, tried to tidy her hair, and threw over the drab costume a rabbitfur pelisse. She did have a few articles of jewelry; she selected a silver necklace studded with cabochon amethysts. A little ostentatious, perhaps? But it was all she had. She looked at her reflection against the glass and the snow. Perhaps, she thought, I could be more attractive. In the window I seem to be a governess, only a governess ... but I have dark dreams for a governess, dark and daring thoughts.

Presently a serving maid, perhaps fourteen, in a uniform came, curtseyed, said, "Für den Knaben." Speranza assumed she had come to watch the boy, and left; the manservant was waiting to conduct her down the corridor. A moment of intense cold as the footman helped her across the precarious coupling beween the two cars, and then it was warm again, stiflingly warm, inside the domain of the Count von Bächl-Wölfing.

The first thing she felt was gloom. The curtains were tightly drawn, and the only light was from a gold candelabrum in the middle of a table of dark Italian marble. The candles were black. The servant showed her to a fauteuil, overplump, dusty, dark velvet; a second servant poured wine into a crystal goblet. Were it not for the

ceaseless motion of the train, she would have thought
herself in a sumptuous, if somewhat ill-kept, apartment
in Mayfair.

The servant, seeming to address the empty room, said,
"Euer Gnade, das französische Fräulein, das Ihr einge-
laden habt." He bowed.

"Welcome," said a voice: liquid, deep, suggestive,
even, of some hidden eroticism. At first she saw only
eyes; the eyes glittered. Strangely, they reminded her of
Johnny's eyes, when he had undergone that eerie metamorphosis into his other, demented self; clear, yellow,
like polished topazes. Now she saw the face they were
set in: a lean face, a man clearly middleaged yet somehow also youthful. His hair, balding, was silver save for
a dark streak above his left temple. His upper lip sported
the barest hint of a mustache.

He said, "Ou est-que vous préférez que je vous parle
en français, peutêtre?" His pronunciation was impeccable.

"It doesn't matter," Speranza said, "what we speak.
But perhaps you can explain to me ... oh, so many
things ... who are you, why do you seem to know so
much about the child and me."

"I am but a pilgrim," von Bächl-Wölfing said, "I
journey to the same shrine as you, my dear Mademoiselle Martinique—or perhaps you will permit me the liberty of addressing you as Speranza. Your name means
hope, and without hope our cause is doomed, alas."

"Your cause?"

The Count moved closer to her, and seated himself in
a leather armchair. "Ah yes. We are all going to see Dr.
Szymanowski, are we not?"

"I am to deliver the boy to him."

He sighed; she felt an almost unbearable sadness in
him, though she could not tell why. It was as if his
emotions were borne on the dust in the air of the car-

riage, as though she could smell his melancholy. "And after?" he said.

"I do not know, sir. Perhaps I shall return to my family in Aix-en-Provence." A maid was serving a fish course; the Count nibbled distractedly, but Speranza was more hungry than she had thought. "Something your servant said . . . that you *felt* that Johnny had gone to sleep . . . in your heart. What did that mean?"

"We have a secret language."

"But you did not even see him."

The Count wrinkled his nose. "I most certainly smelt him, mademoiselle! Still that odor lingers in the air . . . ah, but you cannot smell it. Some of us are more . . . deprived . . . than others."

"If you are referring to Johnny's unfortunate . . . accident . . ."

"It was no accident!" the Count said, laughing. "But he has much to learn. A youngling cannot usurp the territory of a leader merely by baptizing his environment with piss! Ah, but you are shocked at my language; I forgot, you have been in England for a long while. Seriously, mademoiselle, the boy knows only instinct at the moment; soon he will combine that instinct with intelligence. To be able to help mold his mind, so malleable, yet so filled with all that separates our kind from—"

"I have no idea, Count, what you are talking about."

"I apologize. I begin to ramble when the moon waxes. It makes up for the times when I am robbed of the power of human discourse."

Why, Speranza thought, he is as mad as the boy is! Who was this Dr. Szymanowski? Surely the purveyor of a lunatic asylum. And they were going to use Johnny. Experiments, perhaps. Speranza had read *Frankenstein*. She knew what scientists could be like. She wondered whether the young serving girl who was alone with the boy was really—

"She knows nothing," said Count von Bächl-Wölfing.

"You read minds, Count?"

"No. But I *am* observant," he said softly. "I know, for example, that though you appear to me in the guise of a prim, severe governess, that is merely a shield behind which hides a woman of passion, a woman who can take agonizing risks; a dangerous woman, a woman fascinated by what other women shy away from; a woman capable of profound, consuming love."

Speranza's heart began to pound. "Count, I am perhaps a more modern woman than many of my occupation; but I hardly think the first few moments of a meeting, even when the difference in rank between us is so great, is a suitable time for—"

"You are quite wrong, Speranza. I do desire you, but . . . some things one can perforce live without. The boy is important, though. He is a new thing, you see, a wholly new kind of creature. But I see you do not understand me." He sighed; again she seemed to sense that perfume of dolorousness in the air. "It is all so unfair of me . . . but believe me, I would not say these things about you without having first ordered a thorough investigation into your character."

"My character is unassailable!" Speranza said, feeling terribly vulnerable, for the Count had ripped away the mask, so painstakingly assumed, and exposed it for the flimsy self-delusion that it was. "How dare you pry into my life, how dare you have me brought here! I think that under the circumstances I should depart immediately."

"Of course. But before that there is something I ought perhaps to tell you."

"We have nothing to say to each other—"

"Except, Mademoiselle Martinique, that I happen to be your employer."

"You! Who communicated with Lord Slatterthwaite—

who sent Cornelius Quaid to Victoria Station—'' She was trembling now; she felt as lost and bewildered as poor mad Johnny Kindred, who did not know if he was one person or two.

The Count merely smiled, and offered her another glass of wine.

Speranza had left the Count's private coach as soon as she could. She had found the child awake, picking at the light supper which had been brought in for him: a little pâté, a bowl of soup, a loaf of black bread, a goblet of hot spiced wine. The maid, seeing her approach so soon after she had left to join von Bächl-Wölfing, curtseyed and departed, smirking . . . or was Speranza only imagining the worst?

"You stink of him," the boy said. It was the other one. The one with the tongue of a guttersnipe. "You reek of him, he's bursting with animal spunk, he's been wanking all over your cunny, did you let him get inside?" Speranza did not attempt to respond, but waited for the fit to end. At last Johnny Kindred emerged long enough to say, "I'm glad you're back; stay with me always." And then he fell asleep in her arms.

The night passed uneasily. Moving, the train seemed to breathe. She was in the belly of a serpent, slithering over the snow, towards . . . towards . . . she could not tell. She blew out the lamp, eased the boy onto his back on the seat opposite hers, and stared at the passing snowscape. Dark firs, silvered by the moon, stretched as far as she could see. Cold, dappled, the light streamed into the compartment. She tried not to think of the Count von Bächl-Wölfing. But her dreams were of being pursued by him through the dank forest, the stench of earth and wolf-piss burning her nostrils, the wind sharp and ice-cold . . . in the dream she remembered thinking that they had left the German forests behind, that this was some quite alien forest of leviathan trees and unfamiliar animals, a forest in some strange new world.

In the morning the same servant appeared with an invitation to breakfast. "You should bring the child," the man said. She looked at Johnny. He seemed contrite; he offered no resistance as she dressed him from the clothes they found in the trunk. For herself she again selected dark colors; again she wore the silver necklace, although she was afraid he would think poorly of her for wearing the same jewelry two days in a row. Then she castigated herself for her foolishness. The Count was immeasurably wealthy, and, more to the point, far above her station; she was only a governess, and of dubious legitimacy at that!

The curtains in the Count's car were still closed. She could not help noticing the smell; she recognized it from last night's dream. The boy began to growl. "Quiet, Johnny, quiet," she said softly. Some daylight seeped in between the closed draperies; dust swam in the rays. She could see the Count's back; he was seated at a writing desk, paying them no heed. She took in details she had missed before; the car was partitioned by a curtain of heavy purple velvet bearing the wolf-crest; perhaps there was a sleeping area behind. Suddenly she was afraid the boy would start pissing on all the priceless furniture. But his growling seemed more for show; soon he became withdrawn, fidgety, his eyes following a dust-mote as it circled.

The Count moved, shrugged perhaps; abruptly the divider drew open, and music played from the adjoining section, soft-pedaled chords on a piano. After a few bars, a clear, sweet tenor voice joined in with a plaintive melody in the minor key. Sunlight streamed in.

The boy's attention was drawn immediately to the music. At last, for the first time, he smiled.

"Schubert," Speranza said, for the song cycle *Win-*

terreise had not been unknown in the Slatterthwaite household, though His Lordship had sung it in his cousin's stilted English translation, with little Michael pounding unmercifully on the family Broadwood. She had not known it could be so beautiful.

The Count said: " *'Fremd bin ich eingezogen, fremd zieh ich wieder aus.'* Do you know what it means, Speranza? It means, 'I came here a stranger; a stranger I depart.' How true. Look, the boy understands it instinctively. He is no longer annoyed with me."

He clapped his hands. The music stopped; the boy's smile faded. "Shall we have breakfast now?" He got up and beckoned them to follow; as he crossed the partition, he nodded and the music resumed almost in mid-note. She took Johnny by the hand and led him. As they passed the desk where von Bächl-Wölfing had been sitting, she saw that he had been writing a letter in English. She had already read the salutation—"My dear Vanderbilt"—before realizing her appalling breach of manners. Of course she would never normally have contemplated scrutinizing another's correspondence; it only showed how powerful an effect the Count had had on her. She resolved to be more prim, more severe in her demeanor. She would not step one inch over the line of propriety—not one inch!

They had a pleasant enough breakfast of pheasant pâté, egg-and-bacon pies, and toast and marmalade. Coffee was served in blue-and-white Delft demitasses. She admired the china. She admired the cutlery, whose ivory handles were carved in the shape of lean wolves, each one with tiny topaz eyes. Throughout the meal the Count said little. He stared at the boy. The boy stared back. They spoke without words. She became aware that she was babbling, trying to fill an uncomfortable silence with chatter. She stopped abruptly. The music filled the air. Schubert's song cycle dealt with beauty and desolation. And so it was here. The windows had been opened a crack, driving out the musky animal odor. The train moved out of the forest, past frozen lakes and somnolent villages. There were mountains in the distance. In a few hours they would enter the empire of Austria-Hungary, teeming with exotic peoples and dissonant languages. She sipped her coffee, which was flavored with nutmeg and topped with whipped cream, and watched the wordless communion of the deranged boy and the worldly aristocrat.

At last the Count said, "You seem to have made quite an impression on the boy, Speranza. He loves you very much, you know. You have a certain magic with children . . . and even, I may add, with the middleaged."

He smiled disarmingly. She blushed like a schoolgirl even as she forced herself to purse her lips and respond with unyielding decorum. "You are pleased to flatter me, Count," she said.

"You shall call me Hartmut," he said expansively.

"I would not make such a presumption," Speranza said. Her pulse quickened. She steadied her hand by meticulously buttering a slice of toast and applying the pâté to it, patting it into place and making firm, precise ridges with the pâté-knife. Before she could finish, he had reached across the table and was grasping her hand firmly. His hand was hairy and slick with sweat. She felt as though her hand had been plunged into a furnace. Quickly she snatched it away. The Count smiled with his lips, with the contours of his face; but his eyes betrayed an untouchable sadness.

"What are you thinking? That you should touch that sadness?" How strange, she thought, that he could read her mind so accurately. "Ah, but you have not yet learnt the impossibility of the task you set yourself. You are young, so terribly young. Can *you* cage the beast within, Speranza, even though you are fully human?"

"Sir, you are forward."

"It is because you wish it."

There was danger here, though the compartment was awash with light. Speranza decided that she might as well be direct. "Why, Count von Bächl-Wölfing, have you had us brought here? Why do you keep hinting of mysteries? There is an air that you affect, a feeling almost of some supernatural being. I do not think that it is merely the result of your high birth, if I do not overstep—"

"Everything you have imagined, mademoiselle, is true."

But she had not yet imagined . . . the boy was growling again. He was toying with his food. He leapt onto the table on all fours. The Count turned to him. In a second his face seemed transformed. He snarled once. The boy slid sullenly back into his seat. The Count's face returned to normal. Speranza studied him for some clue as to its metamorphosis, but saw nothing.

"What did you do to make him stop?" she asked him.

"We have a way with each other."

"To return to this subject . . . why are we playing at these guessing games, Count? I am a modern woman, and not fond of mysteries."

"I am a werewolf."

They rode on, not speaking, for some moments. The train clattered harshly against the Schubert melodies. Her rational mind told her that the Count was once more entertaining some elaborate fantasy to which she was not privy. Once more she considered the notion that he might be as mad as little Johnny. But another part of her had already seized on the statement. She could not deny that it was intriguing. Though she hardly dared admit it to herself, she even found the idea glamorous.

"Noch was Kaffee, gnädiges Fräulein?" the manservant said, smoothly gliding into position on her right. She nodded absently and he poured.

"I hear no reaction, mademoiselle, to what must constitute a most singular revelation." Was he laughing at

her? But no, he seemed all seriousness. "Perhaps I
should go on about wolf's bane, about nocturnal meta-
morphoses under the full moon, about silver bullets, and
so on. But you will only say, 'I am a modern woman,'
and dismiss with that specious argument the accumu-
lated knowledge of millennia. Let me suggest, instead,
that you ask the boy. He knew at once. He knows now.
By the way, he's a werewolf, too."

She turned to Johnny. She knew at once that the boy
believed at least part of what the Count was saying. But
there was something not quite right about Johnny's place
in this scheme. "Perhaps you, Count, are suffering from
some dementia that convinces you that you are . . . other
than human," she said. "But Johnny's troubles are far
less simple."

"True," said the Count. "How quickly you have di-
vined, mademoiselle, the dilemma that is at the very
heart of my involvement with him!" He did not seem
to want to expand on the subject, and turned his attention
instead to a snuffbox which his manservant had brought
him on a silver tray.

She was bursting with curiosity and frustration. Instead she asked him, "And Dr. Szymanowski? Who is
he?"

"A visionary, my dear mademoiselle! Whereas I . . .
I merely pay the bills. By the way, what is your opinion
of America?"

Taken aback by his change of subject, she said,
"Why, very little, Count! That is, I know that it is a
wild country of savages who are ruled by renegades
scarcely less savage than the *Indiens peaux-rouges* themselves."

The Count laughed. "Ah, a wild country. Perhaps you
will understand why it calls to the wildness within us.
In humans, but especially in us, who are—humor me at
least for the moment—not entirely human. It cries to us
across the very sea." Almost as an afterthought, he

added, "I have been making a number of investments there. They are, I think, shrewd ones."

Speranza had the distinct impression that he was attempting, in a roundabout manner, to answer her questions; at the same time he was testing her, daring her to reveal the darkness inside herself. There was also something in him of a small boy with a secret . . . the frog in the waistcoat pocket . . . the Latin book coded with obscene messages in invisible ink . . . he wanted to know if he could trust her with the truth, but the truth excited him so much that he could hardly restrain himself from spilling everything. Even the sadness in his eyes seemed to have lifted a little. This in him she could understand, for she well knew the minds of children.

She had an idea. "But the cutlery . . . is it not silver? And if it is true that you are indeed what you claim to be . . . is not silver a substance that might cause you distress?"

"My dear Speranza, heft my spoons and forks in your dainty hands! Are they not of unwonted heaviness? I have no cutlery on my dining table that is not purest platinum." He grinned, as though to say, "I was ready for that one; ask something a little more tricky."

"And the full moon. . . ."

"Will soon be upon us. Oh, don't worry, my dear Mademoiselle Martinique. You will be quite safe, as long as you observe certain conditions which I will spell out to you before moonrise. Ah, I see that you are skeptical, are you not? You think little of these extravagant claims?"

"Only, Count, that you are possessed of a powerful imagination." She felt uncomfortable, since both man and boy were staring intently at her, so she continued, "Oh, come, sir! Here we are sitting amidst brilliant sunshine, doing nothing more supernatural than eating a pheasant pâté; how can you expect your ghost stories to have their full effect?"

"Ghost stories! Is that what you think they are?"

"Is it not what they are?"

"You mistake me, Speranza. I do not believe in ghosts. Nor spirits, nor demons, nor any of the trappings of damnation. How can I allow myself to believe in such things? I would fall prey to the utmost despair, for in the Christian hegemony in which we find ourselves, such as I dare hope for no salvation, no redemption from the everlasting fire; we are damned already, damned without hope, damned before we are ever judged! Quindi, Speranza, quindi bramo la speranza!"

He spoke to her in her mother's tongue, the tongue of gentleness and warmth; she felt as though he had violated her final, innermost hiding place. She did not yield, but continued in English, to her the coldest of languages: "And why, Count von Bächl-Wölfing, why is it that you so ardently yearn for hope?"

"But I forget myself." The Count's passion had been but fleeting; now he was all correctness. "I apologize for inflicting my religious torment on you, mademoiselle; I trust you have not been too disturbed by my words?"

"On the contrary, the fault is mine," Speranza said automatically, thinking nothing of the kind. "I should perhaps be going now?"

The sun hung low over the snow.

Johnny sat with his nose pressed against the pane.

"What do you think?" he asked her suddenly. "Shall we trust him? Shall we run with him in the cold cold forest?"

"I don't know what you mean."

"You're going to go to him tonight, aren't you? He'll invite you. Maybe he won't, but you'll find some excuse. Because you're dying from curiosity. You want to know if it's true. And you want to fuck him."

"Johnny, I really must insist—" But she knew that

all he said was true. He understood her so well, this lunatic.

"My language. I can't help it, though, I'm possessed by demons, you see. Everyone says so."

"Johnny, there aren't any demons. Even the Count says so."

"I don't want to be this way."

"You don't have to be, Johnny, because I'm going to help you, I'm going to pull you out of this sickness of yours somehow."

"Will you love me, Speranza?"

"Of course I will."

"Then you must fuck me, too, mustn't you?" The words no longer offended her; she knew it was part of his illness. Somehow these things had become terribly confused for him. How could she blame him? Even she was confused, and she was a sane woman, was she not? She tried to pry him from the window, thinking to comfort him; he resisted at first, but then threw himself into her arms with a hunger that was like anger, and it frightened her, how so much passionate anguish could come in so frail a package; and as she hugged him she heard him wailing, with a desperate concern for her and for his own future, "When you go to see him tonight, you have to wear the silver necklace, don't ever take it off whatever he says don't you ever ever *ever* take it off!"

The inner world of Johnny Kindred was like a forest: not the picture-book forest of fairytales, but a forest of gnarled trees knotted with rage, of writhing vines, of earth pungent with piss and putrescence, of clammy darkness. At the very center of the forest there was a clearing. The circle was the center of the world, and it was bathed in perpetual, pallid moonlight. When you stood in the circle of light, you could see the outside world, you could hear, touch, smell. You controlled the body. But you always had to fend off the others. Especially Jonas.

And when you were tired, they gathered, surrounding the circle, thirsting for the light. Waiting to touch the world outside.

Waiting to use the body.

Right now the circle was empty. The body slept.

"Let me through," Johnny said faintly.

The darkness seethed. Vines shifted. And always the wolves howled. There were unformed persons in the depths of the forest, their strength growing. Johnny could smell them. He could smell Jonas most of all. Jonas hanging head downward from a tree. Jonas laughing, the drool glistening on his canines. Calling his name: "Johnny, Johnny, you silly boy, you're just a fucking figment, you're just a dream."

"Let me through—" He had to step into the light before the body wakened. Because the moon would be rising soon.

"Through? You don't even exist. I'm the owner of this body, and you're just a little thing I made up once to amuse myself. Get back, get back. Into the dark, do you hear? Or I'll send for—"

"No!"

"Our father."

"Our father in Hell," Johnny whispered.

"In Hell." He could see Jonas more clearly now. The other boy was swinging back and forth, back and forth. He looked like one of the cards in their mother's tarot deck . . . The Hanged Man. "Fuck you! Why did you have to think of our mother, simple Johnny? Do you want to go back to the madhouse? Perhaps you have fond memories of your mudlarking days, my little mad brother?"

"I forgot. That you can read my mind." The thought of their mother could still hurt Jonas. Johnny tried to think of her again, but he saw only a great blackness.

Jonas had been at work, striking out any bits of the past that displeased him, tossing them aside like the offal that lined the banks of the Thames, like the rubbish piled up against the walls of their old home. Jonas used to bully him all the time at the home. Whenever the beatings started he would push Johnny out into the clearing so that Johnny would feel all the pain. Even though it was always Jonas who had done wrong. "Get out of my mind!" Johnny screamed, despairing.

"Our mind. No. My mind. It's *my* mind, you're in *my* mind. Why can't you be more like me? I'm not a snivelling, snotty-nosed boy who's afraid of the truth. Our mother never could face the truth, could she? You're weak, like *her*, weak, weak, weak!"

Johnny started to run. The mud clung to his toes. Brambles slithered around his ankles. Thorns sliced into his arms, opening up fresh wounds. The clearing didn't get any nearer. He leapt over rotted logs and mossy stones. He had to reach it first, he had to. Dread seeped into him. He knew that Jonas was swinging from tree to tree, his animal eyes piercing the dark. There it was! He was at the edge now, all he had to do was step inside—

He fell! Twigs and leaves flurried. He was at the bottom of a pit. He breathed uneasily. His hand collided with something hard. Pale light leaked in from the clearing. He saw who was in the trap with him . . . a skeleton, chained to the earthen walls with silver that glinted in the light, cold, cold.

"Let me *out*—"

Jonas stood above him. "The body is mine," he said slowly, triumphantly. Johnny could see that he had already begun to change. The snout was bursting from flaps of human skin . . . the eyes were narrowing, changing color.

Desperate, Johnny beat against the wall of his prison. And Jonas cackled. His laughter was already transforming itself into an inhuman howling.

• • •

Speranza watched the boy as he slept. The moon was
rising. She had half believed the Count's insane suggestion that the boy would now transform into a wolf . . .
but he lay peacefully, his eyes closed, curled up on a
woollen blanket.

Speranza watched the moon. She knew she would
soon go to him. Since crossing the Austro-Hungarian
border she had felt dread and desire in equal measure.
They were moving into a thick forest. Bare trees, their
branches weighed down with icicles, obscured the moon.
The train rattled and sighed and seemed almost to
breathe. She steadied herself and watched the trees go
by. Soon, she thought, I will lose the child . . . I will be
free of these madmen. What then? Obscurity in Aix-en-
Provence?

The boy stirred. He moaned. Beneath closed eyelids,
his eyes moved feverishly. She touched his hand. Recoiled. The hand was burning. Burning! It must be a
fever, she thought. And remembered little Michael's
consumption once more. Gingerly she touched his forehead. It was drenched with sweat. She shook him. He
would not waken. "Johnny," she whispered, "Johnny."

He moaned.

"Johnny!" Why am I panicking? she thought. This
dread is quite unreasonable . . . I must cool his brow.

She opened the door of the compartment. The servant
girl who had looked after Johnny before was sleeping in
the corridor. She awoke instantly. "I am sent . . . by the
Count, gnädiges Fräulein."

The Count. . . .

"Has he done something to the boy?" Thoughts of
cruel scientific experiments . . . potions in the food . . .
mesmerism . . . "Fetch some water. Quickly."

"Jawohl, gnädiges Fräulein." The maid hurried down
the narrow walkway. Speranza watched her disappear.
Wind from an open window whipped at her and left

sprinkles of snow on her black dress. She was still wearing the necklace of silver and amethysts.

She expected the maid to return any moment. Time passed. A powerful odor was wafting into the corridor . . . the reek of animal urine. She heard a trickling sound from within the compartment. The poor child, she thought. He is wetting himself. She went back in.

She looked at him in the moonlight. His nightshirt was stained. The urine was running onto the floor of the compartment. His eyes were darting back and forth beneath squeezed lids. His whole body was slick with sweat. She held a handkerchief over her nose, but still the stench was suffocating. Where was the maid? Could they not understand that the boy was sick? She went out into the corridor once more. The cold blasted her. The dread came again, teasing at her thoughts. The maid, she thought, the maid . . .

"At last!" she cried, seeing the girl come back. She was clutching something in her arms . . . a small bottle and a book . . . a Bible, Speranza saw. "I sent you to get water!"

"Holy water," the maid whispered. The terror in her face was unmistakable.

"What's the matter with you?" said Speranza angrily. "Come inside and help me with the child." She went back into the compartment and put her arm under the boy's neck to lift him into a sitting position. The boy was limp, lifeless-seeming.

The maid stood at the door.

"Come and help me—"

The girl made the sign of the cross and looked down at the floor. The train rocked and clattered. The girl held out the holy water and the Bible—

"This is nonsense, purest nonsense!" Speranza cried. "Superstition and nonsense! This Count of yours has you all under the diabolical influence of his mad illusions . . . you must calm yourself, girl.'' How much did the servant understand?

"Ich habe Angst, gnädiges Fräulein."

"Stop chattering and—" She tried to seize the bottle from the girl. It smashed against the seat and broke. Still the boy slept. "You can see quite clearly that the boy is not a werewolf," Speranza said, trying to keep calm. "Stay with him. I'm going to bring the Count. We'll settle this matter once and for all. Stay with the boy, do you understand?"

The girl had thrown herself against the wall and was sobbing passionately. "What's the *matter* with you?" Speranza said. She was losing all patience now. It was one thing to take charge of a child for a few days . . . quite another to be made to cope with an entire trainload of madmen. The maid's hysteria grated on her ears. She could endure it no longer. She stalked out into the corridor and slammed the door of the compartment.

In that moment Jonas leapt into the clearing, seized control of the body, forced open the child's tired eyes, which glowed like fire in the light of the moon.

And howled.

Speranza felt the dread again. It must be the wind, she thought, the desolate relentless wind. It was howling down the hallway. The walls were damp, and snow glistened on the threadbare carpet.

She had to see him. She had to unmask his terrible deception, had to allay this dread that gnawed at her and would not release her . . . she made her way to the end of the corridor, stumbling as the train lurched. She opened the door.

The wind came, whistling, abrasive. She grasped a handhold. There was no one to help her step over the coupling mechanism, which groaned and clanked between the two cars. An animal's cry sounded above the pounding of the train and the clanging of the couplers. The forest stretched in every direction. They were moving downhill. She took a deep breath and skipped across, feeling frantically for a railing. The howling came again. So close . . . it almost seemed to be coming from the train itself and not the forest.

She peered into the Count's private car. Black drapes shrouded the window. "Let me in!" she cried, banging on the glass with her fists.

Abruptly the door opened. She fell into utter darkness.

She heard the door slam. She could see nothing. The air was close and foul. Even the clerestory windows had been covered up. "Count . . ." she whispered.

"You came."

His voice was changed. There was a rasp to it. She stood near the doorway. She could see nothing, nothing at all.

"Come closer, Speranza. Do not be afraid. The utter darkness does tend to impede the transformation a little. You see, I do have your interests at heart."

She hesitated. The stench filled her nostrils. Its fetor masked a more subtle odor, an odor that was strangely exciting. She backed against the door. The train's motion made her tingle. She was sweating. Still she saw nothing. But she could hear him breathing . . .

"You're driving the boy mad," she whispered. Though it's true that I am being paid, I ought perhaps to dissociate myself from—"

"You did not come here to discuss business, Speranza. Am I wrong?"

The smell was seeping into her . . . she felt a retching at the back of her throat . . . and a stirring, a dark stirring beneath her petticoats . . . "No, Count—" she said softly, at last admitting her shameful desire to herself.

"Only the king wolf mates," said the Count, "and he takes for his consort a female from another tribe. . . ."

Something furry had reached up her skirts. It touched

her thigh. It was searing hot. She whimpered. The hand stroked her, burned her . . . moved inexorably up towards her private parts . . . it caressed them now, and she cried out in pain, but there was pleasure behind the pain, and the warmth burst through her body as it shuddered, as it vibrated with the downhill movement of the train . . . "You must not . . . you ought not to . . ." she said . . . she felt something moist teasing at the lips of her vagina, and she felt her inner moisture mingling with sweat and saliva . . . I must resist him, she thought, I would be ruined . . . yet she made no move to escape, for the fire was racing in her nerves and veins . . .

The hands roved, brutal now. Something lacerated her thighs . . . she moaned at the sharp pain . . . were they claws or hands? My imagination is running wild, she thought. The madness is infecting me. The cloth was tearing now. She felt hot blood spurting. "No," she said, trying to tear herself away, "no, don't hurt me." The Count did not answer her with words but with a growl that resonated against her sexual organs. She tried to inch away, but the hands gripped her thighs tighter. She could see nothing, nothing at all, but the railway car smelled of musk and mud and rotten leaves, the air was dank and clogged with the smells of rutting and animal piss . . . at last she managed to free herself. She groped along the wall . . . the wall was clammy, like a earthy embankment . . . her feet were sliding in damp soil . . .

I'm dreaming! she thought. It's because of the darkness, I'm starting to imagine things—

Her hand touched something soft now. Curtains. I have to let in the light, she thought. She tugged at the velvet. A sliver of moonlight lanced the darkness and—

The Count's voice, barely human, "You should not have—not the light—I will change now—change—"

The curtain fell away and the moonlight streamed in across glittering fields of snow. . . .

The Count . . . his face . . . his nose had elongated into

a snout. Even as she watched he was changing. Bristles
sprouting on his cheeks. His teeth were lengthening, his
mouth widening into the foaming jaws of an animal. The
eyes . . . bright yellow now, slitty, implacable. His
hands, already covered with hair, were shrinking into
paws. With a snarl the Count fell down on all fours. His
teeth were slick with drool. The stench intensified. Her
gorge rose. She tasted vomit in the back of her throat.
Then the wolf leapt.

She was thrown back. She fell down into the patch of
moonlight. The beast was ripping away her dress now.
It still desires me, she thought. The wolf's spit sprayed
her face and ran down her neck. She tried to beat it back
but it straddled her now, about to sink its teeth into her
throat—

It touched the silver necklace—

And recoiled, howling! Speranza scrambled to her
feet. The wolf watched her warily. Where its snout had
touched the necklace, there was a burn mark . . . an impression of the silver links in the chain. The wolf whined
and growled. There was a smell of charred fur. Her heart
beat fast. The trickling drool scalded her neck, her exposed breasts.

She found the door, flung it open, ran, clambered
across to the next car, entered. As she slammed the door
shut, she heard an anguished howling over the cacophony of steam and iron.

For a long moment she stood. The howling died away,
or was drowned by the clatter of the train. She stood,
her arms crossed over the front of her tattered chemise,
the chill air numbing the places where the wolf's touch
had seared her.

She touched the silver necklace. It was cool to her
fingers. She thought: impossible, it's all impossible.

Could it have been done with conjurer's tricks? With
pails of animal dung, with suggestive disguises, preying

on a mind already primed to expect a supernatural metamorphosis? Moonlight streamed into the corridor. They
were emerging from the forest now. There were mountains in the distance. In the middle distance was a
church, enveloped in snow, its spire catching the cold
light and softly glittering.

She thought of Johnny.

Whatever the Count was, he was trying to make
Johnny into one, too. Perhaps it was all some inhuman
scientific experiment . . . or some kind of devil-worship.
Had Cornelius Quaid not spoken of mutilations and
atrocities? The poor child!

I must steal him away, she thought. I cannot suffer
him to remain here, succored by lunatics, a lamb
amongst wolves!

Perhaps they had done something to him already . . .

She opened the door of the compartment.

Wind gusted in her face. The window had been
smashed. The floor, the seats, were blanketed in snow.
"Where is he?" she said.

She could not see the young maidservant. Only something lying on one of the seats, covered in a blanket.
Much of the car was in shadow; perhaps the maid was
lurking in a corner, ashamed of something she had done
to the boy! But Speranza did not want to contemplate
it. . . .

"Where is the boy?" Speranza said.

There was no answer.

"Where is he? He was entrusted to your care!"

Still there was no response.

"I have had enough of these enigmas!" Speranza
said. Anger and frustration deluged her. She strode into
the compartment, meaning to slap the servant's face.

Slowly the blanket slid away. Beneath it was a small
boy, naked, disconsolately sobbing. There was blood
everywhere; the seat looked as though it had been
painted with it. It was clear that the maid had tumbled

to her death—that is, if she had not been dead *before* she was cast out.

"Johnny!" She was too shocked to feel revulsion at first.

Slowly the boy's cries ceased. Slowly he lifted his head up. His mouth, his cheeks were smeared with blood, black in the silver moonlight. His hair was matted with it. He said, "I tried to stop Jonas from coming. I *tried*, Speranza. Oh, I didn't want you to know, I threw her out of the window, but I didn't have enough time . . . Oh, Speranza, it's hopeless, I'm never going to be like you and the other humans."

Speranza remembered what the Count von Bächl-Wölfing had said to her also: "Therefore, Speranza, I long for hope." She knew she could not abandon the boy now. Even though he had killed. It was a sickness, a terrible sickness. She swallowed her dread and allowed him to come to her arms. "Oh, Johnny, you must have hope!" she cried out.

"Yes, I must, mustn't I?" said the child. And he wept bitterly, as though the world were ending, the tears mingling with coagulating blood.

Speranza did not sleep at all that night. She held the child firmly to her bosom, and allowed him to sob until he was quite spent. Little Johnny trembled in her arms, and behind the clatter of the train and the wind whistling through the broken window pane she could hear a faint and plaintive howling from von Bächl-Wölfing's private car. She dared not close her eyes; no, she told herself, I cannot, not until I am sure that the moon has set behind those snowy mountains.

It was cold, unconscionably cold; but a feverish heat arose from the boy's body, and now and then he seemed different, his arms dangling at a strange angle, his nose oddly distended, his cheeks covered with silvery down. Each time she thought he had somehow transformed

himself she would look away, her heart pounding; but
when she looked back he was always a little child again.
And she thought: I am mad, I am imagining everything.
After some hours there came a dank odor of putrescence
from the bloodstained seat. Speranza resolutely faced the
shattered window, letting the fresh chill wind mask the
faint stench of decay.

"There are no monsters," she whispered to herself
over and over. "Only bad dreams."

And they reached Vienna the next morning, and drove
to the Spiegelgasse in a carriage with an impressive-
looking footman as their guide.

On the left, twin staircases led up to a baroque façade.
There was a long line of carriages along the side of the
street. Some were the ordinary station carriages; others
were private, and blazoned with various emblems and
insignia. One was an imported American Concord, and
it was this one that bore the von Bächl-Wölfing arms.
People were dismounting from their carriages and being
escorted up the steps by footmen. The air was cloudy
with horses' breath and rank with their manure; two
brawny lads in uniform were sweeping dung off the
snowy pavement, chattering to each other in some Slavic
dialect.

"This is the residence of Dr. Szymanowski?" Speranza asked.

"Oh, no!" Johnny piped up. "This is the town house
of that Count, the one who frightens me so."

"There is nothing to be afraid of. He is a very generous man."

For a moment Speranza panicked, thinking that the
boy would once more attempt to baptize the Count's
dwelling with urine. But there was no invasion from the
mysterious Jonas, and the boy was nothing if not an-
gelic—almost alarmingly so, Speranza thought.

The guide spoke. "Dr. Szymanowski comes from a

little town in Poland—Oswieçim—Auschwitz, we call it in German—and the Count has graciously allowed him the use of an apartment in the town house, along with some basement space for his experiments. He's a harmless old fool, the doctor. Quite round the bend, I'm afraid. He is an expert, you know, in the . . . ah . . . in the mating patterns of wolves.''

Speranza watched as the Count's guests ascended the steps. Each seemed more outlandish than the last. There was a turbaned gentleman now, whose silken garments, stitched with jewels, almost blinded her with their colors: turquoise, shocking pink, lemon, and pea-green. There was a ragged, stooped old woman who looked just like one of those operatic gipsy fortune tellers. There were elegantly dressed men, in top hats and opera cloaks, and there were those whose origins seemed less than aristocratic; but all were accorded equal deference by the Count's retainers.

They entered through the tradesmen's door, concealed from the street by the twin ornamental balustrades of the grand façade.

A kind of soirée was in progress; she and Johnny stood beside the grand doorway of the ballroom and listened to the chatter, the laughter, the strains of a string quartet. Was it her imagination, or was there mixed into that laughter a sound like wild wolves' howling? She beckoned to Johnny and, gripping his hand, stepped out into a vast ballroom, lit by glittering chandeliers, filled with guests in opulent clothes, decorated with marble statues and unicorn tapestries and pastoral paintings, permeated with the faint but insistent odor of canine piss . . .

Johnny clutched her hand tightly as they stood beside the doorway. In her severe black dress, wearing the single strand of silver around her neck, Speranza had never felt more out of place. The guests paid her no regard at all; most were deep in conversation with one another, and a few stood next to the dais beside the French windows at one end of the ballroom, where the string quartet was performing, the four musicians immaculately dressed in tails, starched wing collars, hunched over their music stands. The French windows were shuttered, admitting neither fresh air nor evening light, and although the hall was spacious, the air was dank and close.

An old man in a dinner jacket stood aloof from the others. From the whispered remarks she overheard, she knew it must be Dr. Szymanowski—the man who, according to the Count, was the architect of some grand scheme that would transform the lives of all werewolves. . . .

She stood, a little embarrassed, not quite certain what she was expected to do. Presently one of the guests— the richly attired Indian whom she had seen enter the town house—accosted her. "Mademoiselle," he said, and continued in heavily accented German, "Sie sind also auch beim Lykanthropenverein—"

"I have no German," she said with a smile.

"Oh, I am jolly glad," he said. "It is good to be encountering a fellow subject of her Britannic Majesty, isn't it?" He surveyed her haughtily, twirling one end of his moustache as he spoke, and extending to her, with his other hand, an open snuffbox made of gold and inlaid with amethysts, emeralds, and mother-of-pearl. "You will perhaps be caring for snuff?" When she demurred, he clapped his hands and a little Negro boy, costumed in an embroidered silk tunic stitched in gold thread, sidled up to him and took the snuffbox from his hands. "Perhaps you will be preferring a cigarette? I know that amongst you people cigarettes are considered more becoming in a woman than the more vulgar incarnations of tobacco. But where we are going, cigarettes are very costly, so I understand."

"We are going—" She noticed that Johnny was sniffing the air and glancing shiftily from side to side, and held on to him even more tightly. "I am not quite sure what you mean."

"Ah, but let us not be speaking of the stark, pioneering future! Let us revel in our past while we may. I will jolly well be missing my homeland. You are, from your manner of dressing, an Englishwoman, isn't it?"

"I'm French actually. But I have lived in England. And this boy, who has at present been entrusted to my care, is English, as he will tell you himself."

"Nevertheless—for we cannot all be fortunate enough to be born beneath that destiny-laden Britannic star—I salute you, madam." He bowed deeply to her, and the peacock plumes that adorned his turban quivered. Johnny reached out and tried to touch them, and laughed when they tickled his fingers. "And, young sahib, I salute you most humbly. I am called Shri Chandraputra Dhar, and was once Lord High Astrologer to the Nawab of Bhaktibhumi, before I was sent away in disgrace and shame, for reasons which no doubt you will already have guessed."

"I'm sure I don't know what you mean," Speranza said. They all seemed to assume that she was one of them, that she knew their secrets. Were they all mad?

The young Negro page reappeared as if by magic with a tray, some glasses of champagne, and a small dish of caviar, and Chandraputra idly ran his finger through the boy's curls. "I no longer serve the Nawab, but his Grace the Count is being kind enough to allow me a position in his household, for which I am being most humbly and abjectly grateful. But you are doubtless understanding me when I say that blood is thicker than water, especially that blood that runs in the veins of those who walk between the two worlds. You will of course know this from your own experience, Miss . . ."

"Martinique," Speranza said. His talk of blood disturbed her. She remembered her dream of the river of blood. The air seemed thicker now, as though the ball-room somehow had been transported to the edge of a dark forest. "And the boy's name is—"

"James," the boy said distinctly. His manner of speaking was quite different from any she had heard him use before: refined, almost haughty, like that of a servant in a highborn household. "My name is James Karney, if you please, sir."

"Oh, nonsense, child!" Speranza said in exaspera-tion. "Do excuse my charge, Mr. Chandraputra . . . we are both very tired from our journey across Europe, and young Johnny Kindred is very much given to make-believe—"

"Ah! He is the one with many names!" said Shri Chandraputra. "Now I understand everything." To Speranza's amazement, the Indian fell on his knees be-fore the child and gazed upon him with a humility that would have seemed comical were it not so earnest. He rose, grasped Speranza's hand fervently, and stooped to kiss it. His nose felt curiously cold against her hand, almost like a dog's. "You, madam, you, you . . . all our company is honoring you . . . you, *you* are, in all truth, the very Madonna of the Wolves incarnate! Ah, Count-ess, to have given birth to the one who will be a bridge between our two races . . . permit me to be the first to worship. Boy! Boy! Champagne, mountains of caviar! Or shall I be fetching the gold, the frankincense, the myrrh?"

"Surely, sir, you are making fun of me," Speranza said, laughing out loud at last, for the fellow was making an astonishing spectacle of himself. "This is no Christ, but a poor, half-crazed young child who cries out for affection; and I am no madonna but a mere governess in the Count's employ."

"Then you are not having the privilege of being the child's mother?" said Shri Chandraputra, raising one eyebrow skeptically.

"No," she said, "I am afraid that honor is not mine," and started to turn away.

She was not comfortable in his presence. But he was standing in between her and the doorway into the inner parlor. Since she could not retreat, she steeled herself and dived into the throng, seizing a glass of champagne from a passing footman as she did so. She saw the Indian whispering into the ear of another guest and pointing to her. A couple who had been waltzing stopped and stared with naked curiosity. Speranza turned and saw others pointing, tittering. The music was abruptly cut off as one of the guests rushed over to tell the latest gossip to the quartet players. Frantically she looked down at her dress, wondering whether she had accidentally exposed some part of her person.

For a few seconds there was no sound at all, and the guests stood stock-still, their jewels glittering, their eyes narrowed, like predators preparing to pounce.

The smell intensified. Sweet-sour fragrance of rotting leaves. A dank forest. The rutting of wild beasts.

Then she heard a whisper somewhere in the crowd: "Der Mond steht in einer halbe Stunde auf." And the others nodded to each other and slowly backed away from her. And glanced warily at each other, taking each other's measure, like fellow beasts of prey. And the Indian astrologer growled at her . . . growled, like an angry hound!

"Der Mond steht auf . . ."

Moonrise . . . in half an hour!

"A dance!" A woman in an embroidered gown stretched out her delicate arms and languorously shrilled: "A dance, my dears, before we all turn into ravening beasts!"

The string quartet, joined by a pianist, burst into a rhapsodic waltz, and all around Speranza guests formed couples and swept out to the center of the ballroom.

"Speranza, Speranza, I'm frightened!" Where was

the voice coming from? She thought she saw the boy, scuttling behind a tall man who was doffing his hat to a petite old woman wrapped in a voluminous shawl. She made off in the man's direction, and he turned to her, smiling, his arm outstretched to invite her to the dance, and his teeth were white, and knife-sharp, and glistening with drool. . . .

"Speranza!" It was coming from somewhere else . . . from behind her. The music welled up, and with it the mingled smells of lust and terror. . . .

Where is the child? she thought. I must find the child, I must protect him from these madmen!

There he was, talking to Dr. Szymanowski . . . were her eyes deluding her, or was the professor's face becoming longer, his nose more snoutlike, his eyes more narrow and inhuman? His smile had become a canine leer, and the tufts of hair pushing up through his bald scalp—

No! She rushed to the boy's side and grasped his hand. His palm was bristly, hot. She pulled him from the professor's side. "We've got to get away from these people," she said. "Come on, Johnny. Please." I mustn't let my dread show, mustn't startle the child, mustn't provoke the monster inside him—

"I've killed Johnny forever, I'm with my own people now!" The boy's voice was deep and rasping. Dr. Szymanowski snarled at her, and she saw saliva running down his chin, which was sprouting dark hairs, and she held on to Johnny and elbowed her way through the guests as they danced frantically to the accelerating music, the jewelled gowns and the chandeliers whirled, she lashed out with her free hand and sent champagne glasses crashing onto the Persian carpet with its design of wolves chasing each other's tails in an infinite spiral—

"Speranza, I'm afraid—" Johnny's tiny voice was interrupted by the voice of the other: "Get back inside!"

It's not your turn anymore. Get back inside and let me kill the bitch!''

"Johnny!''

Shri Chandraputra Dhar had torn off his turban now and had dropped down on all fours. He was sloughing his face. He howled as though racked by the pain of childbirth. Pieces of flayed skin hung from his neck, his palms. Blood gushed from his eyes like tears. His nails were lengthening, his hands shrivelling into paws. Speranza could not move, though her heart was pounding, for there was in his transformation a fierce, alien beauty.

The woman in the elegant gown screeched, "Oh, how tedious, my dears . . . it's that hotblooded oriental nature . . . even with the moon shut out he's off and howling. Oh, someone see to him before he sets everybody else off—'' Her words trailed off into inchoate screaming, and fangs jutted from her moist, painted lips, and hairs were poking through her porcelain complexion—

Speranza ran, dragging the boy behind her.

Two footmen guarded the double oak doors that led to the vestibule. They bowed and let her through. The doors slammed shut behind them. Speranza was shaking. The boy wrested himself free of her grip and looked at her.

"Why are you taking me away from them?'' he said softly. "I understand their language a little, I think. And I belong to them somehow.'' It was the voice of Johnny Kindred once again: always afraid, always a little child.

From behind the massive doors came howling, snarling, screeching, growling, to the accompaniment of passionate music. The vestibule was dark. A single candelabrum, at the foot of a sweeping staircase, flickered forlornly. The walls were hung with purple velvet drapes, and the floor was richly carpeted, siphoning away the faint sound of their footsteps.

And Speranza was at a loss to answer him. There was fear here; there was a palpable, brooding evil; and yet she too had felt the allure of darkness. She dared not remain, and yet . . . she thought of the times when, helping the Hon. Michael Bridgewater with his Latin verbs, or pouring tea at one of Lord Slatterthwaite's interminable garden parties, she had fallen into a reverie of thoughts too dark, too sensual to allow of public expression. Even then she had dreamed of being touched, in the midst of a primal forest, by a creature barely human, and of succumbing to a shuddering delight that was laced with pain and death. And she had thought to herself: I am vile, I am utterly without shame, to let such lewd thoughts surface in myself. She knew that it would be best to take the child away for ever. But the abyss at whose edge they both stood called out to them.

So she did not respond; she merely held the child close to herself. He seemed dazed. He moved, scratching her arms and drawing blood. She stared at his fingernails in the half-light. They had lengthened and crooked themselves into the shape of claws. But his face had not changed.

"We'll go away from here," Speranza said. "If you're away from these people, you'll not become one of them."

"Could it be so simple?" said the boy.

Ahead was the massive front entrance she had earlier seen from the outside; the doors, inlaid with ivory and gilt, were shadowed, and she saw only glimpses of the sylvan scene depicted on them.

The doorknobs were the paws of wolves that faced each other in a contest of wills; in the meager light their eyes, which were cabochon topazes set into the wood, glowed with an intense ferocity. She backed away, still carrying the child in her arms.

Behind her: laughter, music, the howling of wolves.

Gingerly she touched the doorknob, turned it—

The portals swung open! Footmen stood on either side. And, framed in the doorway, tall, dark against the driving snow, his cloak billowing in the wind, stood the man she most dreaded: the man who had brought her to the brink of darkness, and who had awakened in her such unconscionable desires. . . .

"Speranza," he said. "I see you have decided to remain with us."

"Your guests—they are—they are changing—becoming wild animals—"

"Tush! Could they not wait for moonrise? Do they have so little self-discipline? They will destroy all that I have worked for! I begin to regret that I called together this gathering of the Lykandthropenverein."

"Lykan—" She had heard the word spoken many times now; it was one of those Germanic portmanteau words, and she had paid it little regard. But now she looked at him questioningly, and he responded:

"The Society of Werewolves, my dear Speranza. Of which I find myself, by right of single combat, the Herr Präsident. Oh, it was stupid of me to arrange for the meeting at the Vienna residence . . . we could be seen, we could be noticed . . . far better to have the gathering at my estates in Wallachia . . . it was a silly gesture on my part, to encourage such openness, such ostentation!" The Count sighed. "But . . . you were on your way out, were you not, Mademoiselle Martinique?"

She summoned up her last reserves of defiance. "I cannot allow you or Dr. Szymanowski to take charge of this child, Count von Bächl-Wölfing. I apologize for my failure to perform my duties, and I shall attempt to repay your generous stipend when I have obtained some other employment—"

"Have you consulted the child?"

"No . . . but of course he doesn't want to stay here! He's a frightened little boy, a lamb amongst wolves. He needs tenderness and warmth, not your mad professor's bestial experiments!"

"Ask him."

"I don't need to ask him . . . I can see the terror in his eyes, I can tell by the way he clings to my side."

"Ask him!"

He clapped his hands. The doors slammed shut, and the footmen, holding their kerosene lamps aloft, entered and stood on either side of the Count. She heard a voice shriek out from the ballroom within: "Only one more minute until the fatal hour—only one more minute until moonrise!"

The boy extricated himself from Speranza's arms. In the lamplight he cast a huge double shadow against the velvet drapes. He shrank away from the Count; and yet there was in his eyes a certain awe, a certain love.

"Oh, Speranza, don't ask me to choose between you. Oh, Speranza, I do love you, but I have to stay, don't you see? I know that now." As he spoke the reek of canine urine became suddenly more powerful, choking her almost. And the boy spoke again, in the deep voice of Jonas: "He is my father."

"You see?" said von Bächl-Wolfing. "The child knows instinctively. Instinctively! He is my son, conceived on an English harlot in Whitechapel, raised in a madhouse, but my blood runs true—he has the eyes of the wolf, the senses, the memory; he knows me for what I am. And, since he has learnt to call me father, I acknowledge him, I embrace him as mine."

"You can't mean—" Speranza began, trying to shield Johnny from him with her arms. But the boy himself pushed her brusquely aside. His eyes glowed now. The feral odor became more rank, more suffocating.

The Count spread his arms wide to receive the child. With halting steps the boy came forward. Through the stained glass moon above the door, Speranza could see the rising of the real moon, pale and haloed by the icy air. The Count's cloak flapped as the wind gusted around it.

The boy stood close to the Count now, dwarfed. The

Count enfolded him in the cloak. Speranza cried out the boy's name, but her voice was lost in the wind's howling and the cacophony from the ballroom. . . .

The Count looked longingly into her eyes. His gaze mesmerized her; she could not move. There was in it a kind of love. The Count advanced toward her, and already his lips were being wrenched apart as the wolf's jaw began extruding itself from within. As she stood transfixed, he began to court her in Italian: "Come sei bella, fanciulla; come sei bella, o mia Speranza." The voice was harsh, guttural, a travesty of her native tongue . . . yet the wolf was wooing her, trying to make love to her. Her blood raced. Her skin tingled. A hand reached out to her from under the cloak: A twisted, furry hand. A claw grazed her cheek. She closed her eyes, shuddering, desiring yet loathing him. Her cheek burned where his paw had touched it. She did not retreat from him, for he held the child captive still, and she told herself that to effect the child's rescue from this brutish destiny must be a sacred task for which she must sacrifice what small chastity she could lay claim to. She met his gaze with defiance.

"I'll save him yet . . . somehow. . . ."

"Will you, my Madonna of the Wolves? I have a fancy to make you one of us this very moment. A bite from me should suffice. Or else I could force you to drink the dew that has formed in one of my footprints; we keep phials of such precious fluids in this house for just such an occasion. Or perhaps you would care to wear the sacred pelt of my ancestors, which being worn can be cast off only by death?"

"I could never become one of you."

His paw continued to stroke her cheek, drawing blood now. She shook her head, loosening the silver necklace from beneath her collar. The Count recoiled. His voice was barely human: "Consider yourself fortunate, mademoiselle, that you are wearing the necklace! The ser-

vants will show you to your room! You are safe until
the next full moon!''

His forehead was flattening now, his brow creasing
and uncreasing as bristles began to shoot out from folds
of skin. He howled, and a uniformed servant emerged
from an antechamber, lantern in hand.

"If the gnädiges Fräulein would care to follow me,"
he said, bowing deeply.

She hesitated. She was about to protest when the
Count cast aside his cloak and she saw the wolf cub leap
from his arms, and she knew that Johnny was beyond
help, that night at least. In the morning she would see
what could be done with him. She could not abandon
the boy now, never, never.

From her little—a garret, more or less—in the attic of
the von Bächl-Wölfing town house, Speranza was able
to see the street below and the private park, for the snow
had abated a little and the moon was full. From below
there came howling: not the cacophony she had wit-
nessed in the ballroom, but something far more pur-
poseful. First came a single note, drawn out, with an
almost metallic resonance. Then another joined in, on
another pitch, stridently dissonant with the first; then
came a third and a fourth, each adding a note to the
disharmony. The window rattled. Her very bones
seemed to feel the vibration.

The howling crescendoed. The floor trembled against
her feet. The chair she sat in was shaking. And suddenly
it was over. She heard a slamming sound, and she saw
the wolves pouring out into the street. They streamed
past the row of parked carriages. She was glad none of
the horses had been left outside.

When they howled they had seemed hundreds, but
now she saw there were only perhaps twenty. They
stood, still as statues, for a few moments, in the middle
of the alley, their breath steaming up the air. Snow

flecked their pelts. Their leader's fur was black and streaked with silver just as the Count's hair was . . . and beside him stood a young pup, the very one she had seen leaping out of the Count's opera cloak . . . and behind them other wolves. Even from this far up she could see how their eyes glowed. The moon was low, and the wolves cast giant shadows across the wrought iron angel *gates* of the park. The leader shook the snow from his fur and looked from side to side. Then they moved. Sinuously, with an alien grace, almost as one. A sharp bark from their leader and they began to trot down the Spiegelgasse. Quite silently, for the deep snow muffled the patter of their paws. At the corner, the wolves turned and vanished behind a stone wall.

She watched a while longer. But at length she was overcome by an intense weariness, and went to her bed. Her sleep was fitful, for she dreamt of the forest, and the river, and the lupine lover waiting for her at its source.

The wolfling sniffed the chill air and shook the snow out of his pelt. At last he had quelled the rebellion in his soul . . . at last he was as he was meant to be: proud, ferocious, one with the darkness. He was unsteady on his feet at first. But he imitated his father's gait and soon fell into its liquid rhythm.

The wolves moved silently. Now and then the wolfling's father paused to mark his scent, arrogantly lifting his leg to urinate on some memorable spot: a stone, a brick wall, the wheel of a cart. They spoke a language of the dark: now and then with a whine or a bark, more often with a quick motion of the head or a quiver of a nostril or a glance.

"My son," said the leader with his eyes, as the pack slipped into the shadow of another alley. "My son. How much I rejoice that I have found you . . . and that you are truly one of us, able to change . . ."

"Why did you not seek me out before?" the wolfing cried out with a shrug and a circular motion of his paws.

"Because," said his father, lashing the snow with his tail, "I was afraid. Your mother was not one of us."

"My mother . . ."

There was another voice within the wolfing's mind, a voice that seemed to cry out: No, I am not one of these . . . I am a child, a human.

Whose was this inner voice? The young wolf followed his father, faster now, darting from shadow to shadow. The voice distressed him. It did not belong here. It was good to be this way. Good to paw the ground and sniff the air. The air was vivid: he could smell the blood of distant prey, racing, already sensing death. The inner voice spoke again, saying, This vision is bleak, gray, colorless . . . but the wolfing did not understand what the voice meant, for his eyes could not see color, only infinite gradations of light and shadow. And the possessor of the inner voice could not seem to grasp the richness of sound and scent he was experiencing, but continually bemoaned the absence of this thing he called color.

He pushed the voice further back into his mind. It was a useless thing, a vestige of some past existence. He followed his father. The pack had split up now. There were the two of them, hunting as father and son.

Hunting! For the pit of his stomach burned with an all-consuming hunger. Not only for fresh, warm meat, but for the act of killing. . . .

Abruptly his father stopped, cocked his head. The wind had dropped. The snow fell straight down. Footsteps, human footsteps. He smelled blood: sluggish blood, tainted with the sour smell of wine. "Come, my son," his father said with an imperious bark. "We will celebrate together, you and I, the mystery of life and death. The quarry is nigh."

He saw nothing. They did not move. The smell came closer. There was a shape to the smell, a two-legged shape. He stood beside his father, tense, waiting. A second shape, much smaller, beside the first. What were they doing in the cold, in the dark? His father growled . . . a faint, ominous sound, like a distant earth tremor.

The snow thinned and the young wolf saw more. The quarry was on the steps of a church. There was a woman and a child, perhaps four or five years old. A half-empty bottle lay next to them. There was a small puddle of wine on the snow. They were shivering, huddled together under a man's greatcoat.

The woman was muttering to herself in some Slavic tongue, and rocking the child back and forth. She wore a woolen shawl; beneath it he could see wisps of gray hair. She had a drawn, pinched face. The child was sullen, distracted. He could not smell what sex the child was; it was too young.

"They are street people," said the wolfling's father. "They have strayed from the herd. They have sought the desolation of the cold and dark. They belong to us."

And loped up the steps, his jaws wide open, while his son followed closely behind.

At first the woman did not even seem to notice. The wolf circled her several times. Then he pounced.

She let go of the child. The child began to whine. Its scrawny shoulders showed through the torn nightshirt. It began to clamber up the steps towards her. The wine bottle rolled away, chiming as it hit each step. The wolfling watched his father and the woman. For a few seconds they gazed at each other, neither of them moving, oblivious to the bawling of the child. In those moments it seemed almost as though they were exchanging vows, each choosing the other as partner in the ritual of death.

Then his father leapt. He tore out her throat with his jaws. There was an eerie whistling as the wind left her. The child, crying, was pummeling at the wolf's side with its fists, but the wolf ignored it. The woman's

shawl, pinned between her torso and the steps, fluttered
in the wind.

The wolfling smelled the child's fear. It maddened
him. He rushed at the child. The child's eyes widened.
It backed away, up the steps. Then it turned and began
to run. The wolfling followed. The child's blood smelled
warmer than the woman's.

There was a door at the top of the steps. The child
pounded at it with tiny fists. It did not budge. The wolfling jumped up, clawing at the nightshirt, gouging out
great gashes in the child's chest and arms. Suddenly the
door gave way. A rusty bolt, perhaps. The child ran inside. Through the rips in the nightshirt the wolfling saw
its tiny vulva, and knew its gender for the first time.

He smelled incense. And dust. And sweet fragrance
of over-varnished, rotting wood. In the distance there
was an altar. A painted stone Pietà stood guard in the
antechapel. There were candles everywhere.

The girl ran. He followed the sound of her footsteps,
shoeless on the stone floor. She was hiding somewhere
among the pews. She was panting. He could smell her
exhaustion, her desperation. It was only a matter of time.
He felt his heart pounding. He heard her heartbeat too,
and paused to pinpoint it.

There! He scurried down the aisle. She was under the
altar. He ripped the altarcloth with his jaws and found
her huddled, clasping a leg of the altar, sobbing.
Roughly he threw her down, hulking over her, teasing
her face with his tongue and the edges of his teeth, urinating on her to show his possession. And gazed at her,
as he had seen his father gaze into the eyes of the
woman.

He saw her fear. And behind her fear he saw something else, too . . . a kind of invitation . . . the dark side
of desire. He sensed that what they were doing together,
hunter and quarry, was a sacred thing, a dance of life
and death. The girl trembled. Pain racked her body. He

spoke to her in the language of the forest, asking her forgiveness; and she answered in the same language, the language that men believe they have forgotten until such moments as these, giving him permission to take her life.

He was about to tear her apart when a long shadow fell across them both. He looked up and saw his father. Blood dripped from his jaws. There was a trail of blood from the antechapel all the way up the nave. His eyes glowed. His breath clouded the musty air.

"Now," said his father. "Kill. Feel the joy. Feel the spurting blood. Bathe in its warmth."

"I feel no joy," the wolfling said, "only a strange solemnity. I feel a kind of kinship with her."

"Good! You understand the law of the forest well, my son! Men see us as unreasoning, ravening beasts, but that is not all we are. We are not simply Satan's children. There are some of us to whom the killing is nothing more than the exercise of lust. Perhaps most of our little society are like that. But with you it is something more. Good. You are truly my son. To lead the Lykanthropenverein you must be more than a crazed creature of death . . . you must also feel a certain love for your victims. Now kill quickly. Shock her nervous system so that she will no longer feel pain."

The wolfling bent over the girl, ready to despatch her. Then he heard the inner voice: "Get away! Go back into the darkness! I want the body!" There were several other voices, too. Voices of humans. There was a mutiny going on inside his mind! The other personalities were seizing control! He struggled. But he was losing his grip. The girl was fighting him. And there was something going wrong with the vibrant layers of scents and fragrances around him . . . he was losing his sense of smell . . . the shapes were shifting too, darkening, becoming fringed with garish *colors* . . .

Johnny Kindred snapped into consciousness beneath an altar inside a huge church, with a little girl in his

arms. Her eyes widened. She began jabbering away in
a foreign language. She pointed. There was a black wolf
in the church. Staring at the two of them. Its fur was
matted with bright red blood. Blood and drool dribbled
from its teeth, which glistened golden in the candlelight.

"Jonas won't harm you," Johnny said to the girl.
"I've sent him away."

The wolf growled. Johnny felt that he could almost
understand what he was saying. If Jonas were nearby he
could translate, but Jonas was being held down by the
others. He was not being allowed to go anywhere near
the clearing.

"The big bad wolf won't harm you," Johnny said,
stroking the girl's curly hair, "he's . . . my father."

At dawn she drifted into sleep. And dreamed.

There was a forest. She ran among thick trees. She
wore no corsets, no confining garments. Her hair was
long and free to fly in the hot wind. She was naked but
she felt no guilt because she was clothed in darkness.
The air reeked of a woman's menses. Her feet were bare.
They trod the soft earth. Moist leaves clung to her soles.
Twigs lacerated her arms, her thighs, but the pain was
a joyous pain, like the pangs of a lascivious passion.
Worms crawled along her toes and tickled them and
made her laugh. She laughed and her laughter became
an animal's howling.

The primal atmosphere put her in mind of a witches'
sabbath, or perhaps one of those bacchanalian orgies of
the ancient Greeks, with the wild women who used to
dance around and tear wild animals to pieces with their
bare hands.

A brief memory surfaced: she was helping young Michael Bridgewater with his Euripides one day, only to
come across passages which she could not in all decency
translate . . . at least not into English, for in that language
things that could be made to sound elevated in Italian

or French were rendered intolerably crude. It was this enforced crudity, she had reflected at the time, that gave the English their preoccupation with prurience. And then they had lowered young Michael into the ground and it seemed as though it had not stopped snowing, as though she'd never escape the snow, not even by fleeing across half Europe . . .

Here there was no snow.

No snow at all. There was moisture that dripped from the branches overhead, that oozed out of the earth, that was wrung out of the very air. The ground was slippery. She slid, glided almost, cried out with childish delight as the very earth seemed to carry her along. And always came that pungent scent of menstrual blood.

Light broke over leaves streaked with black and silver. Moonlight over a stream. She sat at the edge, bathing her feet. The water warm, like fresh blood . . . the ground trembling a little, with the regularity of a heartbeat . . . and she heard the cry of a wolf, distant, mournful. The sound was both repulsive and somehow alluring. She knew it might well be a love song, if she could but understand its language. . . .

And in the dream she knew, as by a profound inspiration, that the howling came from the waters' source. The beast was waiting for her upstream. And that she was drawn to the beast as the beast was drawn to her . . .

And when she awoke she saw the Count von Bächl-Wölfing standing at the foot of her bed, and the boy beside him, clutching his cloak, as the rays of dawn broke through the high window.

The Count said: "Speranza, these are the last days of the old world. You know why we have gathered here. Dr. Szymanowski's grand scheme is this: in the spring we, the werewolves, will travel to America. There is wilderness there. There is ample food—thousands upon thousands of acres of land untouched by civilization,

where only the savages live, and they will be our quarry.
We will build our own kingdom, our private paradise.
We will hunt by night and by day we will sing songs.
America will be our utopia and you will be its queen,
my Madonna of the Wolves."

She had sworn to herself that she would never leave
the child. Now she understood at last all that that meant.
She had been chosen. Beneath her black dresses and
austere demeanor, she too harbored a beast within. A
passion that could only be slaked by darkest love.

"The boy has no mother now," said von Bächl-
Wölfing. "And he has come to love you."

"And I him," she said.

"We must guard him well. He is a completely new
kind of child—he is very special—the first link between
my kind and your kind. You understand that, don't
you."

"It is a pity about his mother. . . ." He did not look
at her, and she got the impression that he was remembering some past unpleasantness. "Some of the wolves
think of him as a savior, a redeemer. Because he is a
link between the two species—proof that we are of man,
and man is of us. That's the real reason I want to go to
the New World. A new world for a new idea—a new
world for a new kind of being—a bridge between the
natural and the supernatural, between the divine and the
animal within us."

She took the child to her bosom, and embraced the
Count, whose cloak enveloped the three of them, and
said, "I will."

*Only the king wolf mates, and he takes for his consort
a female from outside his tribe. . . .*

RED

SARAH CLEMENS

> *"Red" was purchased by Gardner Dozois, and appeared in the June 1998 issue of* Asimov's, *an impressive debut sale here for new author Sarah Clemens. A legal medical illustrator and a some-time book reviewer, Sarah Clemens has also made sales to* Ripper!, Little Deaths, Twists of the Tale, *and elsewhere. She lives in Florida.*
>
> *Here she offers us the bittersweet and moving story of a child in the 1950s South who stumbles across a family secret of a most unusual kind, and discovers that there's much more to the world than there seems to be. . . .*

Red came to a dead stop at the edge of the garden. "I don't know who you think you are," she said, her voice firm. "But those are Miss Lydia's strawberries."

"I'm Virginia," said the colored girl, getting up and brushing off her dress. "Matilda is my mama, and Miss Lydia said I could pick 'em anytime I wanted."

They stood facing each other in the pounding August heat, and Red's temper wilted as she wiped her freckled face with her sleeve and pulled off her hat to use as a fan. "Well, I guess that's okay." She shoved the straw hat back onto her head and sat between rows, picking a particularly juicy berry and plopping it into her mouth.

The strawberry patch at the back of the property was shut out from the rest of the world, hemmed in by stately hedges.

"Are you Yvette?" asked Virginia. She was a gravely pretty girl with dark brown skin and braids all over her head, clipped with colorful barrettes.

Red grimaced theatrically. "I hate that name. Call me Red."

"It fits. You here for long?"

"Through the end of this month and into the first week of September," said Red, getting up and joining Virginia on her row.

"You'll be here for Miss Portia's next spell," said Virginia matter-of-factly. "Her last one was something! The lions over at the zoo roared all night and the wolves howled."

"They *did*?"

"Yeah, and Miss Lydia and my mama were with her all night."

Red picked a berry and cautiously handed it to Virginia. "How old are you?"

For the second time they sized each other up.

"Twelve."

"Ten," said Red. They ate strawberries for a while, a few making it into a bucket Red had brought with her. "I've never talked to anyone colored my own age," she said finally.

Virginia grinned. "Me either. No white girl, I mean. But my teacher says this is 1963 and things are going to change."

"You mean like going to school together and stuff?"

"Yeah. Last year a black man tried to get into a college in Mississippi. Someday—" she broke off and lifted a finger. "Listen. You hear that?"

It was a deep *Aaaaauh . . . Aaaaauh*, filling the heavy air between them and the Memphis zoo. The lions roaring, bringing the outside world into Lydia's isolated garden.

"Feeding time," whispered Virginia.

"Yvette! Yvette? Where are you!"

Red squinched up her face. "It's my grandmother. I'll talk to you later. G'bye."

She ran to the house with her few strawberries and Lydia, her grandmother, closed the screen door behind her.

"How can you run in this heat, child? Put your bucket down and let's sit in the dining room."

That meant it was serious.

"Do you know why you're here?" asked Lydia, her hands reflected in the rich depths of the mahogany table. Red could see heavyset Matilda pass by the door, listening. Matilda, Virginia's mother, who smelled of Clorox and sweat, whose dark, round face was framed with wisps of gray hair that flew loose from her tight bun. She seemed aloof to Red, as if she owned the house, rather than cleaned it. Lydia didn't seem to know she was there.

Red put both elbows on the table. "Uh—because my parents are moving us to New York and this summer'll be my last chance to learn any manners, because God knows they don't have any up there."

Lydia cocked an eyebrow. "If I didn't know better," she said in her refined drawl, "I'd say you were repeating something you heard."

Red shrugged.

"Well," said Lydia, "we've never been all that close, you and I, and that's why I told your mother I'd keep you here in Memphis while they move. I *am* your—grandmother. And you haven't seen much of your great-grandmother Portia. She'll be down with one of her spells while you're here, at the end of your visit, but that shouldn't be a problem. As to manners . . . I'll start by calling you by your Christian name, Yvette. Red sounds like a cowboy.''

"I hate Yvette."

Lydia just looked at her from beautiful, drooping eyes, her fine lips curving up on one side. "Well, you'll just have to get used to hearing it, because I won't call you Red. I was educated at a good school where they taught you manners."

Red's face brightened. "Daddy says that back before the Punic Wars you went to Randolph-Macon."

Lydia's eyes narrowed. "How kind of him to fill you in."

Through the screened windows, covered with drifts of white curtain, Red could hear the lions.

"Do they roar very often?" she asked.

Lydia frowned. "They're lions. They roar when they roar." She looked elegant in the gardening workshirt and khaki pants in a way Red feared she never would.

"Great-grandmother Portia wants to see you tomorrow, Yvette. She's very happy you've come."

Red smiled, but it came out more a wince.

She slept on a narrow twin bed that night, listening to the fan huff hot air, and to the leaves outside her window, caressing each other in the faint breeze. A tear fell, hot against her skin and the starched pillowcase. This room was so different from her own, and she missed having her mother tuck her in and her father read to her. They had just gotten into Howard Carter's *The Tomb of Tutankhamon* and she longed for the sound of his voice, the way he turned the book around so they could share the pictures.

Then, the night held its breath, and so faintly, so faintly, she heard a new sound—the wolves howling at the zoo.

"Did you wash your face and comb your hair?"

"Uh-huh." Red never washed her face if no one was

watching, and her shock of red hair didn't take much
maintenance.

"Say yes, not uh-huh," smiled Lydia.

They breakfasted and went out back, into the dappled
light of dogwood trees and beyond to the irises, nodding
in ruffled and multi-hued splendor.

"When your mother was little," said Lydia, "she
would always pick out a blue iris. I started breeding
them to get the bluest ones I could for her." She cut
one and, carefully, Red took it from her.

"Now, we'll go see Great-grandmother Portia." She
led her into a tunnel of trees and hedges to the house
next door. Lydia didn't have a lot of money, compared
to what the Tucker family had had when she was young.
When she had married Grandfather Earl, they had purchased two shotgun houses, side by side on Crump Circle, the other one for Great-grandmother Portia.
Grandfather Earl died years before Red was born. What
was left of the Tucker estate brought in just enough to
go without working, which suited Lydia fine, because
her life was devoted to horticulture. She combined both
backyards to create a seamless melding of formal garden
and English herb garden, to plots of irises and vegetables, to the cool tunnel of trees that led from Lydia's
house to the back door of Portia's house, because no
one ever went in the front door. Red had been here several times, but she couldn't help gaping at the denseness
of the foliage in the tunnel. It was as if she had entered
Sherwood Forest itself, thick and primeval. They
emerged at the back of the house and Great-grandmother
Portia stood behind the screen door, a still gray shape.
Red would have given anything to bolt from these old
people and their remote, decorous lives.

"Why, you've brought me an iris." Portia swung the
squinching door open and ushered them in. Portia
Tucker was dressed like a picture out of a book, in a
blue skirt that went all the way to the ground and a

white, high-necked blouse with full sleeves. Her face
was gaunt and very wrinkled and her thin hair lay piled
in a braid on her head, the pink from her scalp showing
through.

The leafy tunnel had brought Red to more than another house; it seemed another world, for there was no
washing machine or dryer on the back porch, no modern
appliances in the kitchen, not even a refrigerator. Red
noticed kerosene lamps here and there, storm covers
lightly blackened with use.

"Could I trouble you to put the iris in a vase?" The
request was directed at Lydia, who knew right where the
vase was; and as she drew the water and dropped the
flower in, Red realized her grandmother had command
over this house. It was spelled out in small gestures, the
way Lydia shook out a towel and wiped the vase, how
she went forward into the dining room and set it down
where she chose.

"Let's sit in the dining room," said Portia. Lydia was
already pulling out chairs. "The front parlor is far too
dark and *hot*."

The magnificent table, china cabinet, and sideboard in
the dining room were oversized and forlorn, refugees
from an antebellum mansion. Every step made the floorboards creak and the ancient china rattle. The living
room at the front of the house was dark and thickly
curtained and its dark mahogany furniture, too, seemed
to loom uncomfortably in the cramped space.

"I believe this is the bluest iris I have ever seen,"
said Portia. It was a soft voice, honeyed with a southern
accent. She looked at Red with eyes far younger than
her face, with fine wrinkles that turned up into smile
lines.

Red felt the dread lift a little as she sat next to the
old woman in the still, cramped room where doilies covered every surface.

"I am pretty old," confessed Portia. Her accent was

different than Lydia's, more courtly; and her eyes were
the palest blue Red had ever seen, as if time had
bleached them out.

"I'm pretty young," grinned Red.

Lydia adjusted a fold in the curtains. "You two have
a little talk, while I go out back and pull some weeds. I
won't be long." Her eyes met Portia's for only a moment, in what looked like a warning frown.

Portia was silent until she heard the back screen door
slam. "You're no sissy, are you?"

"I—guess not."

"I mean, you're not one of those little girls who wears
flouncy dresses and has sausage curls and sits under a
tree on a blanket and plays with dolls."

"Oh, definitely not." Lydia had made Red wear a
dress for this occasion, but both skinned knees poked
out from under the hem.

"Lydia has her good qualities," said Portia. "But she
isn't big on adventure. When I was younger, I had a lot
of adventures. Have you ever been to Vicksburg?"

"No . . . ma'am."

"Like Memphis, it looks down on the Mississippi
River. They dug trenches and tunnels during the siege.
And I used to prowl through them, and oh, would the
soldiers be surprised when I would come upon them!"

Red had no idea what Portia was talking about. "All
I do is watch Tarzan movies," she said wistfully.

Portia gave her a strange look. "Well, you shall find
adventure someday. I am sure of it."

The bang of the screen door announced Lydia's return. "How are you two getting along?" she asked at
the dining room door.

"Just famously," said Portia. "In fact I would like to
give Yvette a little something."

Lydia froze.

"Oh, honey, just a little box! Something my mother
gave to me when I was a little girl. It's in the chifforobe

in my bedroom, in that drawer where I keep all my trinkets.''

Lydia went around the corner and Red heard the sound of drawers opening. She came back holding up a wooden box. ''This one?''

''No dear, the one with the boullework.''

Lydia came back and handed the small box to Portia, who turned it over in her bony, blue-veined hands. She gave it to Red. It was ebony wood, inlaid with brass and red tortoiseshell. Opening it, she found a little key on a tassel, which fit into the keyhole.

''This is really neat,'' said Red. ''Thank you, thank you very much.''

''My mother gave it to me when we still lived up the river from Vicksburg at Fairgrove. I shall tell you about her sometime.''

''But right now,'' Lydia cut in, ''Great-grandmother Portia needs her rest. Maybe you two can visit again in a few days.''

Portia leaned over and whispered to Red, ''This box holds secrets.''

''Pretty fancy,'' said Virginia.

They sat on a bench across from the herb garden, taking advantage of the shade as the cicadas tirelessly whirred their song of summer heat.

The black girl opened the box and looked inside.

''She said something kinda funny,'' said Red. ''That it holds secrets.''

''Old people say things like that. Maybe she was talkin' about memories.''

''I dunno. It was funny the way she said it. Oh! And you know what else? She whispered it to me, like she didn't want Lydia to hear.''

They stared at the box.

''Maybe . . .'' said Virginia, suddenly excited, ''maybe it's like something I saw on Miss Lydia's TV, on *77 Sunset Strip*. You know, a secret compartment."

Red took the box back and turned it over carefully. "Well, the bottom's awfully heavy."

Together they picked and poked at the box. It was Virginia who accidentally pressed the inlay on one side, causing the bottom to come loose at one edge. With careful prying, the bottom swung out, revealing a shallow compartment filled with a mashed scrap of cloth. Red pulled it out and a key fell to her lap. A modern brass key.

"Do you recognize it?" asked Red.

Virginia shook her head. "Mama has lots of keys for the houses, and I can't tell."

"Your mother knows a lot about things around here, doesn't she?"

"Yeah. She's been working here since before I was born. Miss Lydia's been good to our family. She helped us a lot when my papa died."

"Your father died?"

Virginia's face was very still. "He had cancer and he died when I was eight."

It was an overwhelming concept for Red, who felt enough pain just being separated from her father for a few weeks.

"Wow, that's bad," she said lamely.

"Yvette!"

They both jumped, then fumbled frantically with the key and the cloth and the box. The bottom snapped shut just as Lydia came around the corner.

"So! What are you two up to?"

Red burst out laughing and Virginia covered her mouth as she giggled.

"Nothing," said Red. "Just looking at the box."

"There's lemonade in the house. Virginia, could you pick us some strawberries, and we'll have them with cream?"

"Yes, ma'am."

"Yvette," said Lydia as they went into the house, "There's a girl your age whose mother is a member of the Garden Society. She'd love you to come over."

"No, that's okay. Virginia and I have stuff to do."

"Getting too friendly with Virginia might not be a good idea."

"Why not?"

Lydia said starkly, "Virginia is like a member of this family, but she's colored, and that means we mix only so far. Do you understand?"

"I guess," said Red.

The next day, Red waited impatiently until Virginia came to Miss Lydia's house. "My mama's taking a nap over at Miss Portia's."

"Great. Let's get started." Red pulled the key from her pocket. It didn't fit the padlock on Lydia's basement. It didn't fit the back door or the front door.

"How long does my grandmother take when she goes to a garden club meeting?"

"Usually a couple of hours, sometimes more."

She and Red stood in the living room, and Red peered about, as if she could see through the walls. "There aren't any more locks here, are there?"

"No. I *told* you we should check Miss Portia's house. That makes more sense."

"But we had to be sure," said Red, leaving unspoken that they really didn't want to go next door. They traced their way back through the trees, edging past the creaking screen door and into the bleak kitchen.

"I'll check on Mama." Virginia was gone only a moment. "As far as I can remember," she whispered, "there's the front door, the back door—" she ticked them off on her fingers. "The basement, and Miss Portia's room."

"*Miss Portia's room?*"

Virginia shrugged.

Red took a resolute breath. "Is your mother a heavy sleeper?"

"Yeah . . ."

They tiptoed past the dining room, wincing at each creaking board. Matilda sat back, breathing heavily, her work-worn hands draped over the arms of the rocker, a half-finished doily in her lap. Portia looked like a corpse, engulfed in featherbeds and lying on a canopy bed that nearly swallowed the small room. Red crept toward the open door, ready to bolt. She slid the key from her pocket, and placed it against the lock. It bumped in half-way, then it resisted. Red pressed the key harder, to make sure. Nope. This wasn't the lock.

She shook her head for Virginia's benefit, then tugged. The key wouldn't budge.

Fear lanced through her and she yanked hard, pulling the key free and bumping the glass doorknob. Red and Virginia froze, staring at the sleeping women. Matilda's snoring never broke rhythm. But for one second, Red thought she saw Portia's eyes, open and clear, then shutting quickly as they retreated, quaking in their sneakers.

"Something tells me this key won't fit the front door or the back door," whispered Red.

"*You* just don't wanna *be* here."

Red giggled, and so did Virginia, cupping a hand over her mouth.

"Well," said Virginia, "we could try the basement. It's outside."

It wasn't such an adventure now, and Red stood for a moment before nodding. "Yeah. We've come this far, right?"

They nodded together and went to the back of Miss Portia's house. There were steps leading down to the door, and it struck Red as odd that the steps were swept clean and well used. Lydia's basement steps were grimy. Just out of curiosity, Red turned the knob on the door, and to her surprise, it opened.

"Try the key anyway," said Virginia.

Red pushed the key against the lock and shook her head.

They crept down the stairs, smelling the mustiness of an underground room—but it wasn't a room, it was a short passage with a door off one side. It was dark, so dark all Red could tell when she put her hand against the door was that it was smooth metal, cool to the touch. A *snap*, a light came on, and her heart nearly leapt out of her chest. It was only Virginia, her hand on the light switch.

"Look at this!" said Red. There was a rocking chair next to the door, and a small table which held a ring of keys and a quietly ticking clock. On the floor next to the chair was a small basket, filled with yarn and knitting needles.

"That's my mama's knitting," said Virginia very quietly. "I have a lot of sweaters."

The metal door was dull gray with a peephole, several heavy bolts, a handle—and a lock. Red put her weight against one of the bolts and it shot back easily. Oil glistened on the workings. It was the same with the other one . . . and then she tried her key, which went in easily, turning with buttery smoothness. The door swung in, and she groped for a light. Nothing.

"It's here," said Virginia from the hall. She snapped it on, and they beheld the tiny, stark, concrete room. Against the far wall was a very strange bed with a series of hinged clamps contoured to the shape of a body, each with its own lock. There was a light set into the ceiling, covered with bars.

The walls. Crisscrossed with parallel grooves . . . Red crept into the room and ran her hand over the jagged furrows. "Claw marks," she whispered. She looked back at the door, struck by how thick the wall was at the lintel. A foot deep. And as she drew in breath she felt a pulse of unreasoning fear.

"Let's get outta here," she said.

Virginia stood with her hand poised on the light switch as Red backed out and locked up. She nodded and Virginia turned off that light, and the one for the hall. With their last reserve of stealth, they pushed the basement door shut and dashed for the sunlight.

"White folks can be cruel," said Matilda several days later, in the afternoon.

Red, Virginia, and Matilda sat on Lydia's back porch, stringing pole beans. The tired black fan heaved itself back and forth, its faint breeze hushing by their clammy faces. Matilda had put them to work on the bushel basket that never seemed to get any emptier.

"Miss Lydia isn't the only lady I work for," Matilda elaborated. "The other ladies, they're supposed to serve me lunch, and all they ever have on my day is hot dogs. You *know* those folks only eat hot dogs when I come, so they don't have to serve me anything decent."

Matilda glared and sweated, and Red wondered if it was somehow her fault. It took her a moment to think of something to say. "My grandmother—Lydia—she aways has good food."

"Yes, child, Miss Lydia's a good woman. You think she grows so many pole beans just to feed herself and Miss Portia?"

Red stared down at the beans.

"All summer I put up what she grows out there, and she only takes a few of the jars for herself. The rest is for my folks—hold on there, you missed that end."

Red looked down and snapped the end, peeling the string down the length of the bean.

"Miss Portia, now . . ." Red watched her tired, blunt features as she struggled with the right words. "She's a woman who's mighty tired of life. Mighty tired. I wish Miss Lydia would do right by her."

"Yvette?" Lydia appeared around the corner. "Great-grandmother Portia would like some company while I trim the hedges.''

Red got up a little guiltily, leaving Matilda and Virginia with the pole beans.

She sat across the table in the stifling dining room and couldn't think of a thing to say. Gramma Portia clinked the little spoon against her flowered china cup and sipped her tea. Red looked down at hers and wondered if she dared touch it. Cautiously, she held the handle and took a sip. No match for Coca-Cola. Suddenly Portia looked straight at Red and said, ''I think Lydia's out of earshot. Can you check?''

Red blinked, then crept to the kitchen door and listened. She could hear the snick-snick of Lydia's hedge clippers.

''All clear,'' said Red breathlessly, coming back to her seat.

''Well then,'' said Portia. ''How did you like that little box I gave you?''

Red knew what she meant. ''We found the key.''

''We?''

''Me and Virginia.''

''Virginia and *I*. Go on, then.''

''We tried all the doors we could, until we finally thought about the cellar. And we went down there.'' *And saw the stark walls and clawmarks.*

''They keep me in there when I have one of my spells. No, don't stare at me so, it's not cruel. Just necessary. And I've been in smaller places . . . much smaller.''

''Like what?''

''Did they teach in school about the time General Grant came down to Vicksburg and laid siege to our city?''

''Um . . . only a little,'' said Red, to keep Portia going.

''That Yankee Grant was a daring man, I'll give him that. Crossed the Mississippi and surrounded us. But he couldn't storm our barricades! So he fired his big guns at us, shells were falling every day, but no one talked of surrender.'' Portia's voice had grown softer, her face less wizened. ''There I was, an old maid of twenty, living with Papa and the servants who had stayed, in our house in Vicksburg. A shell hit the roof; nothing as terrible as some of our neighbors, but it stirred Papa to action. 'We shall dig into the bluffs like everyone else,' he said. 'It would probably be better for my little Portia, anyway.' He thought me frail.

''So we had a cave dug for us, and there we were, with furniture from the house and a nice rug on the dirt floor. And I confess, I loved it. It was a great adventure, and I could smell the earth all around us and hear the shells as if they were very, very far away . . .''

Portia's eyes seemed darker, like storm clouds. ''But I was never frail, as Papa thought. It was my colored maid Sophie who knew about me, how I got bit by the big wild dog back at Fairgrove, and how, when the moon is full, I have my spells. And while Papa sleeps, I run out in the streets, hungry, starving, like everyone else in the city, only I can smell what I need, and I find the siege tunnels and trenches where our Confederate soldiers wait for me. So dark in the tunnels, black but for the red-flower scent of their blood, and I find one sleeping by himself, my nails are sharp, they shred him like a soft roll, and my teeth mangle his throat like ivory knives—and the thick nectar bubbles up in my jaws and he tastes *so sweet* . . . and then I give him to the river. . . .

''Sometimes they cry out. But there's so much pain here, men hurt and dying. One scream in the night?''

There was a smell of musk in the thick air. Portia's face was radiant and her eyes drunk with color, shot through with spears of red. ''And that is what I am. Do you understand?''

Red couldn't speak.

Portia looked toward the door. "Why, Sophie, come on in here. Meet Yvette."

It was Matilda at the door, and she took Red by the hand as if she were four years old and led her to the garden, out of Lydia's sight, where they could sit in the shade and look out over the beautiful irises, so still in the heat.

"Did she tell you?" said Matilda. "She shouldn't of done that."

Red's throat ached as tears rose. She was so sweaty she felt as if her skin would melt. She felt horrible, betrayed and utterly alone, and had never wanted her mother and father so much in her life.

"You ever seen one o' them monster movies? They call 'em werewolves. And all the people who saw the movie I went to, they screamed at the scary parts. But they weren't scary to me, because Miss Portia . . ." Matilda pulled out a clean handkerchief from the pocket of her apron. Red buried her face behind it.

"Lord knows what happened to her is bad. But she can't help herself. What she's got is some disease that I don't think us or God understands. And it keeps her alive, when all she wants is peace."

"She gave me the key to the room in the cellar," whispered Red.

"That's where we keep her when she has her spells. She came up from Vicksburg right after the war on that riverboat *Sultana*, and it blew up, and she and her maid Sophie got fished out of the Mississippi. When they made it back to Memphis, Sophie told Miss Portia's people here. And they've kept her hidden in little rooms for years and years. She hasn't been able to get out and do harm. And she's so old now . . . no one from the outside knows she's still alive. *Your own mother doesn't know what Miss Portia is.* When she was a little girl, Miss Lydia sent your mother away to school. Which I can't do with my Virginia," said Matilda in that voice she had used when she talked about the cruelty of whites to their maids. "You're the last Tucker female. You have a right to know."

It was too much of a burden, sitting across from Lydia at breakfast the next morning and pretending to be a carefree little girl. Mercifully, her grandmother didn't notice the haunted look on Red's face, or that she picked at her food because there was a heavy stone at her center. One glance and her mother would have known.

So Red told Virginia.

"Does she really turn into a *wolf*?"

"Yes! Even Matil—even your mother says so."

"Mama's been with this family since before I was born. And my great-great-grandmother was named Sophie. Mama works at other people's houses, but not like here. She practically lives here. She must have known about this for a long, long time."

"And maybe your grandmother before her."

"I'll bet! You know, Mama doesn't laugh a lot. Sometimes she says I better laugh while I can."

"Maybe," said Red, "she just means that your life will be hard . . . your being a negro."

Virginia gravely shook her head. "It's more than that. My Aunt Mary works for some awful mean people. But she still laughs and makes jokes and says you can't let life get you down—and that my generation will have it better. Mama . . . well, if she's known about this all her life, it would explain a lot."

"Our two families go back a long way."

"We're practically sisters," grinned Virginia.

Red grinned back and realized the weight had lightened as she talked to Virginia. Yesterday, between one heat-thickened moment and the next, Red had met a monster, and life was full of dark corners. But now she could bear it, if Portia wanted to see her again.

"I'm not going to be your maid," said Virginia. "When I grow up."

"Well, of *course* you aren't. What are you going to do?"

"Dunno yet. I'll go to college."

They sat in contemplative silence. College was further off than anything they could think of, and for a moment it awed them more than the werewolf next door.

Red drifted thoughtfully into Lydia's kitchen and heard her on the phone, heard a name to make her heart pound. She was talking to Daddy.

"... well, Frank, it was nothing really. I just put in a good word. ..."

Red paused in the breakfast nook, some instinct making her hold back and listen.

"I think you got the job because you're a good teacher, not because the dean of the department is a schoolmate from Randolph-Macon. From back before the Punic Wars."

Red waited out the silent space of her father's response.

"... maybe it is time we were on more cordial footing. Frank—Frank, it comes down to this; I knew you wanted the job, I thought it would be good for the three of you to move—up there ... never mind why ... and Miss Delacourte would never have hired you if she didn't think you were the best man for the job. I just wanted the best for the three of you. Oh, let me go get Yvette, and not another word about it. Yvette!"

Red tiptoed back to the kitchen, banged the door and ran into the dining room.

She was part of the enclave now, at home with the stately hedges, embraced by the emerald tunnel. She had prowled the terrible room, shared secrets with a friend. Crying on the pillow that first night seemed a remote dream as Red sat across from Portia the next day.

"Dear child," said Portia, "have you pulled yourself together yet?"

"I guess."

"I could tell you were a girl with sand."

"Sand?"

"Grit, determination, strength." Portia looked at her with those pale blue eyes and the suggestion of a smile shadowed her mouth.

Portia was beautiful when she was young, realized Red.

"I am a one hundred and twenty-year-old werewolf. But I don't change into a wolf like I used to, because when the full moon comes around, Lydia takes me down to that little room with no windows, and I can't see the moon. I just get wild and sick, and I am told my nails and teeth get sharper.

"And here's the thing: if Lydia gets too old, whose turn do you think it will be to take care of me? Your mother or *you*, and that colored girl."

Red shook her head emphatically. "Grandma Lydia got my father a job up north so my mother wouldn't have to take care of you. And Virginia and me can't do it. We're going to college."

"Virginia and *I* . . . now that's interesting, Lydia sending you up north." She seemed far away and Red fiddled anxiously with her teacup.

Portia slapped the table with the flat of her hand. Red jumped and knocked over her tea, but the old woman didn't notice. "I see it now. She's going to kill me."

"What!"

"Oh, not anytime soon. She wants me to hang on for a long time, because that's her revenge. But when she gets so old that caring for me is a real burden, she'll take me outside on a full moon. I think changing into a wolf would kill me at my age."

Red struggled to comprehend. "Revenge for what?"

Portia wasn't listening. "We will beat her to the punch. I'm going to kill myself on the next full moon, two days off."

Red stared at Portia. "Great-grandmother Portia, I've heard it's wrong—"

"—to kill yourself?" Portia turned her hands over and Red looked at her leathery palms and sharp little nails. "Let the truth be told. I'm not your great-grandmother. Oh, I'm a Tucker, but your line descends from my sister, who moved to Memphis before the war. When you have a monster inside, like I do, you don't love men or bear their children, and people die when they get too near. They say your grandfather Earl fell accidentally, or that the boiler of the *Sultana* blew up accidentally, killing eighteen hundred people, but it's not so. If I hadn't been there, neither thing would have happened."

The hairs on Red's arms were standing up.

"I welcome death," said Portia. "Death is a part of me, like the color of my eyes."

The day of the full moon found Red packing for the next day's flight. She was fitting Portia's small box into a corner of her suitcase when the phone rang. Red heard Lydia pick up and thought nothing of it until she heard her grandmother gasp.

"Matilda! Matilda, come to the phone right away!"

As Red heard the heavier tread in the hall, Lydia came into Red's room, her arms crossed tightly, her eyes blazing. "You might as well hear this, Yvette. Matilda's sister Mary has been hit in the face by a brick. Two white men threw it from their car as she walked home from the bus stop."

From the hall they heard heartbreaking sobs and "Oh, Lord, oh Lord!"

Red felt her stomach lurch. "Is she gonna be okay?"

"They don't know. That was the doctor, calling from

the hospital. I'll drive Matilda over there, you stay here with Virginia."

Red sat on her bed, wondering how she was going to face her friend, but it was Matilda who came to her door.

"I have to go now and I don't know when I'll be back," she said in a choked voice. Red could hardly bear to look at her face, the tears soaking into the weary wrinkles. "Maybe in a couple of hours, maybe not for a while." She pulled a vial of green liquid wrapped in yellowed paper out of her apron pocket and handed it to Red. The paper had words written in a spidery scrawl: *belladonna, henbane, jimson weed, wormwood. Ground and mixed with olive oil, turpentine, and hog fat and the fat of an unchristened infant.*

"It'll have to do without that last part. I've been growing those plants by the tracks, waiting for her to give me the word. You go take that bottle to Miss Portia before tonight. You're the last Tucker and maybe this is the way it's supposed to be."

Matilda left. Lydia was starting the car out front, and Red realized Virginia had come into her room.

"I'm sorry," said Red, and she meant it to go beyond the single terrible incident that sent Matilda hurrying to the hospital.

"Mama says it's because all those people went on that march to Washington last week. If they'd just stayed home nobody would be out throwing bricks." Virginia's eyes seemed to burn. "But what those white boys did was wrong. Flat-out wrong."

"Yes." After a mournful silence Red said, "I have to take this bottle to Miss Portia. Your mother told me I have to."

"She told me, too," said Virginia, swiping roughly at her eyes. "I'll go with you."

In the soft, golden afternoon, Red and Virginia emerged on the other side and mounted the steps to the old house, swinging open the screen door. Portia appeared in the kitchen as silently as a ghost.

"What have you got there?" she asked.

Red held up the vial.

"At long last," her mellifluous voice sounded distant.

"Miss Portia," said Virginia, "it might be hard on Red if she hands that to you by herself." Virginia clasped her hand over Red's and together they placed the vial in Portia's hands.

"What will this do?" whispered Red.

"It will change me into a wolf and I won't be able to change back. It won't be painful, but it will be more exertion than the monster can bear, and she won't last long. Do you want to watch me drink?"

The two girls looked at each other. *We've come this far.*

Portia uncorked the little vial, held it to her lips, then paused. She smiled and held it out, saluting them. Then she tilted it to her mouth, grimacing at the taste.

"Goodbye," she said. "Thank you, with every fiber of my being. Remember me like this when you see it tonight."

They sat together by the telephone, as silent in Lydia's house as Portia was next door. The sound of the bell cracked the air, and Red picked it up before the first ring had finished.

"Yvette, we can all breathe easy. Mary got some bad cuts and had to have some stitches, but the doctor doesn't think there's a concussion. They're going to keep her overnight just to be sure. So you tell Virginia. Matilda and I will be home soon. We'll all eat some supper, then you two can stay at my house while we look after great-grandmother Portia. It's one of those nights when she'll have a spell."

•   •   •

From the abundant foliage the two girls watched Lydia
and Matilda go into Portia's house. Matilda came for
them when it was dark and the moon had risen, and led
them to the cellar. Portia lay on the perverse bed,
clamped in a prone position. She writhed against the
restraints, her tidy braid unraveled, the strings of white
hair lashing across her face.

"My *God*, Matilda, what are those girls doing here?"
Lydia almost dropped the plastic cup in her hands. She
was completely undone, bereft of elegance and compo-
sure.

"They've come to see Miss Portia turn into a wolf."

Lydia leaned stiffly against the wall. "You told
them," she said, and Red was amazed at the pain in her
face.

"They—have—the—right!" gasped Portia.

Everyone turned and looked at her, and Lydia cried
out. Portia's face was growing coarse fur, as were her
hands and feet; all that could be seen peeking out from
an old nightgown.

"I took a draught," she whispered, and then she was
lost to them, shuddering and shaking.

Lydia looked straight at Matilda, who stared back un-
flinchingly, as if she had borrowed some of the red light
from Portia's eyes.

"I see," said Lydia. "It's over, and I had no say in
it." She squeezed her eyes shut and turned away from
them as she wept.

They watched over Portia, silently, as she twisted and
strained against the clamps, the room filling with the
musk of a wolf.

"It's time to leave," said Lydia faintly.

They all backed out of the room and bolted it behind
them.

Lydia wouldn't let Red look through the peephole. They
could hear Portia gasping, scrabbling against the re-

straints of the bed. The silence that followed was hollow, unearthly. Then came a low growl, guttural and coarse as gravel—and an explosive, feral scream, coupled with the sound of wood splintering and metal whanging against concrete. Red found herself pressed against the far wall of the corridor, gripping Lydia like a lifeline. Lydia folded her arms around her, softly. The monster howled over and over, hoarse, lusting wails, and her claws screeched against the walls, sending shivers to the pit of Red's stomach. They waited out the rage behind the walls, exhausted by the time the snarls and thuds of the werewolf's body lessened and stopped. Finally, Lydia released Red and peered through the peephole. She was very still for a moment, then she shot back the bolts.

They found her in the middle of the room, her legs splayed to hold her up. Portia was just an old wolf now, covered with white fur that had a worn yellow luster. Her eyes were blue, stark against black lids, and her bony frame seemed fragile as it heaved breath, making Red want to go forward and hold her up. But caution held her back. And Lydia's hand.

"We can take her outside now, Miss Lydia. She's through changing for good," said Matilda.

They bore Portia into the radiant night, collared and cross-tied, and the ancient wolf turned her muzzle to the moon, drinking in its luminosity. Red thought about the trenches in Vicksburg where this werewolf had savaged Confederates, her eyes glowing as they glowed now, full of moon-magic and bloodlust. She could hear the wolves at the zoo, howling like demons.

They led her to a grassy spot by the hedges and she stood silhouetted against the moonlight.

"She killed Earl when your mother was very young," said Lydia. "He got careless on the night of a full moon. *That's* why I kept her alive all these years, she killed my *husband*."

They listened to the wolves howl frantically against the counterpoint of deep lion roars.

Portia's breath came out in wheezes.

"She's dying, at last," said Lydia, and Red could hear sorrow in her voice.

Portia drew herself up, her coat bristling with bright needles of light. She threw her head to the moon and gave one last howl, harrowing and rich, then she fell. It took Red a moment to realize that the wolves at the zoo had become silent. Then, they started again, taking up the dirge; farewell to a fearful and mighty one.

Lydia was in the breakfast nook, the gloves she used for heavy digging laid on the counter. She was going at *The Commercial Appeal* with the kitchen scissors. "Article in the paper says people all over Overton Park were calling in to complain about the wolves and lions. No doubt the *Press Scimitar* will run something this afternoon." She put the short article inside a leather-bound book.

Red slid into the chair opposite her grandmother.

"My whole life revolved around taking care of her, stretching her miserable life out as long as I could," said Lydia, her eyes distant. "I should have let her go years ago. I was so angry when she killed Earl. He was a good man, Yvette, but I don't think he ever really believed, and he got careless. And now, I don't feel angry, just . . . sad. Maybe I'll take a little vacation, visit you all in New York."

Daddy will love every minute of *that*, thought Red.

Lydia leaned forward to get up, then sat down again. "Yvette. Portia left a diary. She kept it faithfully up until the end." Lydia's hand was resting on the little leather-bound book.

A hunger swept through Red.

"When you're older, it's yours," said Lydia. "You've learned a lot already, but you've got some growing to do before most of this will make sense to you. Goodness, it seems like a long time ago that we sat talking at the dining-room table . . . right now, I think you should go say good-bye to Virginia.''

How old was older?

Virginia was waiting at the bench.

''Portia had a diary!''

Virginia's eyes were wide. ''A *diary*? Did Miss Lydia give it to you?''

''No . . . she said I had to get *older*.''

They sat back, frustrated.

''I'll have to go to college up there,'' said Virginia finally, ''so that when Miss Lydia gives it to you, we can read it together.''

''Yes! And we can go to the same school and walk around knowing we have this big secret. And we won't tell *anyone*. Not even our boyfriends.''

''Deal?''

''Deal!''

They never said good-bye.

AN AMERICAN CHILDHOOD

Pat Murphy

"An American Childhood" was purchased by Gardner Dozois, and appeared in the April 1993 issue of Asimov's, *with an interior illustration by Laurie Harden. Murphy doesn't appear in Asimov's as often as we'd like, but she has had a string of important stories here throughout the years, including the classic "Rachel in Love," one of the most popular stories of the decade, which won her a Nebula Award in 1988. In the vivid and powerful novella that follows, one of her very best pieces of work, she takes us to an evocatively portrayed American West, and introduces us to a very unusual family living alone on the distant frontier, a family that soon finds that even their remote wilderness home might not be remote enough to keep it safe from the savagery of the world outside. . . .*

Pat Murphy lives in San Francisco, where she works for a science museum, the Exploratorium, and edits the Exploratorium Quarterly. Her elegant and incisive stories have appeared throughout the eighties and the nineties in Asimov's Science Fiction, The Magazine of Fantasy and Science Fiction, Elsewhere, Amazing, Universe,

Shadows, Chrysalis, Full Spectrum, *and other places. Murphy's first novel,* The Shadow Hunter, *appeared in 1982, to no particular notice, but her second novel,* The Falling Woman, *won her a second Nebula Award in 1988, and was one of the most critically acclaimed novels of the late eighties. Her third novel,* The City, Not Long After, *appeared in 1990, as did a collection of her short fiction,* Points of Departure. *Her most recent book is a major new novel,* Nadya: The Wolf Chronicles, *a book-length expansion of "An American Childhood."*

Nadya Rybak was five years old when she realized that her family was not like other families. She was in the crossroads store, staring at the jars of candy on the high shelf behind the counter and wondering if her father might buy her a peppermint stick to suck during the wagon ride home. It was late spring in Missouri, and the wooden floorboards were warm against her bare feet.

She liked the store. The clutter of boxes and barrels intrigued her. Interesting smells clung to them: jerked beef, clarified butter, pickles, and spices. Her father leaned against the wooden counter in the back, talking with Mr. Evans, the storekeeper, about Indian trouble up north. Two fur traders had been killed the month before. Mr. Evans blamed all the trouble on whiskey and whiskey peddlers, and Nadya's father agreed.

Nadya's mother and Mrs. Evans sat on a bench near shelves that held bolts of fabric and sewing notions. A three-month-old issue of *Godey's Ladies Book*, worn from handling, lay open on Mrs. Evans's lap. Lottie Evans, a wide-eyed three-year-old, sat at her mother's feet, staring at Nadya. One chubby hand clutched her mother's skirt. She was fascinated by the older girl, but had not yet gathered her courage to approach.

A bearded man came in the door and threw a bundle of furs onto the counter. Nadya stared up at him with interest. He was a very shaggy man: his beard was long and unkempt; his hair needed cutting. He was wearing a buckskin coat, homespun pants, and a shirt that hadn't been changed any too recently. There hung about him—mingling with the usual man-smells of chewing tobacco, whiskey, and sweat—a strong smell of many animals. She smelled bear and deer and buffalo and beaver, but what caught her attention was the faint smell of wolf.

The man leaned against the counter, evidently content to wait for the storekeeper's attention. He glanced down at Nadya. "Hello there, young'un."

"Hello." The wolf smell came from the bundle of furs on the counter.

"You know, I've got a little sister back in New York that's not much older than you."

Nadya considered this gravely, but didn't say anything.

"What are you doing here?"

"Waiting for my papa."

"Looked like you were watching those jars of candy back there." She nodded, and the man grinned. "Thought so. Well, maybe when I trade these furs, I'll buy you a piece of candy. Would you like that?"

Nadya nodded solemnly. She watched the man untie the rope that bound the furs together and spread the furs on the counter. She could smell wolf more strongly now. Emboldened by the man's grin, she reached up and touched one of the furs, a soft pelt the color of butter.

"That's a painter," the man said. "A mountain cat." He let her stroke the soft tawny fur, then lifted it aside. "Now here's a beaver pelt. Some fine gentleman in New York City will be wearing a hat made from that soon enough."

The man lifted the beaver pelt aside, revealing a fur that gave off a warm, reassuring scent, the scent of Nadya's mother on certain nights. Nadya reached up hesitantly to stroke the soft pelt. A layer of stiff gray guard hairs lay atop an undercoat of soft fur. She stroked the fur backwards to reveal the soft undercoat, and the long gray guard hairs tickled her hand.

"This 'un, I'll sell for the bounty," the man said. He lifted the fur off the counter and held it down where she could see it better. Where the animal's head should have been, there was a mask with vacant holes in place of eyes. The ears were shriveled; they had been pressed flat by the weight of the other furs.

Nadya stared at the empty eye-holes and took a step back, dropping her hand to her side. "Where did you get it?" she asked, suddenly wary. Until she saw that eyeless mask, she had not thought about where the fur had come from.

"From a wolf bigger than you are." He shook the pelt and the fur rippled. "Saw her prowling around the edge of my camp and got her with a single shot. Right through the head."

Nadya took another step back, glaring at the man.

"What's the matter, young'un? She's dead. Can't hurt you now."

"You shouldn't have done that," she cried shrilly. "You shouldn't have shot her."

She fled across the store to hide behind her mother's long skirt. Her mother put her hand on Nadya's head. "What is it, child? What's the matter?"

"He killed her. That man." Nadya pointed across the store at the bewildered trapper, who still held the wolf skin.

"I didn't mean to scare her, missus," he said apologetically. "I was just showing her some furs."

"It's all right," her mother said. She stooped and put her arm around Nadya's shoulders. She spoke softly. "Come, Nadya. We'll go out to the wagon to wait for Papa."

"Why did he kill the wolf, mama?"

"Hush," her mother said. "Hush now."

Nadya's mother took her hand and led her out the door. Nadya walked by her mother's side, carefully placing herself between her mother and the man who killed wolves. She would protect her mother.

"I didn't mean to scare her," he was saying.

Then they were out in the sunshine, away from the comforting and horrifying scent of the wolf fur. Nadya sat on the wagon seat and her mother explained, very softly, that the wolf the man had killed was not a person—not like Mama or Papa. That wolf was an animal, and it was not murder to kill it.

But her mother's voice trembled when she talked and she held Nadya's hand a little too tightly. Nadya knew that her mother was afraid of the man too. When her father came out of the store, he brought a new ax head, a box of supplies, and a few hard candies to comfort Nadya.

"He's a bad man," Nadya told her father.

"He just doesn't understand," her father said.

Nadya shook her head stubbornly. The world, which had always seemed so safe and secure, was suddenly a frightening place. She sucked on a hard candy and clung to her mother's hand, convinced that her father was wrong.

Dmitri Rybak, Nadya's father, had emigrated to America from a small Polish village. Marietta, her mother, had come from France. They had met in St. Louis, fallen in love, and moved West, looking for land where they could live their lives undisturbed.

At that time, Missouri had been a state for only a few years. According to the unreliable census figures of the time, the state had a population of 66,000 (not counting Indians or Negroes) scattered over its 69,000 or so square miles. Most of the folks were clustered along the Mississippi River. Only a few had ventured westward—trappers and traders and soldiers, for the most part.

Nadya's parents had settled on the Osage River in the southwest portion of the state, a hilly region of creeks and springs and few settlers. When they settled, there had been a trading post located where the river was shallow enough to ford. The Evans's store stood there now.

When Nadya was three, the mountain man who had run the trading post had moved on, selling his ramshackle building to Mr. Evans, who had improved and expanded the store to serve the needs of the farmers who were moving into the area. By the time Nadya was five, a tiny settlement had grown up around the store, including a blacksmith shop, a tavern, and a few houses.

After meeting the trapper in the store, Nadya became more careful of people outside her family, less willing to talk with strangers. On the whole, her new shyness affected her life relatively little—few strangers happened by their farm. And for the most part, Nadya's childhood was happy.

On long winter nights, when the farmyard was dusted with snow and hickory logs burning in the fireplace warmed the cabin, Dmitri taught her to read the *Farmer's Almanack*. They leaned over the book, huddling close to the pool of light cast by a wick burning in a cup of bear oil. Her father stumbled over the difficult words, but he persisted, determined that Nadya learn. While they labored over the book (learning that turnips should be planted in the dark of the moon and that a silver coin, placed in a butter churn, will help the butter come), Marietta watched from the fireside, mending or knitting.

With a pen made from a wild turkey quill, Dmitri taught Nadya to write. By the wavering light, Nadya painstakingly made marks on bark that her father had peeled from the shagbark hickory tree. She learned to write her name in English. Her father could write in another alphabet as well—the alphabet he had learned when he was a boy. But he only taught her the English writing, saying that she was an American and she should write as the Americans did.

When Nadya's lessons were done, she would ask for a story.

"A story?" her father would say. "It's too late for a story." But he always smiled when he said it was too late.

"It's not too late," she would say. "There's time. Please, Papa. Just one story."

"Maybe there's time for one, Dmitri," Marietta would say. Then Dmitri would put aside the pen and the Almanack and he would lift his hands so that the light from the burning wick made wavering shadows on the deerskin that her mother had stretched across the window to keep the drafts out. The shadows that Nadya's father made with his hands were magical.

"Once upon a time, there was a man," her father said, and the shadows of his hands became the silhouette of a man's head—a man with a jutting chin and a big nose. "He lived in a cabin on the edge of the forest. And there was a rabbit who came to eat the vegetables in his garden." The shadows shifted and changed, becoming a rabbit that wiggled its nose and made Nadya giggle. "Every night the rabbit came and ate from the man's garden."

Dmitri told of how the man built a scarecrow to fool the rabbit. The rabbit ignored the scarecrow—it kept on hopping into the garden and eating all the vegetables. The man tried to keep the rabbit away by sitting in the garden all night long, but he always fell asleep. The shadow man snored noisily, and that made Nadya laugh.

"But," Nadya's father said, "on the night when the moon was full, the man changed."

Nadya watched with fascination as the shadow man shifted and became a wolf, a fierce shadow head that snapped at the air and lifted its snout to howl. The wolf chased the rabbit through the forest, growling and snapping.

"All night long, the wolf chased the rabbit and the rabbit ran from the wolf. When the moon set and the sun came up, the rabbit hid in its burrow, afraid to go near the man's garden. And the wolf became a man again."

Nadya watched the shadow wolf give way to the shadow man. Sometimes the shadow man sang a song and sometimes he howled like a wolf. Then Nadya and her mother howled too. If they howled long and hard, the wild wolves that lived in the forest heard them and joined in.

The story was always a little different, but it always involved the shadow man and the shadow wolf. Nadya never grew tired of watching one become the other.

Of course, on nights when the moon was full, there were no lessons and no stories. In the summer, there were romps, where her mother and father, in their other form, would play tag with Nadya in the farmyard by the cabin door. In the winter, the she-wolf would cuddle Nadya, letting the child stroke her soft fur and snuggle against her warm belly. When Nadya was seven years old—old enough to be trusted to stay away from the fire—her mother and father would go running at night, leaving her alone until morning. She was lonely then, sad that she could not go running with her parents. But her mother told her that when she grew up, she would Change when the full moon rose. And then they would run together. She had to be content with that.

Since Nadya had no brothers and sisters, she helped her mother and father in equal part: doing womanly chores with her mother and helping her father with the farming, acting more like a son to her father than a daughter. When she was nine years old, she helped her father plow. Her job was to ride the mule to steady it while her father rode the plow. She loved that—the aroma of the newly turned earth, the warmth of the mule beneath her, the solid shifting of the animal's muscles as it strained to pull the plow through the soil. Her father whistled and shouted to the mule, and sang folk songs in French and Polish.

The summer that she was ten, her father taught her to shoot. As a target, he set a pinecone on a stump in the field. All that first week, he took her down to the field in the early evening. She would hold the rifle to her shoulder and practice pointing it at the pinecone and pulling the trigger.

After a week of sighting on the pinecone, he let her try shooting with powder. The first time she tried, the kick of the explosion bruised her shoulder and nearly knocked her down. But she was not frightened and she tried it again and again, until she could hit the pinecone square with every shot. She hunted squirrels in the forest near the house, aiming for the bark just below the animal's feet. The shot shattered the bark and the concussion killed the squirrel, leaving the meat untouched.

As she grew older, she and her father went hunting for larger game. At night, they hunted deer, mesmerizing the animals with a torch made from a pine knot or a rag soaked in bear oil and lashed to a stick. By day, they hunted turkey or bear, in season.

Nadya's long skirts were a hindrance when she went hunting, rustling against the grass and catching on every burr and thorn. Over her mother's protests, she stitched herself a pair of homespun trousers. "There is no one here to see," her father said. "Let the girl be comfortable."

Nadya was a good hunter—she had a better eye than her father, and she brought in most of the meat for the family table. In the fall of her twelfth year, determined to earn a rifle of her own, she hunted bears for their skins and oil and meat.

She always wore a dress to town—her mother insisted

on that. One Sunday afternoon, Nadya and her father took the bear oil and skins to the store and offered them in trade for a new, muzzle-loading Hawkins rifle. Mr. Evans accepted the trade, but seemed puzzled when Nadya lifted the gun from the counter and sighted along its barrel. He frowned at Dmitri. "You're letting your daughter choose your rifle?" he murmured.

"Her rifle," Dmitri corrected. "She killed the bears. Only seems right she should choose the rifle. After all, she's a better shot than I am."

The men who were lounging by the Franklin stove glanced up. "The girl killed eight bears?" one man asked.

"Ten," Dmitri said. "We kept the skins and meat from two for our own use."

"D'you mind if I try it?" Nadya asked Mr. Evans.

"As you like," he said.

They stepped onto the porch of the store, with Nadya carrying the rifle easily at her side. The men from the store followed: Nadya loaded the rifle, carefully pouring black powder into the barrel, tamping it in place, inserting cotton wadding and a bullet. She looked around then, searching for a target.

"You see that nail in the fence across the way," said one of the loiterers from the store. "I knew a man in Kentucky who could hit a nail like that and drive it home."

Nadya glanced at the man's grinning face. He was laughing at her, and she did not like it. She squinted at the fence across the road, where the rusty head of a nail protruded from a post. "All right," she said easily, lifted the rifle, and fired a single shot. The nail disappeared into the wood, leaving a dark hole where the bullet had struck.

"This rifle will do," Nadya said to her father. They returned to the store, leaving the loiterers staring at the fence.

• • •

In her fourteenth year, Nadya noticed that the world was changing around her. It began when the bargers started calling to her. She had heard people at the store say that the men who steered flatboats down the river were a bad lot—drinking, fighting, and stealing when they could. But Nadya had always liked the look of them. They seemed so much at ease floating down river, leaning back among the crates of apples and barrels of salt pork, playing the harmonica or singing. She had always waved at the bargers, and they had always waved back. But in her fourteenth year, they started shouting when they waved. "Come along with us, little sweetheart!" There was something leering and wicked in the way they said it, and she stopped waving after that.

Then a Yankee peddler stopped at the farm to show her mother his stock of sewing notions and such. He gave Nadya a blue satin ribbon for no reason at all. He said that it would look pretty in her dark hair, and when he held it up so that she could see it, his smell changed ever so slightly. She did not know what to say. He watched her so intently, like a hungry dog with its eye on the hoecakes. When her mother nudged her, she thanked him awkwardly.

After dinner that night, Nadya's mother brought out her cards. She kept them wrapped in a silk scarf on the same shelf with the Bible and the *Farmer's Almanack*. Nadya knew the cards well: when she was a child, she had often played with them, fingering their gilded edges and admiring the pictures of strange people in strange costumes. She would sort the cards according to suit: separating the swords, the coins, the wands, and the cups, and setting aside the special cards that did not fall into any suit. The words on these cards were written in French: *Le Diable*, The Devil; *Le Monde*, The World; *Le Mat*, the Fool.

Her mother did not read the cards often. But when

there was a decision to be made—like whether to plant early or wait—she would lay the cards on the rough wood of the table, studying the bright pictures. She would shake her head over certain cards—a burning tower, a man hanging upside down—while she and Dmitri conferred in soft murmurs.

That night, when Dmitri went out to check on the cattle, Nadya's mother beckoned Nadya to sit beside her. "That trader," her mother said, "You caught his eye." She unwrapped the cards and spread the silk scarf on the table. "What did you think of that?"

Nadya shifted uncomfortably on the wooden chair. "I didn't like the way he watched me."

"He wanted you," she said. "The way a man wants a woman. It's that simple."

Nadya looked down at her hands, suddenly shy. Her mother had always talked of such things matter of factly, without shame.

"I'd guess that the Change will be coming to you with the next full moon," her mother said. She sat back in her chair, holding the cards loosely in her lap. "With the Change, there comes a power. Being wanted—that's part of the power. You need to understand that men will admire you, men will lust after you."

Nadya looked up at her mother's serene face. "What do I do about that?" Nadya asked.

Her mother smiled. "Don't look so worried, *chérie*. This is not a bad thing." She shuffled the cards, her eyes on Nadya. "We will read the cards for guidance." When Nadya cut the deck, her mother restacked the cards and began to lay them face-up on the scarf in a cross-shaped pattern. "You are strong-minded—that's bad and good. Bad because it will lead you into trouble; good because it will keep the trouble from overwhelming you."

Nadya studied the cards. In the center of the pattern was the ten of coins, a card that pictured a happy family gathered together. The ten of coins was crossed and half-covered by *La Lune*, The Moon. On this card, two dogs howled at a frowning moon. There were other cards she recognized. In her future was the knight of swords, charging rashly forward on a gray horse. She saw *Le Diable*, a frightening figure with a man and a woman in chains at his feet; *La Mort*, a skeleton clutching a sickle; *La Maison Diu*, a castle struck by lightning.

"Ah," her mother said softly. "Perhaps this is not the best time for a reading."

"Tell me what it is, Mama."

Her mother stared at the cards. "Pain and destruction."

"When is it coming?" Nadya looked at the door, as if expecting the Devil to walk through it. "What can I do?"

"It is coming with a young man," her mother said. "He charges forward—reckless and brash—and he carries death in his hands."

Her mother dealt more cards, still shaking her head. "We will try again on another day," she said at last. She swept the cards from the scarf and shuffled them together.

That night, Nadya heard her mother and father murmuring softly by the fireside. Nadya listened, but she could not make out the words.

Three days later, when the full moon rose over the forest, the Change came to Nadya. She went running with her mother and father, and life was never the same after that.

Back in 1823, Mr. Hekiziah Jones attended a Methodist revival, a tent meeting that had brought in hundreds of devout Christians and an equal number of curiosity seekers from surrounding towns. Mr. Jones fell into the second category—a hard-drinking young man, he hoped to have a little fun and maybe win a few Christians over to the ways of sin.

Mr. Jones drank a great deal on Saturday night. On Sunday morning, overcome with a hangover and influenced by the persuasive sermon of a Methodist preacher, he renounced the Devil, swore that he would never again touch the demon rum, and, just incidentally, proposed to Cordelia Walker, a twenty-eight-year-old woman who had given up all hope of matrimony. Before Mr. Jones could change his mind, the preacher married the happy couple to the cheers of the crowd.

The first two vows were transitory—Mr. Jones returned to sin and drinking as soon as he possibly could. But the new Mrs. Jones was not so easily dismissed. Determined to save Mr. Jones's soul, she made an honest man of him—a farmer, no less. They emigrated to Kentucky, where he scratched out a living on a poor farm and Mrs. Jones bore him four strapping sons. Mrs. Jones's oldest son, Rufus, took after his father in his fondness for drinking and hunting and gambling and womanizing.

The year that Nadya turned eighteen, the Jones family emigrated again, this time to Missouri. That spring, the Jones family attended the wedding of Zillah Shaw, daughter of a prosperous farmer, to Samuel Prentice, a lanky farmboy.

The celebration was in the barn, which had been cleared of livestock for the occasion. The dirt floor was strewn with clean straw. Rufus Jones stood by the open door with a group of men. They passed a green jug of Mr. Shaw's fine home-brewed whiskey from hand to hand. The sun was setting and Rufus's shadow stretched all the way across the open floor of the barn.

The women were clearing away the remnants of the wedding feast. Children were running around the barn floor, whooping like Indians, and four young dogs were chasing them. At the far end of the barn, a fiddler was tuning his instrument for the dance to come. The air smelled of smoke, venison, and manure.

Rufus took a pull on the whiskey jug to ward off the evening chill, then passed the jug to his father. Hekiziah took a long pull, swallowing several times before he paused for breath. "Those are almighty ugly dogs," he said, squinting his good eye at the young hounds that romped with the children. Hekiziah had lost his other eye in a fight with an eye-gouging boatman before Rufus was born. He wore a patch over the empty socket.

"If they take after their mama, they'll be fine hunters," Mr. Shaw said. "She's as fine a bitch as ever treed a painter."

Hekiziah took another pull from the bottle, then reluctantly passed it to the next man. "That so? You do much hunting in these parts?"

Mr. Shaw nodded, taking the bait. "Not much choice in the matter. Man's got to hunt to keep the varmints out of his stock."

Rufus had heard this conversation before. By the time the bottle was empty, he guessed that his father would have turned the conversation from hunting to shooting and from shooting to who was the best shot. Soon enough, there would be talk of a shooting match with, most likely, a bottle of whiskey as the prize. Rufus was a good shot, and Hekiziah took advantage of that skill whenever he could.

Rufus made himself comfortable, leaning back against the barn wall and watching the girls primp and flutter around the fiddler. Mrs. Jones had taught Rufus to be polite and soft-spoken with the ladies. His father had taught him to get away with whatever he could. The combination was dangerous. In Kentucky, he had courted the sweet young daughter of a nearby farmer, taking her berry-picking in the warm days of Indian summer. He had left Kentucky just in time to avoid the consequences of those berry-picking expeditions.

The fiddler finished his tuning and played a reel. Rufus watched as the dancers formed two lines, stamping their feet in time with the music. Light from the setting sun faded. After the third dance, two of the older Shaw boys climbed into the rafters to light lanterns filled with bear oil. The burning wicks cast pools of yellow light, leaving only the corners in shadow.

It took a bit longer than Rufus expected for talk to turn to a shooting match. Mr. Shaw talked about a painter hunt last fall and about a wolf pack that roved along the river the winter just past. But eventually Hekiziah brought the conversation around.

"I reckon it's the water of Kaintuck," Hekiziah said. "Don't rightly know what else it could be. It must be something that makes the hunters of that state the sharpest-eyed riflemen around."

Mr. Shaw frowned and shook his head. His cheeks and nose were ruddy from drinking. "That just ain't so, Hekiziah. Why my own boys are sharp as any you'll find in Kentucky."

"I'd have to put that to the test before I could agree," Hekiziah said easily. "My boy Rufus is a right fine shot." He hefted the whiskey bottle, which had returned to his hand and lingered there. "Maybe a shooting match could settle the matter."

"All right then, a shooting match," Mr. Shaw agreed. His voice was loud and a little slurred. "With a bottle of whiskey to the winner." He glanced down. Two of the young dogs were wrestling on the barn floor. "And the pick of the litter as well."

"What's the target?" Rufus asked quietly.

Mr. Shaw glanced out the barn door at the dark fields. "A candle-snuffing, I'd say. That sit well with you?"

Rufus shrugged. "One target is as good as another."

In a snuffing contest, the target was the flame of a candle. The idea was not to snuff the candle out—that would be too easy a shot. Instead, the marksman had to shoot away the snuff, the charred part of the candle's wick, without putting out the flame. When the snuff was removed, the flame would brighten. Shoot too close to the candle, and the flame would die. Shoot too far away, and you would miss the wick altogether.

"Boys!" Mr. Shaw shouted over the music of the fiddle. He stamped his feet and shouted again. "Boys, listen here!" The fiddler stopped playing in the middle of a dance. "We're having a shooting match. Mr. Jones here says that his boys from Kentucky can beat anyone from Missouri hands down. Adam, run to the house and fetch a candle. Jack! William! All the rest of you! Get your rifles."

The young men who had been dancing abandoned their partners and scattered to fetch their rifles. When Adam returned with a tallow candle, Mr. Shaw took a flaming torch from the cooking fire and led the way out into the fields. Rufus walked at his father's side. The ground was damp and the air held the scent of spring growth. The sky was overcast. Moonlight illuminated the clouds from behind, creating a silvery patch of light in the eastern sky.

Like many settlers, Mr. Shaw had cleared new land by girdling the trees—removing a strip of bark all around the trunk. Without the bark, the tree died, and the settler cut it down. In the spring, when the ground was soft, the farmer grubbed out the stumps. In Mr. Shaw's field, the stumps of girdled trees—now stripped of all their bark and pale in the torchlight—stood as a reminder of the forest that had once covered his land.

Grass had sprouted between the stumps. Beyond the field, where the uncleared forest stood, the darkness grew thicker. A chorus of crickets, singing in the field and the forest, almost drowned out the fiddle music from the barn.

Mr. Shaw led the way to the far side of the field, where a low, flat-topped stump stood on the edge of the forest. He wedged the candle into a crack in the stump and lit the wick with his torch. He gave Adam the torch.

"Now you stay here, boy," he advised his son. "Call out when the snuff is long enough for shooting, then get back."

The men moved away from the stump, walking toward the barn until Mr. Shaw said, "That'll do." In the still air, the candle flame stood steady, a sliver of yellow light against the darkness of the forest.

"Three shots apiece," Hekiziah suggested, and Mr. Shaw agreed.

Jack, Mr. Shaw's oldest son, took the first shot, standing with his feet spread wide, his rifle set firmly against his shoulder. His shot went high—the distant flame flickered as the ball passed over. The chorus of crickets fell silent for a moment, and then began again, as loud as before.

Jack paused to reload. His second shot was low, cutting the wick and putting out the candle. While Adam was relighting the candle, Jack took a pull from the whiskey jug.

"Move farther away from there," Jack called to Adam when the candle was burning once again. "That damned torch is blinding me."

He took his third shot and the flame flickered and then brightened.

"Dead on!" Adam called.

Jack grinned at his father and the others. "Who'll be next?" he asked.

One by one, the other men shot. Several missed the candle with all three shots. Two others snuffed the candle one time out of three.

Rufus did not shoot until all the others had taken their turns. Then he lifted his rifle and squinted at the candle. In the blue heart of the flame, the charred portion of the wick curled in a long crescent.

He held his breath, steadying the rifle and sighting on that dark crescent. His first shot was perfect: the flame brightened and he smiled as he set the rifle down and reloaded.

"Fool's luck," he said to Mr. Shaw, before Mr. Shaw could say the same to him.

He took a pull from the whiskey bottle while he waited for the candle to burn down. The men around him were quiet. In the field and woods around them, crickets sang in a relentless chorus. "Ready!" Adam called at last.

Rufus lifted his rifle to his shoulder and squeezed off the second shot. The candle flickered—a miss.

"Your luck is passing," Mr. Shaw said in a good-natured tone.

"One more shot," Hekiziah said. "Give the boy a fair chance."

Rufus reloaded and lifted his rifle for the last shot. He braced himself, setting his feet wide apart and sighting carefully. The candle flickered and brightened for the second time.

Hekiziah whooped and clapped Rufus on the back. "Fine shooting, son. Almighty fine shooting. Wouldn't you agree, Mr. Shaw?"

Hekiziah held his hand out to Mr. Shaw, but Mr. Shaw just frowned at him, shaking his head like a bull disturbed by flies. He squinted at the men around him.

"We're not quite done," Mr. Shaw said in a belligerent tone. "There's one other who ought to shoot. One other who ain't here. You just hold on. You all just wait here."

He left them standing in the field and hurried in the direction of the barn. The cloud cover had broken and the half moon cast an uncertain light over the group. Rufus looked around at the others. By the moonlight, he could see them grinning, as if at a private joke.

"Who is he getting?" Hekiziah asked Jack uneasily. "Seems like most every man came with us."

"You just wait," Jack said. "You'll see. Best shot in these parts."

A few minutes later, Rufus saw three figures emerge from the barn and come across the field. As they approached, he realized that one of them was a woman. Her dark hair was braided and the braids were tied with ribbons and coiled on her head. With her left hand, she held her skirt so that the hem did not drag in the mud. She walked with a careful, mincing step, as if she were unaccustomed to wearing shoes. Under her right arm, she carried a muzzle-loading rifle. Another man, a farmer with a broad peasant face, followed behind Mr. Shaw and the woman.

Mr. Shaw performed introductions. "Mr. Jones, this is Miss Nadya Rybak and her father, Mr. Dmitri Rybak. It seemed to me that Miss Rybak should take a turn."

"Pleased to meet you, Miss Rybak," Hekiziah said uncertainly.

She wasn't looking at him. Her eyes were on the distant candle flame.

"Now, Miss Nadya," Mr. Shaw was saying. "You see that candle over there." He explained the rules of the contest and she listened, nodding to show that she understood. Then she glanced at her father and he nodded approval.

"It's ready," Adam called from his post by the candle. In the distance, Rufus could see the bobbing torch as the boy moved to a safe distance.

"Shoot when you're ready, Miss Nadya," Mr. Shaw said.

She planted her feet wide, getting a secure footing on the rough ground. She put her rifle to her shoulder, then frowned and lowered it again. She murmured something to her father—Rufus could not make out the words—and Mr. Rybak shrugged. She handed him the rifle and bent to unlace her shoes. That done, she pulled the shoes off and stood barefoot on the cold ground. She nodded with satisfaction and took her rifle, lifting it with greater confidence than before.

The rifle was barely to her shoulder when she squeezed off the first shot. The flame flickered and then flared brightly.

Nadya took the rifle from her shoulder and waited for the snuff to grow long enough to shoot again. The men waited in silence, looking away into the darkness. Mr. Rybak stood at his daughter's side.

The woman glanced in Rufus's direction, catching him staring. Rather than dropping her eyes, she returned his stare. Her eyes were dark in the moonlight.

"Ready," Adam called out, and Nadya turned to face the candle. Again, she set her feet carefully and lifted the rifle smoothly to her shoulder. A faint breath of wind toyed with the wisps of hair that had escaped her braids. In the distance, the candle flame flickered and threatened to go out. She waited with the rifle at her shoulder until the flame steadied. Her second shot was as good as the first. The flame brightened and burned white.

She did not fidget as she waited for the flame to burn away the wick so that she could shoot again. She lowered the rifle and stood at ease, ignoring the men around her. The whiskey bottle passed from hand to hand. Mr. Rybak took a pull, then touched Nadya's arm. She wet her lips, glanced at the candle, then accepted the bottle and drank. She handed the bottle to Rufus. Her fingers brushed his as he took the bottle—a warm touch in the cool night air.

The candle burned low and Adam called out that she could shoot again. Rufus watched her lift the rifle a third time.

Her third shot was perfect—straight through the snuff. "Good shooting," Mr. Shaw exclaimed. "Fine shooting. Well worth a jug of whiskey, Miss Nadya."

The men returned to the barn in a knot of excitement and noise. Rufus walked with the others, avoiding his father. Hekiziah did not like to be disappointed and Rufus thought it just as well to stay out of his way for a time. He also wanted to get a look at Nadya Rybak in a better light.

In the barn, the table had been cleared away and the fiddler was just starting a tune. A line of couples was forming for a reel, but Nadya was not among them. Rufus looked for her, strolling around the dance floor and peering into the shadowy corners. He tipped his hat to the group of young women who had gathered in one corner. There were some pretty girls there, but he had his mind fixed on Miss Nadya. He made his way to the corner of the barn where the men were drinking.

"I don't see Miss Nadya," he said to Tom Williams, the son of the man who ran the blacksmith shop in town.

Tom shrugged. "I don't believe I've ever seen her dancing. I suppose she doesn't care for it."

"Have you ever tried to persuade her to change her mind? She's a handsome girl," Rufus said.

Tom looked startled. "I never thought of that. I reckon she is. But I expect that trying to change her mind is a waste of time. She's an odd one. Standoffish."

"You think so? I'd wager that I could change her mind."

"You think so? I doubt it."

"How about betting four bits on the proposition. If I don't have her out there dancing by the end of the evening, you win."

Tom nodded. "I'll take you up on that."

"Than I guess I'll see if I can find her." Rufus took a gourd cup and a bottle of cider, crossed the barn to the open door, and stepped outside.

The barnyard was crowded with the farm wagons that had carried the guests to the celebration. He strolled among the wagons. On the far side of the barnyard, he saw a woman leaning against the split rail fence, gazing into the empty field. She turned her head as he approached, and he recognized Nadya Rybak.

"How do, Miss Nadya," Rufus said. "We haven't been properly introduced. I'm Rufus Jones. My father just bought some land by the river not far from here."

"How do," she said politely.

"That was fine shooting. Congratulations."

"Thank you." Her voice was even; she did not seem particularly interested in talking with him.

"I've never known such a pretty girl to be such a fine shot." He poured cider into the cup. "Would you care for a drink of cider? Shooting is thirsty work."

She studied his face, then accepted the cup. By her expression, he guessed that she was not used to flattery. He leaned against the railing beside her. "Mr. Shaw was pleased that you won," he said.

She shook her head. "Not at all. He was pleased that you lost. He's a stiff-necked old Yankee."

He grinned. She was plain-spoken enough. "But surely you're no Yankee."

She shrugged. "We're foreigners, by his lights. But he'd rather lose to a foreigner than a man from Kentucky."

"Well, if I had to lose to someone, I'm happy to lose to you, Miss Nadya. Have you picked out your prize yet?"

She frowned and returned the cup to him. "Mr. Shaw gave me a bottle of whiskey."

"He also promised the pick of the litter. You can get yourself a dog."

She shook her head. "I don't care for dogs."

"Mr. Shaw makes great claims for these dogs. Fine hunters, he says. Perhaps your father . . ."

"My father won't have a dog on the place. He likes them no better than I do."

Rufus shook his head, amazed. Just about every frontier farm had a few dogs around—to warn against intruders, to bark when varmints attacked the livestock. "I had heard you were a hunter. I'm surprised any hunter would turn down a dog."

"I hunt alone," she said. "I don't need a yapping dog to scare away the game."

He drained the cup, filled it again, and offered it to her. She took it from his hand.

"I had hoped I *might* have the honor of a dance," he said.

She shook her head. "I don't care to dance."

"That's kind of you. I'm sure if you elected to dance, you'd put the other girls to shame."

She looked away from him, gazing out at the open field once again. He thought he might have overdone the flattery, but then she spoke softly. "Never learned how."

"Never learned how to dance? Why that's foolish. You move with such a natural grace. You could learn all you needed in a minute." He hesitated, then said, "I could teach you right now, if you'd like."

She glanced at his face.

"Right now," he said, setting the cider jug on the ground and balancing the cup on the fence post. He held his arms out to her. "It won't take a minute."

"I can't," she said, standing with her back to the fence.

"Listen to the music," he said, tapping his foot in time to the fiddle tune. "Here now: I'll bow to you." He bent at the waist, grinning at her.

"And you curtsy to me." She bobbed in an awkward curtsy. "Give me your hand and we'll begin."

She reached out and he took her hands in his. Her hands were small and warm, rough from farm work.

"Tap your foot along with the music," he said. "That's good. Now we step forward and back. That's right. Now left hand circle." He held one hand and led her in a circle. "Right hand circle." Again, she followed obediently. "Swing your partner." He swung her, keeping time with the distant fiddle. "Very good. Promenade now." He pulled her into the promenade position and led her around a farm wagon. Her body was warm against his side.

She was a cooperative partner, moving with him easily. "You're a fine dancer," he said when the music ended.

She smiled at him for the first time. Her face was a little flushed, and a few more wisps of hair had escaped her braids. She looked charming. "You think so?"

"Without a doubt. You come to it naturally. Why don't you come inside and we can join the others."

She shook her head. "I don't care to."

The music started again, a slow tune in a waltz time. He cocked his head to listen. "I'll teach you a dance that's all the rage in Paris," he said. "A dancing teacher who was passing through Kentucky taught it to me. Would you like to learn it?"

He smiled at her. The dancing teacher had told him that the waltz was a fine excuse to hold a girl closer than propriety would ordinarily allow. She held out her hands, and he pulled her close, slipping one arm around her waist and holding her other hand in his.

"Now step as I do. One, two, three; one, two, three; one, two, three. . . ."

She was so close that he could feel the warmth of her body. Just a few thin layers of cloth separated his hand from her waist. Her face was just inches from his.

He stopped counting and began to hum softly along with the fiddle tune. Perhaps he couldn't persuade her to dance with him in the barn. But he might persuade her to spend a little time with him alone. That would be worth losing the wager. He adjusted his hand at her waist, pulling her a little closer.

Nadya stopped in mid-step and pulled away. "I'd best be going," she said suddenly.

"In the middle of a dance?" he said.

She took two steps back. "Yes. I think it's best." She wet her lips. "Thank you for teaching me." She stooped by the fence and retrieved her shoes.

"I would be happy to continue the lesson. I wish you wouldn't run off."

She shook her head and cast a quick look over her shoulder at the barn. "I must be going." She turned away, then hesitated and turned back. "If you would like the dog Mr. Shaw promised to me, you are welcome to have it. You can tell him I said so."

She hurried away then, carrying her shoes. She did not look back. Rufus watched her go, cursing his bad luck. After a bit, he wandered back into the barn. A few moments later, Tom found him in the shadows, watching the dancers.

"No luck," Tom said. "I told you she didn't care for it."

Rufus fished in his pocket and silently paid Tom the money he owed.

A week later, on the day of the full moon, Nadya was in the garden, chopping at weeds with a grubbing hoe and loosening the soil for the spring planting. The breeze was warm and the newly turned soil reeked of rotting leaves and grubs—rich, inviting smells.

"Hello, the house!" She heard a man's voice calling and straightened from her hoeing, grateful for the interruption. She saw a man riding into the farmyard on a gray horse.

Nadya hurried toward the cabin. By the time she reached the farmyard, Rufus Jones had tied his horse to the split rail fence and was greeting her mother politely. "Pleased to make your acquaintance, Mrs. Rybak," he was saying. "How do you do, Miss Nadya?"

Nadya nodded a greeting. Rufus had been hunting and he gave her mother one of the two turkey hens that hung from his saddle. He was saying something about his father feeling a mite poorly and about how Mrs. Evans in the store thought Mrs. Rybak might have a remedy that would ease his stomach.

Nadya's mother nodded, allowing that she had some herbs that might help. She dried her hands on her apron. "I'll get them right away."

"Would you like some tea?" Nadya asked Rufus. She glanced at her mother.

"Don't you want to hurry home to bring the herbs to your father?" her mother asked, frowning at Nadya.

"He was sleeping when I left," Rufus said. "Surely it won't hurt just to stop for a cup of tea. Just to be neighborly."

"Of course not," Nadya said. "Just sit a spell, and then go back."

"Of course," her mother said. There was starch in her voice. "That would be lovely." She looked at Nadya thoughtfully. "Perhaps you'd best go fetch some water from the spring. Mr. Jones, come and sit down."

"Oh, I'll help Miss Nadya with the water," he said quickly.

"Don't be foolish, Mr. Jones," Nadya's mother said sharply. Then she smiled and spoke in a soothing tone. "You are our guest. Come and sit."

"I must insist," Rufus said. "My mother has taught me to help out whenever I visit. If Miss Nadya can show me the way to the spring, I'll carry the buckets."

"Here's the bucket." Nadya picked up the wooden bucket that stood by the door. "I'll show you the way." She started away down the path.

"Fine weather, ain't it?" Rufus said.

Nadya nodded. She had wanted to be alone with Rufus again, but now she did not know what to say. She glanced back to see her mother standing by the cabin door, her hands knotted in her apron. She sensed something waiting under the surface, something surprising and new. When Rufus glanced at her, she felt a flush of warmth on her face.

"Here—I'll carry that." He took the bucket from her hand and she felt his warm fingers brush against hers. The sensation was disturbing. When she was younger, she had walked along the top rail of the split rail fence, balancing carefully. The feeling in her stomach reminded her of the inevitable moment when she teetered, just for a moment, before falling. She was losing her balance, teetering on an edge that she could not even see.

A moment later, he held his free hand out to her, offering to help her over a muddy patch. She hesitated. She walked this path a dozen times a day and never needed anyone's help. But she wanted to see how his touch affected the feeling in her stomach. She took his hand. The feeling in her stomach intensified: a strange fluttering, almost like hunger, but not quite.

She knew about sex. She had seen the hog mating with the sow in the mud of the barnyard and she had seen a stallion mount a mare down at the livery stable. Once, in the dusty road by the store, she had seen the blacksmith's dog and the storekeeper's bitch stuck together. The bitch had snapped and snarled and tried to run away, but the dog had clung to her, hugging her from behind. The two of them yelped and growled and scrabbled in the dust.

Mrs. Evans had shooed Nadya inside just as Mr. Evans threw a bucket of water over the pair. The two animals split up and ran helter-skelter in different directions. Just before Mrs. Evans blocked Nadya's view, she caught a glimpse of the dog's shiny penis, bright red between his bowed black legs.

When Nadya had asked her mother about the dogs, her mother had explained. She told Nadya about men and women, giving biological details about what goes where. Nadya had thought the whole thing quite unlikely: why would anyone do such an odd thing?

Just a month after the incident with the dogs, Nadya's friend Lottie Evans had loaned Nadya a book in which a young man carries off a young woman and does something scandalous to her. Unlike her mother's talk, the book lacked all details. But it made up for the lack of details with its breathless tone and florid language that spoke of dark passion and hot love and fevered kisses. Lottie had told Nadya to hide the book from her mother, and so she did. She read it down by the river. When she read the book, she found herself curling up her legs and rocking to and fro. Something was happening. Her nipples grew tight and she felt a new warmth between her legs. She did not understand why that should be.

When her father stripped for the Change, she had seen his cock and balls, hanging softly between his legs. She thought little of that, even after reading Lottie's book. She thought all the fuss about nakedness and sin and love was nonsense; it had nothing to do with her. And so the feeling that came when Rufus's hand touched hers took her by surprise. The feeling in her stomach reminded her of reading Lottie's book by the river. Something was happening.

"You're surprised to see me," Rufus said.

"That's so."

"I'd hoped you'd be glad."

She said nothing, concentrating on the feel of the cool dirt beneath her bare feet. Like walking on the fence. She did not want to fall.

"Aren't you glad?" he asked.

"I'm glad," she said. Her voice was soft and she didn't sound sure.

They had reached the spring. A small wooden shelter covered the pool and two log steps led down to the water's edge. "I'd best get the water," she said. "My feet are bare, and you don't want to get your boots wet." She took the bucket from him and went down to the bottom step, where the water lapped at her feet. She stooped to fill the bucket, holding her skirt up out of the way.

"You look beautiful," he said, gazing down at her.

She straightened up, holding the bucket, and frowned at him. "You are a very strange man."

"Why do you say that?"

She stood by the cool water, studying his face. "Because you say I'm beautiful."

"You are."

She shook her head ever so slightly. Her mother was beautiful, Nadya knew that. But Nadya had studied her own face in the looking glass. It was a wide face, like her father's, and her hair was too wild to tame with braids and hairpins. She knew that she was not beautiful.

"You were the prettiest girl at the wedding."

"The best shot," she corrected.

"That too."

She shook her head and climbed the steps. He stood on the path, blocking her way.

Lottie and other girls talked about young men and dresses and dances and maybe getting married. Nadya had listened to the girls talk, but she had always known she was not like those girls.

When she reached the top step, she turned to tell him that he should go and talk to Lottie or one of the others, and leave her alone. Before she could speak, he kissed her. The kiss was awkward at first—lips bumping against lips. But she did not pull away, and he kissed her again, this time lifting his hand to touch her cheek. His lips were soft. His hand moved from her cheek to stroke her neck. The touch, more than the kiss, made her catch her breath.

He kissed her again, and she could feel the warmth of him through the thin calico of her dress. She could feel a trembling deep inside herself, so deep that the vibration did not reach the surface. She lifted her hand to touch his cheek, where she could feel the stubble of a beard, clean-shaven that morning. His smell changed, just as it had when they danced together at the wedding. She knew the smell of sex: a warm muskiness that clung to her mother on certain mornings. She could smell the muskiness in the air. His hand, moving downward, touched her breast, stroking gently over the fabric and coming to rest at her waist.

She stepped back. "Mama will wonder where we have been. We'd best go back."

He grinned at her, showing white teeth.

They had tea, and Nadya listened to her mother and Rufus talk about the weather, the plowing, his father's aching stomach, his family, and their journey westward Rufus's scent overpowered the familiar smell of the herbs that hung from the pegs in the wall. Rufus talked with her mother, but every now and again, Nadya caught him glancing in her direction.

When he left, Nadya waved goodbye and watched him go.

Her mother frowned at her. "You've taken a fancy to this young man, haven't you? Look at me, *chérie*. Let me see your face." Nadya looked up and her mother nodded.

"He taught me to waltz at the wedding," Nadya said. She held out her arms and took a few steps, whirling as she stepped. "He put his arm around me and we danced together."

"Yes," her mother said. "What do you think he wants?"

Nadya dropped her hands. Thinking about Rufus made her cheeks grow hot. "To kiss me, I reckon."

"To kiss you, to hug you, to run his hands over your body, to lie with you." Her mother's tone was matter-of-fact. "I have told you how it is between men and women." She stood in front of Nadya and took her daughter's hands. "And you want him to do that."

"I don't know," Nadya said. "I want . . ." She shook her head, thinking about the warmth of Rufus's body, so close to hers. "I don't know what I want."

"There is nothing wrong with wanting a man," Nadya's mother said. "In our family, the blood has always run hot." She hesitated, studying Nadya's face. "But this man—he is not good for you. This man is dangerous."

Nadya pulled her hands away from her mother's. "What do you mean?"

"Remember the cards? A young man, fair-haired, reckless. He brings misfortune to you and to us. Remember."

"Not Rufus," Nadya said. "He won't bring misfortune."

"Listen to me, Nadya," her mother said. "You must listen. Do not go with this man."

Nadya hung her head, looking down at the porch. "I am listening," she said sullenly.

"Do you understand?"

"I understand." Nadya understood, but she did not agree.

"That's good. Now here is Papa, coming in from the fields. Put aside your work and let us prepare for the Change."

Preparing for the Change was not so different from their regular evening chores. They simply began the work early, so that they would be ready when the sun set. Nadya's father milked the cow and fed the mule; Nadya called the hogs and chased the chickens into their coop for the night. Nadya's mother prepared a simple meal of hoecake and ham; she thought it best to change with a little food in the belly—not too much, and not too little. She put the remaining food out of reach of any varmints that might come to the unoccupied cabin and carefully banked the fire so that she could easily revive it when they returned, weary and cold from the night in the forest.

When the sun dipped near the horizon, Nadya stepped out on the front porch. Their cabin faced east and the porch was already in shadow. Nadya pulled off her dress, hung it from a peg beside the cabin door, and waited for her parents.

She could hear her parents murmuring inside the cabin, but the words were already starting to sound like meaningless babble. She could feel the moon rising, a tugging that she felt in her belly and her crotch.

Nadya rubbed her hands over the goose bumps on her naked arms and shivered. Her father said something and mother laughed. She heard the rustling of clothing.

"The sun is setting," Nadya said, and she heard her mother's hand on the door latch.

"We are here," her mother said. Her hair was loose, falling in dark waves down her back.

The Change came.

It began with warmth, as if the moonlight on her skin carried the heat of the tropical sun. But the warmth came from within her, not from outside. She could feel her heart beating and her blood surging through her body, pounding in her veins and arteries. The moon pulled on her blood as it pulled on the ocean: she was caught in a tide, a riptide that she was powerless to resist. Her body burned with the heat and she breathed faster. There was something she wanted, something she needed—she knew that, though she could not describe what that something was.

She could not tell if the feeling was pleasure or pain. These words did not apply. With each Change, she felt a new intensity (surely it could not have felt like this on the last full moon). She felt like she might be dying or she might, at last, be coming to life. In that moment, the two seemed much the same. And maybe she wanted to stop, she wanted to call out "No, no, no, this is too

much, I can't . . . I won't . . .'' But what it was that she
couldn't or wouldn't do was lost in clouds and darkness,
because no words came. Words were going away, rushing away, a babble that no longer had meaning or value.
She was poised on the brink, on the knife's edge, at the
precipice of the mountain, at the edge of the cliff.

And when the Change came at last, it came with an
inexorable rush. Her body made its decision and the part
of her that thought and talked and planned and believed
that it controlled so much, that part was carried along,
like a straw in the river's current. There was no stopping
the river, no turning back.

That was what the Change was like. And when it was
over, she stood on four legs instead of two; her body
was covered with fur; her ears caught the rustling of a
mouse under the porch. But all that was not important.
What was important was the Change itself, the moment
of shifting, the malleability of the flesh, the decision of
the body.

A family of wolves stood on the porch, gazing out at
the forest. The wolf that had been Nadya sniffed the
breeze, then the handle of the bucket by the cabin door.
The scent that clung to the handle made the young wolf
whimper low in her throat. She explored the farmyard,
stopping to sniff deeply by the split rail fence where
Rufus had tied his horse.

The male wolf trotted to the edge of the forest, where
he lifted his head and sampled the air. He headed along
a deer trail, not looking back to see if the others followed. The older female started after the male, then
looked back at the young female and made an encour-
aging sound in her throat. The young wolf ignored the
older female and continued sniffing at the grass by
the fence. The older female whimpered again, but the
younger wolf set off on her own path, following the
scent in the grass. The wolf that was Nadya was old
enough to wander away from the pack if she would, and

the female let her go, following her mate and letting her daughter find her own way.

Nadya came back to her human form on the porch of the farmhouse. The taste of blood was in her mouth. She rubbed her hand across her face, and looked at it. Flecks of dark brown dotted the skin. Dried blood. She could hear her mother in the cabin, breaking kindling to add to the fire.

Nadya blinked in the morning light, trying to remember the night. Memories of the Change faded like dreams; memories of the Change did not fit well in the human brain. The colors were wrong; the smells didn't match the human memory of smells. At best, she could recapture only fragments of the night.

She remembered sheep, bleating sheep that ran from her. She could not help but chase the clumsy creatures, so fat and foolish and warm. She cut a fat ewe from the herd and chased it along a fence, tearing at its haunches and tasting its blood. It cried out, a silly bleating that made her heart beat faster, and she tore at it again. Dark streaks of blood colored the pale fleece, and still the ewe ran. She tore at its legs until it stumbled and then she was on it, bowling it over and ripping at its belly. The blood was warm on her face, splashing over her body, filling her nose with its dark scent.

She remembered a sound—the sharp crack of gunfire, the acrid scent of gunpowder, cutting through the alluring aroma of blood. She heard shouting and more gunfire. She ran then, her fear overcoming her taste for the hunt.

Nadya sat on the porch, the taste of blood still on her lips. Her father stood in the doorway to the cabin. "Little one," he said to her. "Where did you go last night? You left us." His tone was reproachful.

Nadya hung her head. "I guess . . . I reckon I must have followed Rufus home."

Her father wet his lips, looking worried. "I smell blood. That's not good. Not good at all."

Her mother came from the cabin, carrying a basin of water, warmed on the fire. She stood on the porch, watching as Nadya splashed the warm water on her face and arms. She put her arm around Nadya's father. "She's home safe, Dmitri. That's what's important."

He shook his head. "Did they fire at you?" he asked her.

"I think so." Nadya kept her eyes on the water. The blood had colored it pale pink.

"They will come for us with guns," he said. "They will hunt us through the forest with dogs and guns."

"No, Dmitri," her mother said. "Don't be so excited. It will be all right."

Nadya's father turned away and went back into the cabin. Nadya's mother stroked her hair. "It will be all right, *chérie*. I think it will be all right." But the smell of her father's fear lingered in the air.

Just two weeks later, Mrs. Evans had a quilting bee to make a new quilt for Lottie's older sister, who was engaged to Judd Collins. Nadya's mother woke that morning feeling poorly, and so Nadya went alone, riding the mule the five miles to town.

Lottie greeted Nadya in the yard. "Nadya," she called. "I'm so glad you're here. They've been teasing me so." She tucked her hand companionably into the crook of Nadya's arm. "They've been teasing me about when I'll be getting married."

Lottie had grown up to become a rosy-cheeked young woman with blonde hair that invariably escaped her ribbons and pins. Wisps of hair curled at the nape of her neck. The youngest of three sisters, she came in for more than her share of teasing.

"Didn't your mother come?" she asked Nadya.

"She's feeling poorly," Nadya said. "I came by myself."

"You're so brave," Lottie said. "I wouldn't want to come so far by myself."

Nadya shrugged.

"There'll be a dance at Mary Sue's wedding," Lottie said. Lottie lowered her voice. "I asked Mary Sue to make sure Silas Whitman was coming. I danced with him at Zillah's wedding. And Mary Sue told Mama and now they're all teasing me. You won't tease me, will you?"

Nadya shook her head. She never had to say much around Lottie; Lottie did the talking for both of them.

"Is there anyone you're sweet on, Nadya?"

"Rufus Jones came visiting a few days back," Nadya admitted softly.

"He came visiting?" Lottie's eyes widened with excitement. "Oh, Nadya, he didn't."

Nadya nodded. "He sure did."

Lottie wet her lips. "Mrs. Jones is here, helping with the quilting." She made a face. "She doesn't approve of dancing at weddings. I don't think she likes anyone to have any fun."

"Nadya!" Mrs. Evans called from the doorway. "How nice to see you. Isn't your mother with you?"

"My mama was feeling poorly," Nadya said softly. "She told me to give you her love."

"You came all this way alone?" Mrs. Evans shook her head and clicked her tongue. "My goodness—this is no time for a girl to be gallivanting about alone. Now you come on in and sit down here."

The Evanses had a fine house, with four separate rooms and a puncheon floor in the parlor. Mrs. Evans had a dozen store-bought chairs and a mantelpiece clock. On the wall of the parlor there was a looking glass and a hair wreath that Mrs. Evans had woven from the tresses of departed relations: from each of her three chil-

dren who had died young, from her own mother and
father. The puncheon floor was covered with a real
machine-woven carpet, not a rag rug.

The quilt frame stretched the width of the parlor, leaving just enough space at the sides for women to sit beside it. The room was already crowded: Mrs. Shaw and
her daughter Zillah sat on one side of the quilt, Mrs.
Whitman and her daughter sat on the other. Mrs. Jones
sat at the far end of the quilt frame, enthroned in one of
Mrs. Evans's best chairs. Mary Sue sat beside her. Lottie
sat on a stool at one corner and Nadya sat beside her
and Mrs. Evans.

The quilt, an intricate design of bright calico dia-
monds, was stretched on the frame. Nadya threaded a
needle and began stitching the brightly colored patch-
work to the padded lining.

"Nadya rode from her house alone," Mrs. Evans announced to the others.

"Oh, dear," Mrs. Whitman murmured. "Hadn't you
heard about the wolves?" The Whitmans had moved to
Missouri from Connecticut just a year before, and Mrs.
Whitman was still very nervous about wild animals and
Indians.

Nadya shook her head. "What about wolves?"

Mrs. Whitman clapped her hands. "Wolves attacked
the Jones' farm! Mrs. Jones, you must tell the child."

Mrs. Jones looked up from her stitching and smiled
grimly. "I woke in the night to the sound of our sheep,
bleating in terror. A pack of wolves had attacked our
flock. Ravening beasts from the depths of the forest
dragging down the innocent lambs. Rufus chased them
away with a shot, but not before the wolves had killed
our fattest ewe." She shook her head. "The poor de-
fenseless creature never had a chance."

Nadya ducked her head and kept her eyes on her
stitching.

"Oh, you must have been so frightened," Mrs. Whitman said. "When I hear wolves howling, the sound sends chills up my spine. It's as if the Devil himself was out there, crying for blood."

"I put my faith in the Lord," Mrs. Jones said staunchly. "The Devil has no power over a true Christian."

Nadya neatly stitched around a red calico diamond. It seemed to her that rifles would do a better job of driving a wolf away than Mrs. Jones's prayers, but she did not think it would be wise to mention that.

"So you can see that this is no time for you to be wandering about by yourself," Mrs. Evans said to Nadya. "I'll have one of the boys escort you home."

"I heard that there was a preacher down river in White's Landing a few days back," Mrs. Shaw said, changing the subject. "Reverend William Cooper is his name. They say he can exhort the bark off a tree. He'll be here next Sunday."

The last great wave of camp meetings had ended back in the 1820s, but even in the 1840s, the Methodists had their circuit riders, preachers on horseback who traveled from one frontier settlement to the next, calling the wrath of God on sinners, warning of the coming Judgment Day, and saving souls where they could. A preacher with the power of exhortation could call the Spirit of the Lord upon the Assembly, causing men and women to jerk wildly to and fro, to fall on all fours and bark like dogs, to weep and cry and shout in languages that no American could understand.

The women talked for a time about the preacher.

"I don't know if Mr. Shaw will come to hear a preacher," Mrs. Shaw murmured. The last preacher to visit the community had been a Baptist, traveling by flatboat. He held a Sunday service by the riverside and dunked half a dozen farmers. Mr. Shaw's dunking had given him a fierce case of the grippe.

Mrs. Jones straightened her back, looking even more

formidable. "It's our Christian duty to attend this meeting," she said. "I will bring all my boys."

The mention of Mrs. Jones's boys brought the conversation back to Mary Sue's marriage. As they worked, the older women talked about the dress Mary Sue would wear and about the latest fashions in *Godey's Ladies Book*. Mary Sue talked about all the people who would be coming to the wedding and the dance.

They chatted amiably until teatime. After eating, they returned to their work.

"Take smaller stitches, Lottie," Mrs. Evans admonished her daughter. "Look at Nadya's stitches. See how small and tight they are."

Nadya glanced up at her friend with a sympathetic expression. Her own hands were tired from the careful work.

"Maybe Lottie and Nadya should fetch some water for another pot of tea," Mrs. Shaw suggested kindly. "I'll finish up that corner."

Lottie and Nadya wasted no time hurrying out of the house. They took two buckets from beside the door and strolled down to the pump. "So now that you know about the wolves, aren't you scared about riding around alone?" Lottie asked.

"Nope," Nadya said. "A wolf ain't going to bother with me."

Lottie shook her head. "You'd best be careful, Nadya. One of my brothers will ride home with you."

Nadya frowned. "What's your brother going to do that I couldn't do myself?"

"Well, he'd shoot any wolf that came after you."

"So? I'm a better shot than any of your brothers. I could shoot a wolf myself, if it came to that."

Lottie shook her head at Nadya's audacity. "I'd be so scared."

Nadya shrugged. "I've shot deer. I've shot bear. I can take care of myself."

"I guess so," Lottie said doubtfully. Then she brightened, changing the subject. "Do you reckon that Rufus will come to fetch his mother?"

Nadya shrugged. "I reckon so." She had wondered that herself. The thought of Rufus alarmed her more than all the talk of the wolves. She looked down at the path.

"When he came visiting, what happened?" Lottie asked.

"He talked to my mama for a while about herbs for Mr. Jones. And he came with me to the spring to fetch water."

Lottie stopped and stared at Nadya. "Nadya, you're blushing. I've never seen you blush before."

Nadya scuffed her bare foot in the dust.

"What happened? Did he hold your hand? Did he kiss you?"

Nadya nodded. "He held my hand. And then he kissed me."

"Oh, Nadya. Was it like in the book? Did you swoon in his arms?"

Nadya remembered the moment by the spring. "It's more like standing on top of the barn roof, wondering if you're going to fall."

"I've never done that," Lottie said.

"Or standing on the bluff over the river, looking at the current below. That current could sweep you away and you'd never get back again." Nadya shook her head. "Don't know that I like it."

"It's so exciting, Nadya. I hope that Silas Whitman comes visiting me. What did you say to him?"

"I hardly talked at all," Nadya confessed. "I didn't know what to say."

"That's all right," Lottie said. "My sister Mary Sue says that you don't have to talk much. I asked her, and she said that all you have to do when you're sitting with a man is to tell him how wonderful he is, and that's enough. Like this." They had reached the pump. Lottie

set down her bucket and took Nadya's hand in hers.
"Oh, Rufus—I feel so safe with you here. You're so
strong and brave."

Nadya frowned at her. "That's silly, Lottie. He
doesn't make me feel safe."

"But you could say he did, couldn't you?" Lottie
held the bucket while Nadya pumped the water. "Mary
Sue says that men like to hear things like that."

Lottie set down her bucket and held Nadya's under
the rush of water. Nadya continued pumping, consider-
ing what Lottie had said. She had nothing against lying,
but this seemed like a foolish thing to lie about. "I don't
know why he would make me feel safe," Nadya said.
"I can shoot as well as he can. Seems like he ought to
tell me that I make him feel safe."

"Oh, Nadya, don't you go around saying things like
that. He tells you that you're pretty and you tell him that
he's strong. That's what Mary Sue says," Lottie spoke
with the superior wisdom of a girl who had older sisters.

"My mama says he's dangerous," Nadya said hesitantly.

"How exciting!" Lottie danced in a little circle. "I
don't see how you can be so calm about it. If it was me,
I'd be beside myself."

"We'd best get back with the water," Nadya said.

As they walked back toward the house, Lottie did
most of the talking. "I can help you fix your hair for
Mary Sue's wedding. We can put it up like the picture
I saw in *Godey's Ladies Book*. You'll look so fine. But
you have to promise that you won't get into a shooting
match or anything like that."

Nadya walked at Lottie's side. Her friend's excitement made her uneasy. She was not sure how she felt
about Rufus, but Lottie seemed certain that she should
be happy.

They returned to the cabin and built up the fire to boil
water for tea. The quilt was almost done—all that re-

mained was the edging, and Zillah and Mary Sue and Mrs. Evans would manage that.

Lottie had just made a pot of tea when the dogs began barking outside. "Hello!" A man's voice called from the farmyard. "Hello, ladies!"

Mr. Whitman had come to escort Mrs. Whitman and her daughters home. He had a cup of tea with the women, and while they were drinking it, Mr. Evans and his sons returned from fishing, carrying a string of catfish. Then Rufus Jones and his brother Moses appeared in the doorway. Rufus took off his hat and smiled at all the women. It seemed to Nadya that his eyes lingered on her.

Mrs. Evans insisted that Nadya accompany Mrs. Jones and her sons to the fork in the trail that led to the Rybak house. Then Rufus would escort Nadya to her door. "We just can't be too careful," Mrs. Evans said.

Nadya protested, but Mrs. Jones hushed her with a wave of a hand. "Of course you will come with us. I'll have no more said about it."

Nadya rode with Mrs. Jones in the farm wagon for the first few miles. Her mule was tied on behind the wagon. As they bumped over the rough trail, Mrs. Jones lectured Nadya on the dangers of wandering through the forest alone. Nadya remained silent, watching Rufus's back. He sat on the driver's seat, eyes on the trail ahead.

At the fork in the road, Moses took the reins. Rufus swung down from the driver's seat and untied Nadya's mule from the back of the wagon. Nadya jumped down from the wagon before he could help her, not wanting to touch his hand.

"You hurry home, Rufus," Mrs. Jones said to her son.

Rufus touched his hat to his mother and waved as the horse pulled the wagon down the main trail.

"It's a pleasure to have your company again so soon," Rufus said. The wagon reached a bend in the trail and Rufus waved to his mother as the trail took her out of sight. Then he reached out and took Nadya's hand. "I had hoped I might see you today."

"I was glad to see you too," Nadya said. She wasn't certain of the truth of her words until after she said them. He squeezed her hand.

"Come on," he said, and they started in the direction of the Rybak farm.

The trail followed the river, more or less. Sometimes, it ran alongside the water, and sometimes it snaked between the trees, avoiding the brambles and thickets at the river's edge.

Nadya walked silently at his side. It was strange, having his hand in hers. Overhead, squirrels chattered and barked at them.

"Here—stop a bit," he said. He let go of her hand and stepped to where a dogwood tree was blooming. He picked a pale blossom and returned to her side. "These would look nice in your hair," he said, and reached up to tuck the flower behind her ear. He stepped back and looked at her. "It suits you," he said. "You look very pretty."

She returned his stare, still silent.

"You're such a quiet one," he said. "Don't you like flowers?"

"I like flowers."

He hesitated. "I know a place not far from here, down by the river, where there's a beautiful patch of flowers. Would you like to see it?"

His scent had changed—she could smell the muskiness of sex. "All right," she said. "I'd like to."

He took her hand again, holding it tighter than before, and led her off the main trail, along a deer path that led through the trees and downward toward the river. Partway down, out of sight of the trail, he tied the mule to a tree.

The path led to a secluded hollow where the grass

was already thick and green. A redbud tree bloomed on the river bank, its flowers brilliant against the spring greenery. He held her hand and led her to where the sheltering branch of a willow blocked the view of the river. The tree formed a great room, carpeted with ferns and perfumed with the fragrance of the flowers and plants.

"I found this when I was hunting," he said. "It's a beautiful place, isn't it?" He looked down at her and wet his lips. "I hoped you would come here with me." Then he reached out and put his arms around her.

She could feel the warmth of his skin through her dress; she could smell his sweat—a complex musky smell mingled with the aroma of tobacco. She tilted her head to look up into his face and he kissed her as he had at the spring.

She sensed the thing that waited beneath the surface, like the currents that boiled in the river. There was a mystery here, something that went beyond the farm animals mating in the barnyard. She had listened to the cats yowling at night. The female in heat made a low moaning sound that contained both pleading and threat. She understood that sound now.

"Here," he said, releasing her. "Let's sit in the grass. That would be fine." He led her to a place where the grass was soft. She sat there, her bare feet pulled up under her dress and her arms wrapped around her knees. He sat beside her and put his arm around her shoulders.

"I should have known you would come here with me," he said then. "You aren't like the other girls."

She nodded. She knew that was true—the other girls didn't hunt and shoot—but she wondered what that had to do with sitting beside him by the river. He kissed her lightly. His arm dropped from her shoulder to her waist. His other hand caressed her thigh through the fabric of her dress and her petticoat. He lifted his eyes to her face.

"I love you, Nadya." His hand continued to stroke her thigh.

"My mama says that you're dangerous," she said.

"Your mama doesn't like you playing with the boys. But I think you like me." He kissed her again. "Don't you believe that I love you, Nadya?"

She ignored the question. "Your mother told me about the wolves that killed your sheep the other night."

"Ah, sweet Nadya—are you afraid of wolves?" He tightened the arm that encircled her shoulders. "I'll keep you safe. I'll kill any wolf that comes near us."

"No!" she said, starting to pull away. "You mustn't."

"What is it, Nadya?" He reached out and held her tighter. "What is it?"

"You mustn't kill wolves," she said. "You've got to promise me that."

He laughed. "Does it worry you that I hunt for wolves? Well then, I won't go hunting for wolves if that makes you unhappy." His face relaxed and his hand resumed its movement on her thigh. "Now don't you believe that I love you, Nadya?"

Her body believed him. When he kissed her, she responded. She felt his hand on her thigh, lifting her dress so that he could stroke the bare skin. He kept kissing her, giving her no chance to answer his question, but she did not mind that. There was a warmth in her body, a kind of tingling that felt like the coming of the Change, only different. His body pressed against hers, pushing her back on the grass. One of his hands fumbled at the buttons of her dress; the other slid higher between her thighs. She was not wearing any underwear, and his hand explored the warmth between her legs. She made a sound—almost a growl like the cats in the barn—and he pressed his fingers harder against her.

"Oh, Nadya, I can't stop myself." He was on top of her now, fumbling with the buttons of his trousers. His hand was fumbling with the buttons on the front of her dress. The tingling was growing greater, spreading through her body. He moaned, pressing against her.

Rufus pushed his leg between her thighs, spreading her legs apart. The movement of his leg made her squirm as the tingling grew stronger. It was frightening, this feeling, but she welcomed it at the same time. She wanted something that she could not name.

Abruptly, he shoved himself between her thighs and thrust into her. She cried out, startled. There was a sensation of tearing and wetness and a sudden pain that mingled with the warmth and tingling. He thrust again and then came quickly, collapsing against her with a moan. She moved her hips against him, trying to shift him so that the tingling sensations would return, but he did not move, lying atop her like a dead man. "Oh," he moaned, "Oh, Nadya."

He rolled off her and lay in the grass, staring up at the sky. His penis glistened in the late afternoon sunlight. Streaked with semen and blood, it had started to droop. She reached between her own legs, and her fingers came away touched with blood. But even so, there was still pleasure in her own touch.

He looked over at her, propping himself up on one elbow. The top of her dress gaped open and her nipples were crinkled and brown in the sun. Her skirt was bunched around her waist. He reached over and tugged on her dress, pulling the fabric so that it covered her breasts. "You'd best cover yourself," he said.

"Why?"

He shook his head as if she should not have asked, and frowned. As she watched, he started to button his trousers.

She put her hand on his to stop him. "No," she said. Her dress gaped when she moved, exposing her breasts once again. She slipped her hand beneath his and into his trousers. He made a sound, the beginning of a protest, but it died in his throat. His cock was warm in her hand; the skin so soft and smooth. She slid her hand lower, cupping his balls and feeling his rough pubic hair against her fingers. One hand was on his cock, the other was between her own legs, teasing the slippery folds, pressing into her body.

Rufus moaned and his eyes half-closed. He put one hand on her breast and started to move toward her, as if to roll on top of her again.

"No," she said. "Not that way." She pushed him so that he lay flat on his back. Before he could move again, she threw a leg over his and straddled him. His cock was erect now, and she rubbed it against herself, directing its movement with her hand.

With her free hand, she lifted Rufus' hand to her breast, relishing the feel of his rough skin against her nipple. His eyes were open now; he looked surprised, a little confused. She rubbed herself up and down, then lifted herself and slipped his cock inside her. With her hand, she continued to rub the hard knot of flesh in the midst of the folds where the tingling seemed to center. She growled, a sound that rumbled from her throat without her thought or will. She squeezed her eyes closed, shutting out the brightness of the sunlight that filtered through the willow leaves. She bent so that her breasts rubbed against his chest and she nipped at his shoulder, rocking back and forth faster now, still faster.

She arched her back, and the pleasure was so intense it was nearly pain. She felt him inside her, squeezed by the spasms of her muscles. A great wave pulsed within her, beginning between her legs and spreading outward. Pleasure, urgency, darkness, and warmth—a confusion of sensations that left her gasping and limp.

"Ah," she said. "Ah, Rufus." She opened her eyes then, and looked down at him.

His eyes were open and he was watching her. He wasn't smiling; she could not read his expression. His cock was growing soft within her, so she slipped off him and lay beside him in the grass, where she could watch his face. He looked up at the sky.

"What are you thinking?" she asked him.

He kept looking at the sky. "You're not like the other girls."

She smiled. "That's so. You already told me that."

"It's not proper. You shouldn't . . ." He hesitated. "You oughtn't act like that."

"Like what?"

He shook his head and frowned at her. "Girls don't act like that. You're very bold."

She continued to smile. "And so are you."

He reached out and tugged her dress down so that it covered her. "We'd best be getting home."

She watched him sit up and hurriedly button his trousers and tuck his shirt. He did not look at her again. She made no move to dress herself, just studied him, trying to understand his expression. He smelled of sex and anger and fear. She did not understand the anger or the fear. What had frightened him?

He glanced down at her. "Button yourself," he said roughly. "Cover yourself and act decent."

She sat up then, pulling her skirt down to cover her legs and slowly buttoning her dress.

"Come along," he said, and led the way back up to where the mule was tied. He did not take her hand. He accompanied her home, but did not linger to have tea or talk with her parents, leaving her at the doorstep and hurrying away into the forest as if he were suddenly afraid of her.

The next Sunday morning, Nadya and her family went to town. The mule had thrown a shoe and her father was taking it to the blacksmith.

The bench in front of the general store was crowded with loafing men: trappers, come to town to trade and drink; a rough-looking crew from the barge that was tied at the crossing; a few farmers. Nadya saw Mr. Jones among them but looked for Rufus in vain. A green jug was passing from hand to hand, and Nadya could smell the sharp scent of chewing tobacco.

Nadya's father pulled the farm wagon to the side of the dirt street. He stopped by the bench to chat with the men, while Nadya and her mother went into the store.

Mr. Evans was counting out nutmegs and cinnamon sticks for Mrs. Walker, and the spices perfumed the air. Mrs. Evans was helping Mrs. Jones, who had just purchased a length of plain red calico for new shirts for her sons. "Those boys are almighty rough on clothes," she was saying to Mrs. Evans. "I pity the girl that marries Rufus. She'll be sewing her fingers to the bone just to keep him in shirts."

Mrs. Evans looked up and greeted Nadya and her mother. "Morning, Mrs. Rybak, Miss Nadya. How are you today?"

Mrs. Jones studied the pair of them. "Morning, Mrs. Rybak," Mrs. Jones said. "How nice to see you again. Did Nadya tell you that the tea you sent was a great help to Mr. Jones?"

"I'm pleased to hear it, Mrs. Jones." Nadya watched in silence. She knew that her mother did not care for Mrs. Jones, but she smiled as if Mrs. Jones were a friend. "It is really the simplest thing to make. If you like, I can show you the herbs that I use."

"Mr. Jones won't be needing the remedy again. He told me that very morning that he had sworn off the demon whiskey and would drink only healthful beverages from that day on."

Nadya wondered at that. She was certain that Mr. Jones had been among the loiterers on the porch. In her experience, a jug being passed on the porch of a store rarely contained healthful beverages. But she held her tongue and listened while her mother murmured polite congratulations.

"I do hope that you and your family will be attending the services by the river this afternoon," Mrs. Jones said. "Reverend William Cooper, a preacher of fine repute, has come to speak to us of the ways of sin. My family will be there."

"What denomination is the preacher?" Nadya's mother asked. Nadya knew this was simply politeness. If the preacher were a Baptist, Nadya's mother would claim to be strictly Methodist. If he were a Methodist, she might declare herself a Baptist. One way or the other, she would politely evade the preaching.

"He is a man of God," Mrs. Jones declared. "I don't know more than that. But that is all I need to know. All Christians are brothers under the skin."

Nadya's mother nodded thoughtfully. "Thank you so much for telling us about it. Perhaps we will see you there."

Mrs. Jones took the calico that Mrs. Evans had folded neatly. "Now I must be going, to tell others that we are blessed with a preacher this Sunday. Perhaps some of those who prefer dancing to praying will come and see the evil of their ways. I will see you by the river." She left the store without looking back.

Nadya's mother and Mrs. Evans exchanged glances. "She's enough to give being a Christian a bad name," Mrs. Evans murmured, and Nadya's mother laughed.

"I hear that she scolded Mrs. Shaw for allowing dancing and drinking at the wedding," Nadya's mother said softly.

"I hear the same. But Mr. Jones and his sons were drinking and dancing with the rest of them."

Nadya's mother smiled and shrugged. "Ah, but you heard what Mrs. Jones said. Mr. Jones has declared he will only drink healthful beverages."

Mrs. Evans laughed. "Ah, but whiskey can be medicinal, and surely that's a healthful thing.''

"And dancing is fine exercise, and that is needed for health as well," Nadya's mother replied.

"Of course," Mrs. Evans said. "I should have thought of that. And all Mr. Jones's gasconading about what fine shots his boys are, that's exercise for the lungs.''

The women laughed softly.

"And so what is it that brings you to town?" Mrs. Evans asked.

"Nadya thought she'd sew a new dress to wear to Mary Sue's wedding, so we have come for calico.''

"A new dress?" Mrs. Evans smiled at Nadya. "Miss Nadya, you're not buying black powder and lead shot? You're becoming a lady.''

Nadya blushed and looked down at her feet.

"Here now, Nadya, I have some lovely cloth to choose from." Mrs. Evans pulled bolt after bolt from the shelves, placing them on the table for Nadya's examination. Nadya favored a length of fine dark blue cloth, patterned with tiny red roses.

"The color complements your complexion," Mrs. Evans said. "And it won't show the dirt.''

Nadya's mother fingered the cloth, testing the weave. "It seems quite sturdy," she said.

"Oh, it will wear well, I'm sure of that.''

While Mrs. Evans was cutting and folding the cloth, Lottie came into the store from the back. The mothers remained in the store, chatting about remedies and recipes, but Nadya and Lottie escaped to the outside.

Nadya's father was sitting on the porch. The two young women lingered for a moment, to see if the men were talking about anything interesting Mr. Walker was holding a penny paper that had just come in from Philadelphia. "It's a brand new party for new times," he was saying. "Call themselves the Native Americans. They have no use for Papists, and I'll go along with that. Take those Irishmen, fresh off the boat. You can scarcely understand a word that comes out of their mouths." He slapped the paper against his thigh. "Keep America for Americans. That's what I say."

"Keep America for the Americans," Nadya's father said slowly, repeating the words as if he had not heard them right. His Polish accent grew thicker, as it always did when he was upset. "Twenty years, I have been in this country. I would guess that I am an American. But these people would say I ain't." Mr. Walker started to interrupt, but Nadya's father kept going. "America is for all types of men from all different countries. That's what makes this country strong."

"Next thing you know, you'll be saying we should set free the slaves," Mr. Jones said.

"Come on," Lottie whispered to Nadya. "They're just talking politics. Let's go." They walked down the dusty street, and Lottie companionably linked her arm in Nadya's.

"Do you want to go down to the river?" Lottie asked. "Mrs. Jones said there'd be a preacher talking about God."

"I don't know," Nadya said, looking doubtful. "I'd better ask my mama."

"Oh, come on. Let's just go. Your mama will be glad you are hearing the word of God. Besides, maybe Rufus and Silas will be there."

"All right," Nadya said. "I'll go."

Arm in arm, they strolled to the river crossing. As they grew closer, they could make out muddled singing. The tune was familiar, a popular song modified to match a holier set of words.

They followed the sound to the river bank, where a small hollow created a natural amphitheater. William Cooper stood above the crowd, on the stump of an oak tree. A group of farmers and folks from town stood near the stump, watching the preacher with anticipation and doing their best to sing the hymn. Mrs. Jones was in the front of the group, her raised hand beating the rhythm of the hymn in the air, like a dutiful singing teacher. Her voice rang above the others, a sturdy contralto that made up in volume what it lacked in grace. "He comes! He comes! The Judge severe! The Seventh Trumpet speaks him near. His lightnings flash; His thunders roll. How welcome to the faithful soul." Nadya didn't see Rufus anywhere.

On the far side of the hollow there was a clump of rivermen. They weren't singing. Rather, they watched the preacher in silence, chewing tobacco.

The hymn droned to a close, Mrs. Jones singing the last line as a determined solo. The preacher lifted his Bible and read in a sonorous voice. "Serve the Lord with gladness: come before His presence with singing. Know ye that the Lord He is God: it is He hath made us; we are His people and the sheep of His pasture."

Nadya frowned at that—she did not think much of sheep and she would rather not be called one. But no one else in the crowd seemed to mind.

The preacher closed the book with a snap and looked at the people gathered around him. "Brothers and sisters," he said to them. "We are the people of the Lord, we are His sheep. But I see many sheep that have strayed from the flock, lambs that are in danger from the wolves of Satan that linger outside the pasture gate. I see men who gamble, and men who curse and take the name of their Lord in vain, and men who lie and cheat and steal. I see women who wear gaudy clothing, women who are proud of their outward show, caring not for their inner beauty. How many of you could hold your heads up and walk through the pasture gates into Heaven?" He looked out at the crowd, and a man in the front row spat a stream of tobacco juice over the river bank.

"Brothers and sisters," the preacher said. "I was a sinner too. Listen to me, brothers and sisters, for I was once like you. And then I found the love of the Lord."

"I'd sooner have the love of a good woman," called out one of the rivermen in the back, and his companions laughed.

"That way lies the path to Hell," the preacher shouted back.

"That way lies the path to glory," called the man, and again his friends laughed, slapping him on the back. "Have you ever walked that path, Preacher?"

"I walk the path of the Lord," the preacher said. "I follow the word of the Lord. You must listen to me." He brandished his Bible over his head, swayed as if he were about to fall from the stump, and he steadied himself. His eyes were blinking furiously. "You must listen," he cried, but Nadya could barely hear his voice over the catcalls of the rivermen.

"Listen," the preacher shouted. Then he tilted back his head and howled, a piercing wail that cut through the laughter of the hecklers. Mrs. Jones took a step back, startled by the howl, her hands suddenly still, clasped together as if in prayer. The preacher tilted back his head and howled again. When he stopped, the crowd was silent, watching him to see what would happen next.

"I hear you howling like the beasts you are," he snarled at the rivermen. "I hear you growling and snapping like the wolves of the forest. I hear you and the Lord hears you, and He judges you, as I am not fit to judge.

"Why have you come to this barren wilderness, brothers and sisters? Why have you come to this howling land, where wild beasts shriek in the night, where savage Indians lurk in the darkness?" He waited a moment, then filled the silence with a shout. "You have come here at the command of the Lord!"

"Not likely," yelled a riverman, but the preacher lifted his hands up over his head, waving the Bible as if it were a club.

"The Good Book commands us to be fruitful and multiply, to replenish the earth and subdue it," the preacher cried. "Our Lord commands us to have dominion over every living thing that moveth on the face of the earth. The Lord asks this of us, he sends us into the wilderness to claim it for His own. You have come to take this land for the Lord."

"Amen!" called a farmer who stood near Nadya. "Amen!"

"This land, this wild and desolate land—it can strike despair into a man's heart." The preacher's voice dropped. "I know it, brothers and sisters, for my own heart has been laid low by loneliness and fear. My own heart has ached for the comforts of civilization." He lowered his hands, bringing his Bible to his chest. "Just a few nights ago, brothers and sisters, when I lay shivering in the cold and the rain, I thought of turning my back on this land. I thought of returning to my home in Connecticut, of seeking an easier life, a life where a man can eat a fine dinner and sleep in a warm bed." His head was bowed and his tone was that of a man confiding his secret thoughts. "And I prayed to the Lord to send me a sign. Tell me what to do, oh Lord. Help me find the way."

He lifted his head. "In the darkness, wolves howled— a dreadful howling, like the shrieking of the souls burning in hell, doomed for all eternity to be wrapped in sheets of fire and brimstone."

Nadya glanced at Lottie, who was listening with rapt attention. "I always thought the wolves sounded nice," she murmured to Lottie. "Like singing."

"Hush," Lottie said. "I'm listening."

"You have heard the beasts, brothers and sisters, I know you have heard them," the preacher said. "Damned souls, spawn of Satan—they howl their anguish at the sky and turn, in anger, on the righteous children of the Lord. Imagine this sound—but imagine it near to you, as near to you as I am standing. The beasts were all around me, shrieking in anger and calling for blood."

Half a dozen stragglers joined the crowd, attracted by the howling and shouting.

"I lifted my head from my prayer, brothers and sisters, and I saw the eyes of wolves—great yellow eyes that flashed in the firelight, the eyes of devils glaring from the darkness. Demons from Hell, clad in the guise of wolves. Each as big as a man, grinning at me, showing their teeth and snarling."

Mrs. Jones fell to her knees, clasping her hands in prayer. "Save us, Lord, from the demons of Satan," she wailed.

"What did I do, brothers and sisters?" the preacher was saying. "What could I do against the demons of Satan?" He lifted his Bible, to remind them of its presence. "I trusted in the power of the Lord."

A chorus of fervent "Amens" drowned out the hooting of the hecklers.

"Here it is, brothers and sisters, here is my weapon— the word of the Lord. I lifted this Holy Book so that the beasts could see it, could tremble before the truth of the Lord. And I called out to the Lord. I called to Him: 'May the spirit come down, may it come like a fire, may it come in streams of fire, fire of the Lord come down and free the earth of this pestilence.' "

Three more women at the front of the crowd knelt together, rocking back and forth in time with the preacher's words. Whenever he paused for breath, they chorused "Amen." The men in the front were shifting from foot to foot, swaying in time with the kneeling women.

"The very air around me trembled," the preacher said. "I felt the power, the power, the power of sanctification. In the light of the burning fire, I saw a great figure—an angel standing in the flame with a sword that was also a flame.'' He spoke with unshakeable confidence, lifting his hand as if to show the Lord's angel to anyone who could see.

"The angel lifted his sword, holding it high so that it blazed and lit the forest all around, bringing the glory of God to the darkness. And the demon wolf leaped to do battle with the messenger of the Lord. I could hear the sword crackle as it passed through the air, I could smell the brimstone when it touched the demon wolf. And the monsters fled, banished into the darkness.

"I stood in the darkness before the angel and I heard the angel speak to me. 'Take this land for the Lord,' the angel said to me. 'Drive the Devil from this wilderness.' "

"Praise the Lord," Mrs. Jones shouted, and the others took up the words. "Praise the Lord!"

The preacher raised his voice, thundering over the moaning and shouting. "Take this land, brothers and sisters! Drive out the Devil! You must kill the demon wolf wherever you find him. Kill the spawn of Satan. Drive him from this fair land that it may belong to the Lord."

"Drive out the Devil!" Mrs. Jones cried. "Drive him out!"

The preacher glared at the crowd, sweeping Nadya and Lottie with his gaze. "Listen to the message of the angel of God," he cried. "There are some among you who have not accepted the power of the Lord. They think that they can make peace with the Devil. I tell these sinners that Hell stands ready to receive them. Hell opens its yawning mouth to receive them. Repent, or you will spend your eternity burning in the pit. Repent!"

Two women in the front row had been taken by the Holy Spirit—they lay on the ground, jerking and moaning uncontrollably. Others were falling to their knees, calling out to the Lord to save them.

"There is no peace with the Devil! There is no concord between the wolf and the lamb. Let us pray, brothers and sisters, let us pray that the spirit of fire will come to us and set us ablaze with the glory of the Lord.'' He bowed his head, lowering his voice. "Let us pray that we triumph over the demon wolf, let us take this land for the Lord, let us bring civilization to this howling wilderness. Pray with me, brothers and sisters. Pray with me and bring the power of the Lord to this land.''

He bowed his head for a moment, then began a hymn, a sweet slow song that asked Jesus to watch over the wandering sheep. Nadya watched as the preacher walked among the men and women who knelt on the grassy ground. He laid a hand on one woman's head, patted another man on the shoulder. The two women who had been taken by the spirit lay in the grass, resting quietly now.

"Come on,'' Lottie said. "Let's go and get him to bless us.''

"I don't want to,'' Nadya said, hanging back.

Lottie glanced at her. "What's the matter? Come on.'' She looked back toward the preacher. "There's Silas. We can go talk to him.''

Nadya shook her head. "I have to go find my mama,'' she said. "She won't know where I am.'' She was trembling. She turned away from her friend, hurrying up the slope to the store.

On her way back to the store, Nadya met her father. "Papa, they are talking of hunting wolves.''

She thought he might be angry—angry with the people for talking of hunting, angry with her for killing the sheep at the Jones farm—but he just looked at her sadly and took her hand. "We'd best be going home, Nadya. This is no place for us just now.''

That week, Dmitri began building a wagon to carry his family West. Marietta protested, saying that the madness would pass, but she could not dissuade her husband. He said that they had lingered too long already. There were too many people in Missouri. They needed to go West, where there was open land and forests.

Midway through the week, Hekiziah Jones stopped by the Rybak farm. "Hello," he called out. "Hello, neighbor."

Dmitri was trimming and smoothing a length of oak to make a spare axle for the wagon that would carry them westward. He had spent the morning reinforcing the wagonbed with oak planks. Dmitri glanced up from his work when Jones rode into the farmyard, reined in his horse, and swung down from the saddle.

"What's all this? You emigrating?" Jones asked, staring at the wagon.

"Soon as we can," Dmitri said.

Jones considered the wagon, then glanced around the farmyard. "I hadn't heard tell that your farm was for sale."

"You're hearing it now," Dmitri said. The man stank of unwashed clothing, chewing tobacco, and alcohol— hard cider, by the smell. "Too crowded here. Time to move on."

Jones nodded and thoughtfully shifted the wad of chewing tobacco that was tucked in his lip. "Reasonable piece of land. Maybe I'll make you an offer. You in a hurry to sell?"

Dmitri studied Jones's face. "Two dollars an acre. Hard currency."

Jones shifted the wad of tobacco again and spat a stream of brown juice. "Ain't easy to come by so much hard currency."

"Ain't easy to be a farmer," Dmitri said.

"I might manage a dollar an acre."

Dmitri continued smoothing the oak shaft. Two dollars an acre for cleared land was already a bargain. Dmitri would need the hard currency once they reached Oregon. He would sell for less only if he had to. "I reckon I'll wait until someone with a better understanding of the value of land comes along,'' he said slowly.

"Suit yourself," Jones said easily. "Suit yourself. I came to invite you for some hunting Saturday next. Me and my boys gonna kill the varmints that killed my sheep. Some other folks will be joining us. We'll be gathering at the saloon. Thought you might like to come along.'' Jones grinned, showing crooked, tobacco-stained teeth. "A little whiskey and a little hunting. And the preacher's coming along to give us his blessing. A fine sporting afternoon.''

The full moon was Sunday night. Saturday's hunt offered no danger to Dmitri's family. He looked up from the axle. "Strange thing, Mr. Jones," he said. "We never had wolf trouble around here before. Maybe you should keep better watch on those sheep of yours.''

Jones's smile faltered. "What's that?" he said.

"Never had any trouble with wolves," Dmitri said. "They never bothered my stock. Maybe you'd be better off bringing your sheep in at night.''

Jones scowled. "What's that you're saying? You saying we shouldn't hunt those varmints?''

"Don't see that you have any call to," Dmitri said. "Don't see the need.''

"You're saying you won't go hunting?''

"I'm saying I'll have nothing to do with your sporting day. Won't slaughter animals that never did me no harm. Won't sell my land for less than it's worth.'' Dmitri was a patient man. He grew angry slowly. But the full moon was near, and this man threatened his family so casually, so confidently, insolently chewing his tobacco and eyeing Dmitri's land. Dmitri shifted his weight, setting his feet wide apart. He hefted the axle in his hands, shifting the heavy shaft so that he could swing it as a club. He bared his teeth in a ferocious grin. "I'd suggest you get yourself off my land. You'd best hurry.''

Jones eyed the axle and hurried to mount his horse.

He jerked on the reins and kicked the horse savagely. Dmitri returned to his work, relieved that the hunt would be on Saturday. They were safe for this full moon.

Over dinner that night, Dmitri told his wife and daughter about the coming hunt. The sun was near setting. Its light shone through the open windows. There was no other light; they were saving oil for the journey. "Hekiziah Jones said they would have a hunt this Saturday," he told them. "They want to kill the wolves that killed their sheep."

Nadya shook her head. "That can't be so," she said. "Rufus said that he wouldn't hunt wolves."

Dmitri studied his daughter's face. "When did he do that?"

Nadya would not meet his eyes. "When I asked him," she said. Her voice had an edge to it, a slight tremor of contained emotion. "He said he wouldn't hunt wolves."

"When was that?" Dmitri asked. "When did you ask him?"

"When he brought me home from the quilting." Still, she would not meet his eyes.

"Look at me, Nadya," he said angrily. "Why won't you look at me?"

"She's upset, Dmitri," her mother said softly.

He looked at his wife. "What do you know about this?"

Nadya stood up and headed for the cabin door.

"Where are you going, Nadya?" Dmitri asked, shocked at her behavior.

"I'd best check to see that the chickens are locked up for the night," she said, and rushed away.

Dmitri turned to his wife, shaking his head. "What is all this about?" He was bewildered by his daughter's tears.

His wife took his hand in both of hers. "She can't hear you. She can only hear the roar of the blood rushing in her ears. She is growing up." She lifted her eyes to meet his. "Do you remember how hard that was?"

"That boy and his family—they're no friends of ours. The father is a drunkard; the mother is a zealot. The son is a gambler. He means her no good."

"I know that. I read the cards. I told her that she shouldn't love this boy. I told her to take care. Might as well tell the river not to flow downhill." She released his hand. "What else can we do? Lock our daughter up? Deny her nature?" She shook her head. "We must hurry to build the wagon and prepare for our journey. She will be very sad when we go, but on the trail to Oregon, she will forget him." She smiled at her husband. "Be happy that we have time to prepare. She will survive the pain of heartbreak as we all have before her."

Dmitri shook his head slowly. He pushed himself away from the table and went to the door. By the light of the moon, he could see Nadya standing at the edge of the forest, leaning against the split rail fence. He went to stand at her side.

"Hello, Nadya," he said softly.

"Hello, Papa."

The moonlight was bright enough to cast shadows.

"Do you remember," Dmitri asked, "when I used to tell you stories with shadows?"

"I remember," Nadya said softly. She kept her face turned away so that he could not see her eyes.

"They were lies, those stories," Dmitri said. He hesitated, wishing that he could see her face. "In my stories, the wolf always wins. That's a lie."

"But the wolf could win, Papa. Don't you think? I think the wolf could win."

"The hunters win. They always have and they always will."

Nadya turned to face him then. Her jaw was set and her expression was stubborn. "Rufus said he wouldn't hunt wolves. He won't let them go hunting," she said.

Dmitri hesitated. "I'm not the only one who lies."

She turned her face to the forest again.

"The Oregon Territory is a beautiful land," he said. "Acres and acres of rich land, with never a person nearby. That's the place for us. We'll be emigrating as soon as the wagon's done."

She didn't answer.

"We will be happy there. Far from all the hunters and fools. Are you listening to me?"

She didn't answer.

At last, he sighed heavily. "Come inside when you get cold," he told her, and stamped back into the warmth of the cabin. When she came back inside to sit by the fire, he ignored her, talking with Marietta about the things they would need for the trip, telling her about the route that they would follow. Nadya climbed to her bed in the loft, but he kept up the cheerful conversation, knowing that she would hear him, hoping that she would listen to reason.

The hunt was to be on Saturday, the day before the moon was full. All would have been well, had it not been for the rain. The rain brought bad luck.

Nadya woke on Saturday to the sound of raindrops rattling against the greased paper windows. A thunderstorm had swept in during the night. The wind shook the branches of the trees and the rain hammered down, filling the ditches and gullies to overflowing.

Her parents tried to act as if nothing were wrong. They went about their work, as if this day were like any other. But Nadya could smell the tension in the air.

Sunday morning dawned wet and cold. In the morning, Nadya watched the sky and prayed that the rain would continue. But early in the afternoon, the rain became a drizzle. Water dripped from the branches of the trees, but the sky was clearing.

Nadya sat on the porch, mending a tear in her father's

second-best pair of trousers. Through the half-opened door, she listened to the murmur of her parents' voices inside the cabin.

"Surely they wouldn't begin a hunt so late in the day," her mother said.

"Depends on how much they've been drinking," her father's voice rumbled. "Depends on how foolish they feel. From what little I've seen of Rufus and Hekiziah Jones, I would guess that they're foolish enough."

Nadya set the mending in her lap. He was wrong about Rufus. He had to be.

"We'd best put some space between ourselves and the town before the moon rises," her father said.

"We can't pack the wagon quickly enough," her mother said. "We haven't time."

"We'll leave the wagon and save our skins. We have no choices."

Nadya knew there would be no hunt. Her father wouldn't believe her, but she knew that Rufus would stop them. He wouldn't allow it. He had said so, down by the river.

But even as she thought about Rufus, she felt uneasy. It would be difficult for him to persuade the others. He might need her help. While her parents argued, she slipped away to the barn, saddled the mule, and headed for town.

When Nadya was eight, her father had built their barn from rough-hewn logs. Neighbors had helped raise the walls and the ridge beam, leaving her father to complete the structure. Nadya's father told her not to climb on the newly erected frame. "It's dangerous," he had said. "You'll fall."

The next day, when her father was out of sight, she climbed to the top of the barn and walked the length of the roof's ridgebeam. She started with confidence, arms extended like a tightrope walker's. She was halfway across when she looked down at the ground far below.

In that moment, she swayed, feeling suddenly dizzy. Just before she recovered her balance, she imagined what it would be like to fall, arms flailing at the beam and missing, body tumbling to break on the ground below. Her legs trembled and she could feel her heart pounding. And then, despite the panic, she continued to the far end of the beam.

As she rode the mule into town, she felt as she had when she stood on the ridgebeam. Defiant and frightened. The ground lay far below her, and she did not dare look down.

She found Rufus in the tavern, playing cards. She recognized the other men at the table, all of them neighbors: Hekiziah Jones, Tom Williams, Mr. Shaw, Mr. Whitman. Their faces looked unfamiliar in the dim light of the tavern, skin slack with drink, eyes rimmed with red.

Mr. Shaw frowned at her. "What are you doing here?" he asked her. "This is no place for a young lady."

"I came to talk to Rufus." Her voice was strained. The smell of the tavern—tobacco spit, whiskey, and sweat—made her feel sick.

"Does your Papa know you're here?" Mr. Shaw said. "I don't think it's proper . . ."

Rufus looked up from his cards and stared at her. She could not read his expression. He tossed his cards face down on the table and pushed back his chair. When he stood, he swayed, unsteady on his feet. "How do, Miss Nadya," he said, his words a little slurred. "I'd be pleased to talk with you. Let's leave these fellas behind."

He took her arm and led her toward the door. Behind her, Nadya heard Tom Williams's voice, but she could not make out the words. All the men laughed—an unfriendly sound containing no merriment.

Outside, the day was clearing. The clouds that had

covered the sun had dissipated. Muddy puddles filled the ruts of the dirt track that ran past the tavern's front porch. The livery stable and store had been washed clean; the white facades glistened in the late afternoon sunshine. The street was deserted.

"Rufus," she said. "I had to talk to you."

"Darling, I've been thinking about you too," he said. He put his arms around her and started to pull her into an embrace. He reeked of whiskey. "We'll go to the hayloft in the livery stable. No one will bother us there."

She pulled back, shaking his arms off her. "My father said that you were going hunting for wolves."

He frowned. "We have time. They won't go hunting without me." He reached out and took hold of her hand. "I've missed you, Nadya."

"You're going hunting?" she asked. The air seemed suddenly colder. She could feel a trembling that began deep inside her. It had not yet reached the surface.

"Not yet. I tell you, we have time." With his free hand, he fumbled at the buttons on the front of her dress. His fingers were clumsy and the buttons did not cooperate.

"You promised," Nadya said, taking a step back away from him. "You promised you wouldn't hunt wolves."

He stared at her, then burst out laughing. "Not hunt wolves? That's the most damn fool idea I've ever heard."

"You said you wouldn't," she said.

"Never said anything like it," he protested.

"Down by the river," she said. "You promised me you wouldn't hunt wolves."

He was looking at her with the same expression he had worn when she climbed on top of him to satisfy her desire. He was astounded and bewildered and disapproving. "Nadya, I reckon I got to hunt wolves," he said. "If we don't kill the wolves, they'll kill our sheep.

What do those varmints matter to you? Come on, now.''
He tried to pull her to him. She jerked her wrist away.

"You mustn't kill wolves," she said. "You can't."

He glared at her then. "Don't you tell me what I can't
do." His voice had lost its wheedling tone. "Just because we've had a little fun together doesn't mean you
can tell me what to do. I'll kill every wolf in the county,
if I like."

"But you said. . . ."

"You're a crazy one," he told her. "You don't act
like a normal woman. I didn't say nothing about
wolves."

"My mother warned me," Nadya said. The trembling
had reached the surface. She was cold, very cold, and
she could not stop shaking. "She told me that you were
dangerous. I should have listened."

She turned away, walking toward the mule that was
tied at the hitching post.

"Hold on there," he said. He grabbed her shoulder.
As she turned to face him, she lifted an elbow and
caught him with a clout on the side of the head. He
stumbled and fell.

"Leave me be," she said. "Just leave me be."

She mounted the mule and kicked the beast into a trot.
When she was halfway down the street, she glanced
back and saw Rufus struggling to his feet.

"The weather's clear," he shouted—to the men in the
saloon, to Nadya's retreating back. "Let's go hunting.
Let's kill some wolves!"

She kicked the mule again. The sun was already low
in the sky. She could feel the pull of the full moon—a
sensation in her belly and her crotch. For the first time,
she feared the Change.

The ride home was long and she felt sick to her stomach, sick at heart. As she came into the farmyard, she
saw her mother, waiting for her on the porch.

Nadya swung off the mule and ran into her mother's

arms. "I saw Rufus," she said. "I saw him and the other men and . . ." Then she wept, unable to stop the tears.

Her father put his hand on her shoulder. "Come," he said. "There is little time left."

They had only gotten as far as the riverbank when the moon rose.

William Cooper came to the tavern and said a prayer before the hunt began. It was clear from his expression that he disapproved of drinking and gambling. But Rufus guessed that he disapproved of wolves more.

"May the All Mighty God give us strength to overcome the forces of darkness," the preacher prayed. "We come in Your name, to do away with the beasts of waste and desolation that devour Your innocent creatures. We call on You to bless our bullets and guide our aim."

The prayer droned on, and Rufus kept his head bowed. He was thinking of Nadya—still angry that she had pulled away, that she had demanded that he stop the hunt. She was crazy, that was clear. A pretty girl, but crazy. There were many other pretty girls in town.

When Cooper finally wound down, Rufus murmured "Amen." They toasted the preacher a few times. Then there was another delay when the preacher had insisted on coming along. They finally got underway just before sunset. It didn't matter, Rufus figured. The full moon would provide the light they needed. They were all accustomed to night hunting.

The air was crisp and cool, but the glow of the whiskey kept Rufus warm. The hounds set out, and the men followed on horseback. They took the trail north along the river, where Rufus had spotted wolf sign, now and again.

The sun set and the full moon rose. With the setting of the sun, colors faded from the forest: the world was black and white with shades of silver-gray.

At the river, the dogs found a scent, and they gave

voice, a deep musical baying that echoed across the valley. Rufus's horse ran ahead of the others, sure-footed even in the darkness. Behind him, Rufus could hear Cooper calling for the Lord's assistance in this hunt against the demons of Satan.

Rufus had never believed in demons, despite his mother's convictions. But he liked hunting and he favored the darkness. He forgot his anger in the excitement. The chill air washed the whiskey fumes away, leaving his head clear.

The river was at flood. The muddy waters swirled around the bases of oak trees that normally stood high on the bank. Once, the dogs lost the trail and cast about frantically, running up and down the riverbank and sniffing the muddy ground. But they found the scent again and coursed along the bank, heading north.

Rufus was in the lead when the hounds' baying grew more frantic. He spurred his tired horse. The dogs had three wolves trapped on a jutting cliff where the river had eaten the bank away. The wolves stood with their backs to the edge, holding off the dogs. As Rufus approached, the biggest wolf rushed the hounds, snapping and snarling.

Rufus waited until the animal broke clear of the pack of hounds and squeezed off a shot. The lead wolf tumbled, somersaulting forward as his front legs went out from under him. Half the dog pack closed in on the fallen wolf; the rest pursued the other two. Rufus reined in his horse and reloaded, then spurred his horse after the pack of hounds.

He caught up with them a short distance away. He could see the two wolves bounding toward the river. He aimed and fired: good shot; one animal fell. The last wolf ran ran toward the river's edge. He could see it clearly, and he struggled to reload, but his horse shied, spilling the powder. He fumbled with the rifle.

Too late: the animal reached the cliff one leap ahead

of the running hounds and launched itself over the edge. The dogs milled in a pack, yelping and snarling. Below, where the river ran like liquid silver in the moonlight, Rufus could see a dark head—the wolf struggling in the current. He did not waste the powder firing at the distant animal, but used the butt of his rifle to club the dogs away from the body of the fallen female.

By the time the other men arrived, the swimming wolf had been carried south by the current. The others built a fire, while Rufus skinned the two carcasses. The two wolves were in fine condition, fat and healthy, with thick fur.

He ran his knife down the female's belly and peeled back the skin, working carefully to avoid spoiling the fur. In the cold night air, steam rose from the body.

The preacher was the last to arrive. He stood by the fire with the others and called for a prayer of thanks. Rufus continued skinning the wolf while the preacher thanked God for their salvation.

After the prayer, Rufus went to work on the male wolf. He could hear the men around the fire talking about the wolf that got away. "It'll drown, sure enough," he heard his father say. The male's body had cooled and Rufus's hands were icy by the time he was done. He bundled the furs, then went to the fire to warm his hands and share the whiskey bottle that was making its way around the circle. Someone was telling a story about another hunt where they had killed four wolves, and someone else told of wolf hunting on the plains. Tales of blood and excitement.

The moon set and they finished the bottle. Rufus strapped the wolf skins behind his saddle, patting his horse when it shied away from the scent. The day was dawning, gray and dim.

Rufus parted company with the others at the turnoff that led to the Rybak farm and his own family's farm.

His father was returning to town to continue the card game they had left. Rufus continued home alone.

Nadya woke to find herself lying by the river at a bend where the current had created a narrow gravel beach. She was naked. Her skin was marked with bruises, streaked with river silt and blood. During the long chase, brambles had slashed her. The dogs had snapped at her feet and legs, leaving bloody gashes behind.

She sat up and hugged her knees for warmth. Early morning: the sun was barely above the horizon. Pale mist rose from the river, shifting and flowing like the water itself. From years of hunting the area, she recognized this stretch of river. She was just a mile or so downstream of the farm.

Her memories were blurred: darkness, panic, pain. Running—she remembered running among the trees, terrified by the baying of the hounds. And shouting— she remembered men's voices, shouting and singing and laughing like devils. Her body remembered the tugging of the river's currents, dragging her this way and that. Her muscles ached—she had fought the current, paddling desperately for this small beach.

She shivered. Where were her parents? That, she did not remember. Perhaps they had been carried further downstream. If that were the case, they would meet her at the farm. Surely, if she found her way to the farm, they would be there.

She clambered up the bank. She was used to going barefoot, but the brambles growing by the river scratched her bare skin and snagged in her hair. Under the oak trees at the top of the bank, the going was easier: last autumn's leaves, now damp and half rotted, were soft underfoot. She forced her tired muscles into a trot, telling herself that she would see her mother and father as soon as she reached the cabin. Of course, they would have to be at the cabin.

She was almost to the cabin when she heard a man shout. She did not recognize the voice exactly. At least, recognition did not penetrate the haze that occupied her mind, a peculiar cloudiness, as if her head were filled with river mist that ebbed and swirled. But the voice sounded familiar—that voice had called out to the hounds the night before, urging them on. The voice called to her again, and she ran faster, ducking through the trees, ignoring the branches that scratched her legs.

"Mama!" she called as she ran toward the cabin. "Mama! Papa!" The mule grazing in the field lifted its head to watch her.

She pushed the cabin door open. The room was empty, but she snatched her father's rifle from its place beside the door and the powder horn from the peg on the wall. She loaded the rifle quickly, her hands trembling in the cold. She spilled the black powder, but did not stop until she had rammed the bullet into place.

Still naked, she held the loaded rifle. With one foot, she kicked open the cabin door.

She smelled blood. Dried blood, mingled with the scent of wolf. She recognized the man on the horse—vaguely, dimly, through the river mist that filled her head—recognized him by his smell. His name didn't come to her—names were not really important yet. Someday soon, maybe they would be, but just then, names had not returned to her.

But his smell—that she knew. It was the smell of passion and the smell of death. Sex and blood and river water and dogs baying as they rushed through the night, chasing wild things that ran and ran and ran, but never escaped. The smell told her what to do, even before she saw the two bundles of gray fur, tied to the saddle behind him.

"Nadya," the man said, and she lifted the rifle and shot him, point blank, not thinking, not thinking at all.

His horse shied at the sound, and shied again at the

sudden limpness of the man in the saddle. The man slumped, then fell, sliding gracelessly to the ground, lying face down with one foot still caught in the stirrup. The smell of fresh blood joined the smell of dried blood, and a brilliant red stain spread across the back of the man's shirt where the bullet had left his body.

Nadya freed the man's foot from the stirrup and let the body lie in the dirt. She spoke soothingly to the horse, murmuring the French endearments with which her mother had once comforted her. She tied the horse to the split rail fence and returned to the cabin. She walked past the body, but did not look at it.

She stirred up the embers and built a fire. She did not think. She built a fire and heated water for tea. She washed herself, using a rag and warm water to wipe away the dirt and the blood. Even when she put on her hunting trousers and a warm shirt, she could not stop shivering. The cold came from deep inside her.

The water boiled and she made tea, carefully measuring the dried leaves into the pot. Her mother liked her tea just so—Nadya was careful to make it properly, and she sat by the fire, sipping her tea. She caught herself listening for the sound of her parents' footsteps. Her mind shied away from the memory of the two bundles of fur on the back of the horse. She had another cup of tea.

Then she took the shovel and went to a place in the woods where the ground was soft. The horse carried the man's body.

She buried the two bundles of fur side by side in a single grave. She stood by the grave for a time, unable to pray. "I'm sorry," she said at last. "I'm sorry. I shouldn't have . . . I didn't mean . . ." But the words stopped. She bowed her head and stood silent again. "Papa," she said at last. "There was nothing wrong with your stories. They weren't lies. The wolf can win.

Just not here. Not now. But somewhere, the wolf can win.''

Some distance away, she buried the body of the man who had killed her parents. Rufus's body. The name had returned to her with the memory of love and betrayal. But she said nothing over his grave. She had nothing to say to him.

Then she packed a few things: gunpowder, salt, tea, a pot in which to boil water, two blankets, her hunting knife, a hatchet, a pistol. Necessities only.

She closed the door on her way out of the cabin. She lifted the gate that kept the pigs in their pen, shooed the cattle and the mule from the stable. Then she tied her small bundle behind the saddle and mounted.

She turned the horse's head toward the wilderness of the Oregon Territory. America was a big country. Out there, the land was empty; the forests were thick and green. Out there, she would find a place where she could be happy.

She kicked the horse into a trot and rode west, leaving childhood behind.

Penguin Putnam Inc.
Online

Your Internet gateway to a virtual environment with
hundreds of entertaining and enlightening books from
Penguin Putnam Inc.

*While you're there, get the latest buzz on
the best authors and books around—*

Tom Clancy, Patricia Cornwell, W.E.B. Griffin,
Nora Roberts, William Gibson, Robin Cook,
Brian Jacques, Catherine Coulter, Stephen King,
Jacquelyn Mitchard, and many more!

**Penguin Putnam Online is located at
http://www.penguinputnam.com**

PENGUIN PUTNAM NEWS

Every month you'll get an inside look at our upcoming
books and new features on our site. This is an ongoing
effort to provide you with the most up-to-date
information about our books and authors.

Subscribe to Penguin Putnam News at
http://www.penguinputnam.com/ClubPPI